DOUBL. PUCKED

LAUREN BLAKELY

ABOUT THE BOOK

When I discover my boyfriend is cheating on me, I move out right away taking what I love most – my dog. As I fly out the door, I make sure to swipe the thing my ex loves best. The VIP tickets he won to a hockey game, complete with the chance to spend an evening with the city's two biggest NHL stars.

I can't wait to snap selfies with my ex's idols and rub it in his face.

Except, when I head out with the two hockey studs, they have something else in mind besides sweet revenge. Would I like to spend the night...with both of them?

Talk about the VIP experience. That's what I get for one knee-weakening, sheet-grabbing night. In the morning, I plan to return to my bestie's house to crash on her couch with my dog.

But when they learn what happened with my awful ex, they ask me to be their temporary roomie for the week. Oh, and one of them needs my help with his grumpy reputation. The other? Well, he wants me to be his fake date at an upcoming wedding.

Looks like I'm about to get double pucked. *Again.*

DID YOU KNOW?

To be the first to find out when all of my upcoming books go live click here!

PRO TIP: Add lauren@laurenblakely.com to your contacts before signing up to make sure the emails go to your inbox!

Did you know this book is also available in audio and paperback on all major retailers? Go to my website for links!

To all the girls who dare to dream—big, dirty, filthy, fabulous dreams!

With gratitude to Dr. Hunter Finn for his Valentine's Day video.

SAN FRANCISCO MAP

Ever wonder where all the places in the books are located in my version of San Francisco? @Makeit-bookish designed this "town map" for my stories! Enjoy!

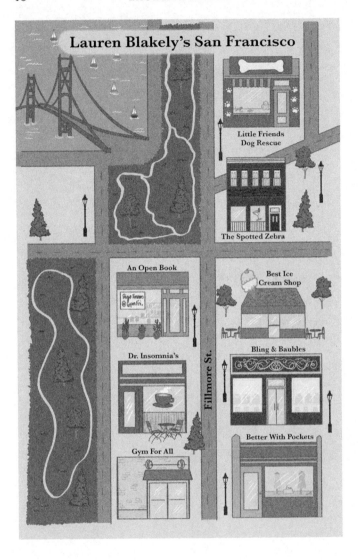

MY HOCKEY ROMANCE BOOK #1

AN MFM ROOMIES-TO-LOVERS SPICY HOCKEY ROM-COM

By Lauren Blakely

1

THE DOG ATE MY UNDERWEAR

Trina

Let me state for the record—I love my dog madly. This little stinker of a Min Pin mix is my baby, with his three legs, slobbery kisses, and burrow-under-my-covers-and-snuggle-all-night soul.

But there's one thing I don't love about my dog, Nacho. He eats my underwear.

You'd think a four-foot-high hamper with a lid that shuts would deter him. You'd be dead wrong.

As a hockey game blasts on the TV next to him, the twenty pounds of trouble lounges in his cuddler cup, licking his naughty lips without an ounce of remorse, the spoils of our lingerie war in his paws. *Again.*

"Seriously? Did you have to make them crotchless?" I ask as I bend down to grab the panty leftovers.

He doesn't even have the decency to look guilty. Just wags his tail. Too adorably.

Gingerly, I pluck the remains of my pink polka-dot boy shorts from his pervy paws while my boyfriend Jasper shouts at the TV, "Are you kidding me? That was cross-checking."

With an outrage only known to the species of *rabid sports fans who wear jerseys of other men*, Jasper jumps up from the couch, barking at the refs, telling them they're blind, he's going to give them a piece of his mind when he goes to the game later this month, and blah, blah, blah.

It's just hockey. Who cares? Well, besides Jasper, though caring is an understatement to describe how he feels about hockey. Come to think of it, so is the word *obsessed*. With the half-eaten undies in hand, I walk behind the couch, not in front of it, so I don't block his view as I head to the trash bin. I don't dare disturb him during a hockey bout. Or match. Or whatever it is the guys on screen are doing with sticks and ice and stuff.

"Guess I'll be shopping for new panties later today," I say to myself as I drop the remains of my dignity in the garbage bin.

"What, babe?" Jasper calls out, and that must mean there's a cross-checking time-out. Is that a thing? Who knows?

As a jingle about chicken wings with burn-your-tongue-off hot sauce plays from the TV, I answer him, "The dog ate my panties again. I'm going to go shopping for new ones. He went on a tear this week."

"Oh, could you get thongs this time? Those are hot."

That'd be a hard no. "I don't want to floss my ass all day long at the bookstore."

"But you'd look so good in them," he says in his *sexy baby pretty please* voice. "You could wear one when we use those VIP tix later this month."

Ugh. Don't remind me. One of my life goals is to avoid *ever* going to a sporting event. Naturally, I had to fall for a sports junkie. But I'll make the game fun by turning it into a gift that keeps on giving. I bought Jasper some jerseys for each team, and some pucks, and I'm going to get them all signed by the athletes as a surprise for him.

"Let me get this straight," I call out as I grab my phone from the counter. "You want me to wear a thong and nothing else to the VIP thingie?"

He wiggles his eyebrows my way. "A thong and a short dress and those hot glasses. Yowzers."

Well, I wear the glasses everywhere. But I don't point that out. "Sounds perfect for a game played on ice," I tease, stuffing my phone in my pocket, then grabbing my purse and keys. But on the way to the front door of our apartment in the Mission District, a terrifying sound catches my attention. A dry heave, then a wheezing hack, and then a horrible gasp of air.

Oh no! My baby!

I spin around. Nacho is puking up panty parts like a priest is conducting a lingerie exorcism of his esophagus.

My heart rockets with worry. I fly over to my darling, scoop him up, and race off to the vet around the corner as Jasper yells obscenities at the screen.

* * *

"He's going to be fine."

I can breathe again.

I press my palms together in gratitude. "Thank you so much, Doctor Lennox. I can't thank you enough." Then I wince, filled with worry. "But what do I do if Nacho does it again? I honestly didn't think he ate that much. I mean, how much underwear is too much underwear? He's done this before but he usually only eats—"

I stop myself before I say the next thing out loud. *The panel.* Seriously. How gross is that? My dog eats the panel of my panties after I take them off and I'm telling the story to the guy who's known online as The Hot Vet, since he shoots helpful tips for pet owners. No wonder my older sister thinks I'm the family *hot mess.*

In this moment, she's not wrong.

I might as well just hold up a sign for his vid that says, *The dog likes the way I taste.*

Gross.

Well, not gross. I'm sure I taste fabulous. But I don't want to discuss my peach flavor with my dog's doctor.

"They usually only eat the panels," he says, and that's not totally embarrassing to hear him say even though he delivers this dog truth nugget with a completely straight face. "But I don't want you to stress, Trina. Dogs eat a lot of non-food items and sometimes they just need their stomach pumped. He's resting comfortably right now and should be able to go home in about thirty minutes." He flashes a warm smile, then sets a hand on my arm. "Besides, it was just a thong."

"Well, that's good," I say, still relieved that Nacho is

fine and that we're no longer talking about the panel of my panties.

Except.

Wait.

Hold the hell on.

What did he just say? "A thong?" I ask. It comes out thoroughly skeptical because there's no way my dog ate a thong. I don't own any thongs.

Maybe Dr. Lennox is just bad at identifying women's underwear. I mean, he wouldn't be the first man who couldn't tell a bikini from a cheeky or a high-rise from a hipster.

"You just mean that that's what was left, right? That it looked like a thong? The pink polka-dot pair? I threw the rest of it out at home."

Dr. Lennox tilts his head, like I'm the one not making sense. "There was a tiny bit of fabric that was pink, and he vomited that first. But then there was a red lacy bit for the floss. That came out in three pieces, but honestly, it wasn't that hard to puzzle the words together."

"The words?" I ask, feeling like he's speaking another language.

The vet has the good grace to look at the counter as he says, "The front had the words *bad girl* written on it."

Somehow he manages to say all this with a straight face. Which tells me that many dogs eat many weird things and that an important skill for a vet is being able to not laugh when he learns what type of underwear you wear.

And I'm not laughing either.

Because my dog did not eat *my* pair.

My jaw hangs open. My heart doesn't want to compute what he just said. But my brain has already processed this awful news. And my momentary shock is laced with hurt and chased with a giant ball of anger.

My boyfriend didn't only screw another woman.

That charmed-my-parents, won-over-my-tough-as-nails-sister and obviously-fooled-me-too *boyfriend* screwed someone else at *our* apartment.

To make matters worse, that cheating scumbag of a boyfriend screwed that *bad girl* in front of my dog.

Wait.

Make that soon-to-be ex-boyfriend.

* * *

"I can explain."

I seethe as Jasper utters those three awful words. They're the kiss of death to any relationship. Not that I had much hope that there would be any sort of reasonable excuse for the presence of another woman's shredded panties in my darling dog's digestive tract.

Still, I'm part investigator (and I can tell you which Enneagram types all my friends are too), so I'm damn curious how Jasper's going to spin this dirty laundry.

I'm back home now, facing off against the man I was sure I'd been falling for. As I clutch my drugged dog, who's still woozy from the meds, I sweep out my free arm, inviting the stinking, no-good cheater to present his case—right here in the living room. His favorite room, since it's got that damn symbol of his real love. The TV that blasts every freaking hockey game.

"Have at it," I bite out. "And bear in mind I've read about five thousand romance novels so I've heard pretty much all the excuses. But by all means, you take the floor."

I've got the evidence though and I confronted him with it when I walked in the door two minutes ago, wagging a ziplock bag and asking him coolly, calmly, "Any idea why another woman's panties were in my dog's belly?" Because damn straight I took that evidence from Dr. Lennox. "I would really, *really* like to know what the explanation for this is."

Jasper backs up against his living room wall, right next to the framed tickets of the first ever hockey game his dad took him to. Hair from his man bun falls loose, framing his guilty face. He gulps so visibly it's like a bullfrog just crawled up his throat.

"I was d-doing laundry," he begins. "The other day. Down in the basement of the building." In case I don't know where the washer and dryer are, I presume. "And our neighbor—you know the redhead from the second floor?"

I growl. The one whose ass I caught him staring at the other week when she walked up the steps in front of us, asking how Nacho's weave-pole classes were going. Gah. I'd been bamboozled by dog talk. "Delilah," I supply, anger lacing my tone, but I'm angry with myself. Why didn't I realize that his ogling of her was a sign? "Continue."

With a rough swallow, he soldiers on. "All the

machines were full so I said that she could wash her clothes with ours."

"How noble."

He breathes a clear sigh of relief, missing my sarcasm. "Right? I just wanted to help her, Trina," he says.

"Naturally. Sharing a washing machine is neighborly."

He hazards a smile. "I'm glad you agree."

This guy. He thinks he's getting away with fooling me. But actually...I think for a few seconds. Yes, maybe this'll work. Yeah, I'll let him think I believe him.

I adopt a warmer expression, like I'm buying this bill of goods he's selling. "So, you opened your washing machine to her. Let her share in a full spin cycle."

"Exactly," he says, a bigger smile lighting up his handsome face. What a stupidly handsome face. It tricked me.

But he's not tricking me now. I'm feeling all kinds of *Law & Order*. "So the dog got the undies from the clean laundry then?" I ask, innocently, leading the witness.

Jasper's smile is so damn bright. "Exactly. I did her laundry. And her underwear must have fallen into our laundry basket at the end," he says, letting out a laugh. Like, can you believe the laundry room shenanigans? Right, right. Those panties had a mind of their own just jumping into our basket. "Then I brought it back upstairs and the dog got it."

I breathe in deeply. I can work with his song-and-dance routine. "So you're a Good Samaritan," I say, affecting my best *thank god my guy isn't a cheater* grin before I sling an inquisitive, "Not a fabulist?"

He blinks, scrunching his brow. "What?"

"Here's a hint. It doesn't mean fabulous. It comes from the word *fable*, and it means you're spinning stories."

Jasper holds up his hands, lip trembling. "I swear she just needed to do her laundry. I was doing her a solid."

"Doing her is right," I say.

He shakes his head, whipping it back and forth. The denial is strong in this one. "I accidentally put it away with your stuff. So then Nacho just went into your drawer and got it out. You know what he's like. He's totally into underwear."

"I do know what he's like. I know exactly what he's like," I say, my anger masking all my hurt. I advance toward Jasper, crossing the living room and setting my sweetheart safely down in his cuddler cup. "And I know beyond a reasonable doubt that you're a liar. Want to know how?"

"How?" He wobbles.

Deep breath. "Nacho only eats dirty underwear."

Jasper's face falls. He gulps visibly, and then the great backtracking begins. "It only happened one time. You were running a signing at the bookstore. We watched a hockey game together. She's a hockey fan too. It won't happen again." He presses his palms together in prayer. "Please forgive me. I just love you so much."

A sob threatens to climb up my throat. It threatens

to make me believe him. That it was a one-time thing, that it was no big deal, that it was a transgression.

But that sob comes from my broken heart, not my head.

When my eyes stray to the framed tickets behind him, to his precious hockey paraphernalia, my head takes over, saying *hold my beer* to my dumb heart. "I'll consider it," I say carefully, evenly. "But I need a few hours alone." I push out my lower lip, letting it quiver. "Can you do that for me, baby?"

He nods immediately, clearly ready to grovel, giving me puppy-dog eyes. "I just don't want you to move out. I mean, we're doing such a great job, making rent together. Life plan and all, babe."

Our life plan did not involve your dick in another woman and her panties in my dog's belly.

By some miracle, I don't say that, though I completely understand every impulse every woman throughout time has ever had to hurl vases, dishes, or mugs at a cheating ex. But I'm not going to do that. I am going to hit him where it hurts. Just like he hurt me right in the heart—through my dog. "I get it. I'm just going to do some yoga," I lie.

"Absolutely, babe. Anything you say. Thank you so much for considering forgiving me. It will never happen again." With his tail tucked between his lying legs, he leaves.

The second the door shuts, I take a deep breath, let a few tears fall, then say fuck off to my feelings.

I spend the next hour calling reinforcements, devising a plan, packing all my clothes, grabbing my laptop, and snagging my books, candles, lotions and potions.

When I'm done, I yank open my closet for a final check and spot a bag with all the stupid jerseys and pucks I bought for him. No way does he get this now. I don't want it, but I am *not* leaving this behind for him to give to Delilah the hockey fan or for him to wear. I grab the bag, something catching in my throat. I'm crying the whole time, wiping my tears under my glasses with countless wads of tissues. They're tears of hurt, and they're tears of rage too.

I gather up all of Nacho's toys, food, and jackets, telling my darling that we'll be staying with my friend Aubrey for a few days. He thumps his tail as Aubrey texts that she's pulling up.

I do one final scan of the bedroom to make sure I took everything, when I spot something white and shiny under his bedside lamp. I walk over, inspecting the black bordered card.

Ohh.

It's the VIP tickets he won to spend an evening with the star center of the San Francisco Sea Dogs and his crosstown rival, the top defenseman of the California Avengers.

With a wicked smile, I stuff them inside my bra and take off with everything that matters to me and the one thing that matters most to him.

* * *

At Aubrey's home that night, we devour a pint of ice cream, and half a bottle of wine—fine, it's a whole bottle. Nacho's tucked next to me on the couch, a little drowsy still, his snout resting on my thigh. While I stroke his soft head, Aubrey sets down the pint and her spoon decisively.

"Wallow hour is over. Let's see who you're going to meet while Jasper cries in the corner."

The image of him sobbing like a big baby over lost hockey tickets is a beautiful sight, so I grab my phone, then Google the names of the two players I'll be meeting in two weeks.

And...oh. How about that? They aren't too shabby.

"Check them out," I say.

Chase Weston is the golden guy center, all warm brown eyes and panty-melting smile, of the Sea Dogs.

Ryker Samuels is the dark-haired, bearded, and broody-as-sin defenseman on the Avengers.

Aubrey whistles approvingly at their pics. "They're snacks," she says, then gives me a naughty look. "You have to wear something ridiculously sexy and take a ton of selfies to make your ex jealous."

"Yes. Yes, I do."

TWO WEEKS LATER

2

SHE LIKES BOTH

Chase

"Oh man. That's got to hurt," I say to myself as I climb toward the fiftieth floor.

I'm sweating buckets, and laughing my ass off as I watch a hilarious vet video on my phone. This is a good fucking way to start a good fucking morning, and it's going to be a great fucking day. My hockey team is playing our crosstown rivals tonight, and my game plan is simple—I'm going to kick their ass.

But first I have to show this video to my bud. I pop my earbuds out and wave a hand in front of the burly dude on the StairMaster next to me. "Samuels," I bark.

My friend, who's also the star defenseman for our crosstown rivals, slowly turns his head toward me, arching a brow. The dude could not be any more poker-faced if he tried. As I climb another floor, I motion for him to take out his earbuds, the fucking jackass.

Like I've asked him to give me a limb, Ryker takes his sweet time removing one. "Better be a good reason for you to intrude, Weston. I was about to learn the etymology of the word avocado."

I roll my eyes. "We get it. Your brain is big. You know what they say about that."

"Yes. There was a study that found the size of a man's dick is directly proportional to the size of his brain. Ergo..."

I shake my head. "I saw that same study and it was the size of his funny bone. Dick to funny bone, and both of mine are huge...Also, I was going to say...*it means you wear a big hat*."

With an unamused stare he's perfected since child-hood—seriously, Ryker made our fifth grade math teacher cower with his intensity—he says, "Anyway, did you want me to put the earbud back in right now and finish my podcast? Because I'd like to."

"First, check this out," I say, waving the phone at him. As I climb another floor, heart pumping, legs burning, I shove the screen at him. "This popular vet posted a video the other day and he said..." I pause to clear my throat. "*It was a good day. I successfully made a dog puke up a pair of panties. But, since they were not the owner's panties, it's safe to say someone is having a worse day than the dog.*" I blow out a long stream of air, shaking my head. "Can you believe that?"

"People are dicks," my buddy huffs, and that's been his mantra since his dad took off.

"Only a handful," I say, since we don't see eye to eye

on humanity, but hey, that's what makes it fun to rile him up.

He narrows his eyes. "Anything else you need to tell me or can I go back to learning about words and you can watch dog videos?"

"I like dogs," I say, defensively. Then in a cockier tone, I add, "And I like winning. Which is what I plan to do tonight when we kick your ass on the ice."

I pop my earbuds back in and proceed to race climb him. It's an unwritten rule of two pro athletes working out next to each other. You must school the other guy. Lift more, climb farther, run faster.

I always do.

With my pulse spiking, I'm chasing the sky as I watch a pack of Border Collies catch frisbees. Someday, I'll be able to adopt a badass dog who can do tricks and shit.

But not too soon, since hockey comes first, second, and third. It's everything to me, and it lets me fulfill a promise I made years ago. A promise I'll always keep.

As I'm nearing the end of my cardio, my phone buzzes. I glance down at the text flashing across the screen. It's from Gianna, the publicist for the Sea Dogs.

> Gianna: Don't forget the VIP event is tonight after the game! Be on your best behavior.

I chuckle at her note, then tap out a reply saying, *I always am*. But before I can send it she's already written back.

> Gianna: JK. I know you always are, Chase.

She's right. I pride myself on my reputation as a good guy. It works well for me. It helps me pay all the bills and take care of my mom and younger brothers. That's why I do everything I can to be the good guy man about town. I spearhead the Hockey Hotties calendar to raise money for both youth sports and rescue dogs, and I've got one helluva smile. It gleams. And I always talk to the press, even though I know firsthand that the media isn't always friendly. That's okay—it's just part of the game.

> Chase: I've got you, G. It's all good.

> Gianna: You're the best. P.S. Tell Ryker to smile. No King of Grunts tonight.

Ouch. But that's what a popular hockey podcaster nicknamed my friend, and if the skate fits...

> Chase: I will definitely tell him. I'm working out with him right now.

> Gianna: I figured as much! But remember, you're rivals on the ice.

> Chase: That's what my Stanley Cup says too.

I finish the exchange and the workout, stabbing the end button on the StairMaster dashboard.

Ryker follows suit. "Did more floors than you."

I peer at his screen. "Dammit," I mutter.

We leave the gym and exit onto Fillmore Street, heading toward Doctor Insomnia's Tea and Coffee Emporium. A good workout deserves a good cup of Joe. And that place is my regular haunt. "Here's the deal. You need to be all sunshine tonight."

He grunts.

"Nope. No grunts. Use those big words in your big brain when we meet our guest."

He narrows his eyes, then drops a pair of aviator shades over them and emits a menacing growl. As if he scares me. "C'mon. You can do it. Be a good guy and say you'll be sunny tonight."

With a death glare—yes, I can tell those are daggers behind his mirrored shades—he says, "I will be so fucking refulgent tonight."

I cringe. "Do not be repugnant. Just be nice."

He snickers. "Refulgent means luminous. As in sunshiney. Like you said."

Like it's happening in slow-mo, I raise my middle finger. "And this means fuck off, word nerd."

"Aww, was it hard for you to learn something? Or did it drive you crazy?"

I scoff. "You know what drives me crazy? When you act like you're an irascible bastard," I say, flinging one of his fancy words back at him.

Ryker cracks a rare grin. "See? My word nerding rubs off on you. Such a surprise for a Golden Retriever."

"Did you mean team captain? Since that's what it says on my jersey."

He growls again. But I'm not fooled by his grumpy routine. Only one thing I've done has ever really pissed off Ryker. A year ago, when he thought I stole his girl. Dude didn't speak to me for a week. But I didn't know Abby was his and I will never do it again. We made a pact after all. "By the way, what's the etymology of avocado?" I ask.

That perks him up. "It comes from a word for testicles."

I cringe. "This is why I don't need to learn your weird words."

* * *

Ten hours later I'm rinkside, in my uniform, and ready to destroy the Avengers. The game starts in twenty minutes. But first, my goalie taps my knee with his stick.

"Listen," Erik begins from his spot on the bench

next to me. "Lisette needs to know if you want to be at the singles table next weekend? She says it'll be fun."

Fun and singles tables don't usually go hand in hand. But that's my cousin Lisette for you. I invited her to a barbecue at my house a couple years ago, and she hit it off with my teammate. "Was the table by the dumpster in the alley unavailable?"

He rolls his eyes. "She wants to introduce you to some of her friends."

Yup. Knew that was coming. My cousin's been trying to return the favor and set me up with someone ever since Erik proposed. "Let me think about it while we play. You do the same," I deadpan.

"Fuck off. This is how I get in the zone," he says.

I smile. "I know, man. I know. Hence, I indulge you."

Erik never talks hockey before a game so we shoot the shit some more till Gianna heads through the stands, coming from one direction, Ryker from the other. Even though he's on the other team, he's joining me over here for the pic, per his agent's orders since the guy is making him do this event with me tonight. I pop up, moving away from Erik and the other guys.

"Our VIP guest has arrived," Gianna says to Ryker and me with a bright smile. "Well, one of them. Her name is Trina and I'll grab her in just a minute. Quick debrief—she's meeting her friend Aubrey here shortly, but we'll do a photo with Trina before the game since she won the tickets. I spoke with the Avengers publicist and Oliver wants you," she says, looking at Ryker, "to lean into the whole *friendly rivalry* thing. Got it?"

Ryker gives a curt nod, but says nothing.

Gianna continues, "Then after the game, you'll both take Trina and her friend to the bar they chose for your favorite thing."

Sex. That's my favorite thing. I don't say that out loud but I fucking think it. "Ping-Pong," I say brightly.

"Pool," Ryker says.

"I meant bar games." Gianna laughs. "Can you two ever agree on anything?"

We look at each other, stony-faced. "Hockey is the best sport," I say.

"But that's about it," Ryker adds, even though the truth is we agree on a ton of things. That you've got to take care of your mom, look out for your little sibs, and play hard for every period, to name a few.

I've known Ryker since we were six and growing up in the same neighborhood in Denver. Our moms were and still are best friends.

But ribbing him is a daily hobby, and I'm devoted to it. Even more so when we face off against each other on the ice. While Gianna retreats to grab our VIP guest, we debate bar games. "Ping-Pong is the best. It's fun, fast, and you can slam the hell out of a tiny white ball," I say, making my case.

"Pool requires strategy," Ryker puts in.

We argue a little more about which hobby rules until a warm, feminine voice lands in my ears, saying, "Pretty sure I'll like both."

I turn to the pretty voice and *shut the fuck up* because...

She's a vision.

A woman with waves of chestnut hair, full red lips,

and a clever smile stands five feet away from us. She wears jeans that hug her hips and cute little ankle boots, along with a Chase Weston jersey and a Ryker Samuels jacket. There's nothing sexier than a woman with my name on her back. Not a teddy. Not a pair of stockings. Nope. My jersey is the hottest thing a woman can wear. She looks damn good in our gear.

Gianna's next to her and makes quick intros. Trina extends her left hand, then quickly switches, offering her right instead.

She's a little awkward, maybe. Which only adds to the instant attraction. After we shake, I nod to her outfit. "You're like a Weston/Samuels sandwich."

She grins, fingering the side of the jacket then the neckline of the jersey. "What do you know? I guess I am. Not a bad look."

"Not at all," Ryker says, and whoa. That's more than I expected to hear from him. He hardly says anything more than *thanks* to fans these days.

But once Ryker says those three words, the beauty swings her gaze from him to me and back again. She has the most curious bright green eyes behind those red cat-eye glasses. I'm such a sucker for eyes.

Then, I blink. Oh, shit. Ryker's staring at her like he can't look away. He thinks she's a smoke show too.

And the great fucking day I'd planned has just been iced.

3

SEX MEAT

Trina

Look, I'm not saying I suddenly like hockey or anything crazy like that. But I definitely don't mind being smushed next to these two big hunks. I mean, fine. There's a lot of gear on them. Shoulder pads and stuff.

But still.

They smell nice.

Is it normal to smell good before a game? No idea, but the bearded one smells like a forest, and the brown-eyed guy reminds me of an ocean breeze.

I inhale them surreptitiously as I smile for the camera, little me wedged between my ex's idols here at the players' bench.

The players' bench.

I am so not going to mind posting this photo on my socials in, oh, say two minutes.

Take that, Jasper.

He's been begging me for the last two weeks to return the VIP tickets. Pleading, crying, and prostrating himself in his pathetic effort to woo them back. But gee, my phone just seems to be broken. It refuses to answer his calls, texts, or emails.

Imagine that.

I'll be sure to tag him in these pics shortly though.

Gianna snaps a few more photos on her phone, then I hand her my phone, too, and return to my spot between the rivals. They sling their arms around me again.

And again, I don't mind one bit. Ryker's arm is so big. Chase's too. Strong arms are just extra *nice*.

"Perfect," Gianna declares when she's done, then holds up a finger. "But let me just check and make sure they'll work."

As Gianna busies herself swiping the screen, the guy with the killer smile turns to me. "So, who's your favorite player, Trina? I'm guessing since you're wearing a Weston jersey that it's me," Chase says, all charm and great teeth. He's friendlier than I'd expected him to be. I'd figured a couple of pampered athletes would just smile plastically for the camera, since they're doing this out of obligation, then focus their attention on the game, no conversation allowed.

I return his smile with one of my own. "Is that a requirement? That I have a favorite?" I ask playfully.

"Nope. But it's likely you will when you see me play." Someone is confident.

But Ryker scoffs.

I turn to him, curious. "Does that mean you think you'll be my favorite instead?"

He scratches his jaw, a little aloof. "I don't play to make favorites. I play to win," he says with a careless shrug, but he's not aloof with his stare, aimed right at me. His dark blue eyes are smoldering with their intensity. With a promise of what's to come.

In the game? On the ice? Or after when we all play... Ping-Pong?

I'm not sure, but it seems like it'd be fun to wind him up. "Then maybe we should make a bet. If you're both my favorite players after the game, I'll buy a round. But it's going to take a lot of convincing," I warn, then shrug casually, ready to surprise these guys with this little nugget. I lean in and whisper, "It's my first time...at a hockey game."

Chase whistles. "Fuck favorite players. We have a bigger mission now for your *virgin* game," he says, a little flirty. "We're gonna make sure hockey is your new favorite sport."

I arch a doubtful brow then say, "Good luck."

There's no way I plan on falling for either team, or for my ex's favorite game for that matter. Still, I have a full night of revenge gloating ahead of me, and I plan to savor every second here at the arena and with these two guys.

"Drinks are on us when you're convinced, and you'll definitely be convinced," Chase adds, full of athlete bravado.

Ryker rolls his eyes at the other guy. "Dickhead, drinks *are* on us. It's part of the VIP package," he says, and this bearded brute might as well have G-R-U-M-P written on his jersey.

But he's not wrong. "You make a very good point too," I say sweetly to Ryker, since grumps don't scare me.

The man's brow knits, like he's taken aback by my comment. That's fun, his reaction.

"I mean, details matter, right?" I add with a smile.

His forehead gets even tighter. "Yeah. They do," he grumbles, but his lips twitch, like he's fighting off a grin.

Ha. I've defused the big bad grump some. Yay me.

"Speaking of good points and details, I'll be expecting a full report over drinks, Trina," Chase says, cutting in and taking over. "Every detail on how *I* convinced you hockey is the best."

I tap my temple and say, "Don't worry. I'll take copious notes for later."

"And we'll have a full review then, Trina," he says, pausing at my name, almost like he's enjoying the way it tastes on his tongue.

That's unexpected, the ramp up. And I don't have a comeback this time. Especially since both men are looking at me with competitive fire in their eyes.

For a few seconds, I feel a little wobbly under the heat of their stares. Like I'm the unexpected object of their desires. But there's no way they'd both be staring at me like that. I've probably read too many books. I'm likely imagining the flames in their irises, mistaking their drive to win for, well, a drive for something else.

Besides, they probably just want to prove their dicks

are bigger than the next guy's. "I can't wait for the full review," I say.

"I can't either," Chase says, then shakes my hand, sealing our bet. As our palms connect, warmth licks my veins again. I'm not sure what to make of this sensation skimming through me. I'm in an icy arena. I should be shivering.

Instead, I'm borderline sweating.

"The pics look great. You guys nailed the friendly rivals brief," Gianna says, interrupting my thoughts and my tingles.

I snap my gaze to her and she's waving, beckoning me over. I let go of Chase's hand, perhaps a little reluctantly. "See you guys later," I say to my VIP hosts.

But before I go, Ryker reaches for my hand, only he doesn't shake it again. He surprises the hell out of me when he drops a whiskery kiss to the top of my knuckles.

"Oh," I say as he lingers just a little bit, and I'm tingling all over again. What the hell is going on with me?

Then he lets go and holds my gaze once more with those midnight blue eyes that look even darker than they did a few minutes ago.

I do my best to not dwell on that whole interaction that ran the gamut from grumpy to cocky to bossy to flirty.

Time to focus on my mission for the night.

Photos.

I have so many more photos to take. Because revenge is the best way to get over an ex.

Even though I have to sit through a hockey game to get there.

* * *

There's stuff happening on the ice. Like big men in bulky uniforms jumping over the boards and flying really fast on blades that look like knives.

I peer at the game from the VIP suite high above the action, where Aubrey and I are enjoying sparkling wine and stuffed mushrooms. We already devoured cauliflower tacos and mini beef wellington bites. The food is ridiculously good, but I'm still in awe of the way they wear those skates. "How do they move on those things, Aub? That is going to be at the top of my list to ask the guys tonight."

It's a bummer Aubrey won't be with me for the VIP hang, but she has an "emergency blowout" tomorrow morning at the unholy hour of seven. She's a hair stylist and one of her clients has a Saturday morning TV appearance.

My bestie lifts her wine, her brown eyes twinkling with doubt. "That's on the top of your list?"

"Yes," I say. "I tried figure skating once and my ankles punished me the next day by screaming in pain. I believe it was a warning that exercise is dangerous, and I do best with light strolls and long savasanas."

"Girl, I think the top of your list of questions for tonight will be...which one of them is going to fight off the other for a piece of you?" She sets down her wine to waggle her phone at me.

"What are you talking about?"

She stabs a polished pink fingernail, decorated with silver bling hearts, on the screen. "Look at the pics we posted."

I scoot closer and peer again at a shot of the guys and me, and *hmm*. She has a point. There's a little smolder there, but still. "I bet that's just a look they teach athletes in smile-for-the-camera school. *Look hot and hot for the fans* I believe is the lesson."

"Sure, the muscles and the million-dollar contracts bump up the hotness factor. But look again."

Fine, Chase does seem to be stealing a glance at me out of the corner of his eye. And Ryker's hand *is* curled tightly around my shoulder. Possessively. "Cameras are funny," I say, a little surprised at what it's revealing.

"Yeah, they're funny how they capture the animals in their native habitat, Trina. They're both staring at you like lions."

"So they want to devour me as prey?"

"Um, yeah," she says.

"And rip me to shreds?" I ask, egging her on.

"To pieces of sex meat," she says salaciously, then burps, which cracks her up to no end. She slaps her phone-covered hand to her mouth. "Oh my god. I've had too much sparkling wine."

I pour her a glass of water from the table next to us and hand her the cup. "No more fancy suite wine for you. No more talk of sex meat. Water, good; sex meat, bad."

"And hockey? Mildly okay?" she asks after she takes a sip.

Right. There's a game going on. I *should* watch it. But I've already learned hockey is super fun in a private suite when they give you buffets of fancy food and fabulous wine.

On the ice, someone with a number fourteen Sea Dogs jersey—ooh, that's Chase Panty-Melting-Smile Weston—races across the blue line. But when he passes the little black disc to another Sea Dog, out of nowhere, Hot Bearded Avenger flies in front of him. Whoa. He whips that puck the other way, sending it screaming down the rink.

I hoot, thrusting an arm in the air, but I don't know who's the good guy and who's the bad guy. Ryker? Chase? "Go...um? Who are we rooting for, Aub?"

"The snack men," she declares, with a salacious lick of her lips. "And also...you. A badass babe who will not be fucked with by losers like dickless Jasper."

I sling an arm around her. "You're the true badass babe. Thanks again for letting me stay with you. I'm going to find a place really soon."

She waves a dismissive hand. "You're welcome to stay as long as you need," she says, but there are real nerves in her voice. She lives in a tiny apartment in a building that isn't entirely dog-friendly.

"I can move back in with my parents or...my sister," I say, nearly choking on that last thought since my sister, Cassie, recently went into full pregnant-zilla mode, planning her upcoming baby shower and maternity leave, while my high school sweetheart parents have suggested each day since I left Jasper that *they* help me find a great new guy I can settle down with and make babies too. Like, tomorrow.

No thanks. I just want to make rent. But I don't want to inconvenience Aubrey and her anti-canine landlord. "I'm sure Cassie would let me stay in her guest room," I offer with a wince, since of course my uber successful interior designer sister has both a fully decorated nursery in gender-neutral pale yellow colors, as well as an extra bedroom, neatly appointed with a flower bedspread and hand towels. She also has a long list of ideas for my life, since I *clearly* need her help to get my career going and reach my full potential as working at a bookstore can't possibly be my endgame.

Aubrey cringes. "Wash your mouth out with soap. You will do no such thing, Trina Beaumont."

Thank god she said that. "I don't deserve you."

"No one does, but I still love you. And that means... can I be the first to hold up the sign?"

Yes! The signs. "Do it."

She reaches for the cardboard signs we made last night and hands one to me. She holds up hers, so everyone can see. I do the same.

It takes a while, but after a few minutes, fans in the stands crane their necks, point, laugh, and snap pics.

Soon enough, the jumbotron operator must notice because our signs are flashing across the big screen in the arena during a time-out.

Aubrey's says: *Hey, cheating ex.*

Mine reads: *How do you like your hockey tickets now?*

Down by the players' benches, Number Fourteen

tugs up his helmet and stares up at our suite, then laughs deeply. Captain Bossy.

The possessive bearded guy on the other team cracks a small smile. I bet that's rare for Mister Grumpy.

I grin, feeling a little victorious in my sweet revenge.

I'm not saying it takes the sting and the heartache away. I still feel stupid. I still have zero interest in ever getting involved with a guy ever again, pretty much for time immemorial.

But tonight? I feel good, and that has to count for something in the healing process.

* * *

When Aubrey leaves at the end of the game with the Sea Dogs winning, she gives me a big hug and whispers, "Have so much fun tonight with those hotties. And don't do anything I wouldn't do."

"Like, what? Burp wine? Oh, wait—you did that."

"Don't do that. But do make them fight for you. Rawr." She makes claws with her hands. Or tries to at least.

I'm so glad she's taking a Lyft home. Glad, too, I only had one glass tonight.

She's off and I'm heading to meet Gianna, who escorts me to just outside the locker room where the two hockey studs wait for me.

When I reach them, she says a quick hello and goodbye, and I just stare stupidly. They're no longer in their uniforms. They're both wearing tailored, trim suits that hug strong butts and snuggle firm arms.

And...whoa. Those thighs.

Chase's are so obviously toned and muscular in those charcoal pants. And Ryker's are bigger and thicker in his midnight blue slacks that match his eyes.

Did I just discover I'm a thighs woman? I didn't know that about myself till just now. *But hello, strong legs. I like you. Both pairs of legs.*

But more importantly, why did no one tell me hockey players wear suits after games?

That is information I would have liked to know before now. Suits are kind of my thing. Well, I've read a lot of billionaire romances.

"Nice suits," I say, recovering from my too-long gawk at last as I stand in the long, chilly hallway at the Sea Dogs arena.

"Are we going to your corner office in a skyscraper overlooking the city?"

Chase smirks. "We can go wherever you want."

Is it hot in here all of a sudden or what?

4

TOTAL BALLER MOVE

Ryker

I hate this shit. More than I hate when someone writes *could of* instead of *could have*.

But there are worse things than a sloppy *they're* or *their*.

Like, say, PR events. Followed by press interviews after games I've lost. And topped by fan meet-and-greets that are actually more like probation for being bad.

Don't get me wrong—I love fans. But I detest public appearances.

I blame my ex Selena, who soured me for the press for all time. Which means I don't like the media or anything related to it. Like...*tonight.*

Trouble is, my agent said I need to be nicer.

Outside the locker room before a game last month, Josh's exact words were, "Lately, you've been coming across like a world-class asshole in the press. Maybe use your words once in a while rather than acting like a caveman. It helps the team. It helps the public image. It helps, gasp, *you*. And your family."

That night, when hockey reporter Bryce Tucker asked me to talk about how I felt after a bad tripping call, I used my words all right. One word. I said, "Shit-tastic."

And I stalked out of the pressroom.

Trouble is that sneaky fucker turned my comment around, reporting that I had called the officials *shit-tastic*. And then he dubbed me the King of Grunts. That was fun.

The Avengers PR guy, Oliver, called Josh, and Josh told me I needed to work on my rep, stat, starting by doing a fan event with the star of the Sea Dogs when we played our enemies on the ice, and ending with a photo op with the same VIP winner at the Hockey Hotties calendar kickoff a few weeks after that. "It's the fastest way to show you're not a dick. By consorting with the rival."

I believe my words to Josh were *kill me now*.

But Chase loves fan events. Chase loves the press. Chase loves everything. Hell, the Golden Retriever even loved high school, and no one loves high school.

So, here I am, slapping on my smile as I hold open the door to the limo for the woman we're entertaining tonight. "After you..."

I trail off because I don't remember her name. Guess I am an asshole.

"Trina," Chase corrects with an eye roll, sliding into the limo right behind her.

Dick.

Besides, I thought some hardcore fan named Jasper won the tix. That was what Oliver told me a couple weeks ago, so I was expecting an amateur hockey analyst type to show up at the bench for the pre-game photo op, giving me super-useful advice, like "Dude! Why didn't you get that goal in the second period in the game the other night? I totally could have gotten that goal. Shoulda skated faster."

But I didn't expect a woman who's *fit.*

A woman I stared at for far too long before, during, and after that photo shoot, so much so that I didn't pay attention when Gianna said her name.

But damn, as she scoots into the limo, takes off her jacket, and sits in the back seat, Trina's hard to look away from with that heart-shaped face and those cat-eye red glasses. Is that a tiny cherry drawing on the frame? That's adorable and sexy at the same time. Translation: my downfall.

Plus, she's got a spray of freckles across her nose. And don't even get me started on those pretty lips.

Except, I fell for Selena right away because of her looks. Where did that get me? Getting crushed by a woman who stabbed me in the back and slashed my heart.

Relationships suck. Romance is a lie. The human race is doomed. Case closed.

But I suppose Josh is right. Can't hurt for me to be *un-surly* now and then. *Un-surly* pays the bills much better than surly does, and that helps me take care of my mom and sisters—something I intend to do always. I will never put my mom in a position where she has to make hard choices ever again.

"Trina's a nice name," I mutter, but I'm not sure she hears since she's busy whipping her head back and forth, seemingly hunting for the seat belt. Then, she finds it as I take the long seat along the side of the stretch limo.

"I didn't expect to see this," she says, strangely delighted at the presence of a...seat belt. She doesn't put it on though. Just kind of regards it. "I didn't think limos had seat belts."

"They weren't required to for a long time," I answer.

That piques her interest. Tilting her head, she asks, "How did they get out of that before? Having a seat belt?"

I strip off my suit jacket and set it on the leather seat. "Technically, a stretch limo was considered a bus for a long time. If it seated more than ten people, or had backward-facing or sideway-facing seats, it was a bus."

"Even if it didn't quack like a bus?" Chase counters.

"But the California Seat Belt Law came along, so here we are," I say, not taking his joke bait.

Trina looks at me like I'm an oddity found in a parlor of the weird. "How do you know the California Seat Belt Law?"

"Looked it up when I got my youngest sister a limo for prom a few years ago. Had to make sure Katie and all her friends were safe, even if the guys they went

with were little shits," I say, shaking my head in remembered annoyance.

"Why were they little shits?" Trina asks. She can't
stop asking questions. Maybe she's a secret reporter.
Ah, hell. I really hope she's not.

I stare her down. "Are you actually a reporter?" I
ask, not answering her question. "Because you ask a lot
of questions."

"Dude. Settle down. She's not a reporter. And don't
be such a sore loser," Chase chides.

I narrow my eyes. "You hate losing too."

"No shit. But not the point. Anyway, *Trina* works at a
bookstore."

How does he know that? Also, *cool*. "Yeah? Which
one?" I ask, intrigued.

"At An Open Book over on Fillmore," she says, a
little defensively. "I'm a manager there."

Love that store. Frequent it a lot. But I'm not gonna
tell her. I don't want to let on that I *am* an oddity. The
defenseman who got all A's in school. Who listens to
grammar and word podcasts. Who reads all sorts of
fascinating shit on how the world works.

I had to do that. I didn't know if hockey would pay
the bills, and I needed a way to take care of my mom
and sisters.

"And while I may not be a reporter, I am just naturally curious. I'm an investigator. And I bet you're the
challenger."

Great. She's one of those personality-test people.
Which means she's a people person. Which means
she'll try to actually understand why I'm a such-and-

such personality. Which means she'll want to know who fucked me up as a kid.

Like I'm going to tell anyone about my dad.

Easier just to answer her question. "Here you go. Teenage boys are little shits because they're horny bastards. Like the guy who took my sister to prom and stared at her chest the whole time."

Chase drops his head in his hand, laughing. "I remember him. You called him Boner Boy."

"He always had a pillow on his lap when he came over," I grumble.

"Well, at least he was trying," Trina says, seeming to fight off a smile.

Chase raises his face. "Also, not all teenage boys are little shits. My little brothers aren't," Chase says, pride in his tone. He looks out for those turkeys like they're his own.

"But I bet they're horny for all the girls. And you've had to give them the 'no means no' and consent talks," I point out, since his dad isn't around to do that either, though for vastly different reasons than mine.

"Well, Jackson is gay, so he's not horny for teenage girls."

"I know, man. But you get my point," I say, exasperated, turning to our VIP guest. "I just don't trust anyone around my little sisters. Ergo, the seat belt law."

"I don't think a seat belt was the protection they needed at prom," Trina stage whispers.

Cracking up, Chase offers her a hand to high-five.

Clenching my jaw, I yank my seat belt as hard as I

can and put it on. "Put yours on too," I bark at my friend.

With his charming smile that wins over fans, women, and reporters, Chase pats Trina's shoulder. "Don't worry about him. He has the manners of a Rottweiler. But I can translate Ryker speak. What he means to say is, '*I'm secretly a softie and I don't want a thing to happen to you especially while you're out with us, so would you please put your seat belt on?*'"

With an amused shake of her head, Trina complies. "Only because Captain Bossy asked nicely," she says to Chase, flashing him a cute grin.

I look away.

"We have nicknames already? Nice. Also, accurate." Chase rubs his palms together, then points to me. "What's his? Please tell me it's Big Bad Wolf."

She lifts her chin a little defiantly as she stares me down, just like I did to her a few minutes ago. "It's Mister Grumpy, but I think Big Bad Wolf works too."

Her boldness is fuck hot too. This is a problem. "Yes, yes it does," I say, staying stone-faced. I tip my chin at Chase. "You too, golden boy. Put it on."

With a sigh, Chase takes off his suit jacket and tugs on the seat belt. "Sure thing...Big Bad Wolf."

Then I tap on the glass and tell the driver to take us to Sticks and Stones, a bar with pool, Ping-Pong and other games. It's the place Jasper picked—which reminds me...As the car cruises through the arena's players' lot, I turn to Trina. "You still want to go there? Some dude named Jasper picked it."

She grins a little wickedly. That's annoying. She's

too damn pretty when she smiles like that, kind of devilishly. "I actually picked it. Jasper asked me for suggestions. And it was my idea since I want to learn how to play both. They sound like fun, and I've been dying to give them a try," she says. "His only idea was to go to a strip club with you two."

I sneer. "Like I said, *little shit*."

Chase snorts. "That'd have been a no."

"Also, that's weak," I add. "Does this Jasper have zero creativity?"

She squares her shoulders. "Considering he banged our neighbor in our bed while I was working, I'd have to say yes, he lacks any and all creativity. I mean, try a little harder, right? Maybe get a room, or get creative and go to, I dunno, Target and pull her into a dressing room or something. Right?" she says, so clearly trying to stay strong and tough, but I can tell it still hurts. Instantly, I hate him even more than I did already. More than I hate the shit-tastic Bryce Tucker, AKA Pompous Fuckface.

"You want us to fuck him up?" I crack my knuckles, ready and willing.

That earns me my first real laugh from her.

"Because we will," Chase says, jumping in. Gone is the charm from his voice. He's all business now, ready to send a message if he has to. "Just say the word."

Trina blinks, then lets out a surprised breath. "Tempting, but I'll pass. Appreciate the thought though," she says as the car weaves into traffic.

"The offer stands. Any time," I add, then scratch my jaw. "But how'd you get his tickets for the game?"

Trina smiles like an Internet meme for the word *sneaky*. "He's obsessed with hockey. You're both his favorite players. So I swiped the VIP tix he won after I caught him cheating. I sent him out of the house, making him think I was forgiving him and just needed some time to cry alone before he came back. Instead, I packed up all my stuff and my dog so I could crash with my bestie, and on the way out I grabbed the bag of jerseys and pucks I bought—as a surprise to him—to have signed by you two. I wasn't going to let him give any bit of gear to his new woman. And as I was about to take off, I spotted the tickets on his nightstand," she says with a wicked glint in those green eyes. "I took them too. The pièce de résistance, as they say."

Damn. I don't want to like her, but...that's just ballsy. "How'd you learn he was the biggest fuckhead in the universe?"

She straightens her shoulders, like she needs to be tough. "My dog ate the other woman's underwear."

Chase's jaw drops, then he points. "Oh, shit. I saw the vet's video. You're the woman with the dog underwear."

And I'm cracking up. So is Trina. We're laughing like loons in the limo.

"Pretty sure it wasn't *dog underwear*, Weston," I correct in between breaths.

With a wince, Chase realizes his error, but then he grins. "Your dog probably doesn't wear underwear. But if he does, that's okay. No judgment." He holds up his hands and looks Trina's way. "Freedom of expression and all."

"My dog does *not* wear underwear. He only has an appetite for it," she says primly.

"But does he wear *other* clothes?" Chase asks.

As Trina tells him about some tartan jacket the dog has for foggy mornings, then whips out her phone to presumably show him the pics, I'm thinking about how she stole Jasper's memorabilia and his tickets, then came to the game and slapped up a sign. And she did it all classy and shit. She didn't reveal who he was. Just his crime. Brilliant revenge. She's smart, and there's nothing hotter than a woman's brain.

I stroke my chin. Then I meet her gaze, and when there's a break in the discussion of dog sartorial choices, I say, "What you did tonight at the game with the signs..."

Her eyes widen with worry. Like I'm about to get on her case for lambasting a straying man when I am not at all. So I quickly add, "It was a total baller move."

She dips her face, maybe a tiny bit shy over the praise. Great. Just great. That's sexy too—the way she's got a bit of a shy side to go with her outgoing, badass personality.

Don't get any ideas. Don't start thinking about taking her out. Nope. She's just a fan and that's all.

I reach across the seat and offer a fist for bumping. There. She's just a fan, not a cutie I want to take home, strip down to nothing, and lick everywhere till she's begging for more. All night long.

She bumps back.

Not to be left out, Chase joins in, the three of us knocking together.

When Trina lets go, she leans back into her seat, but she doesn't seem as playful as she was seconds ago. Or as saucy. Maybe she's thinking about her jerk of an ex.

And that won't do at all. "Trina, we're going to help you make him regret every single second of hurting you." I shift my gaze to my buddy. "Isn't that right, Weston?"

Chase nods, his expression intensely serious, like he is on the ice. "We fucking are."

Trina smiles again, and my chest feels a little strange when she does that. A little good. "I'm liking hockey more and more," she says.

"You'll love it by the end of the night," Chase says, then flashes that winning smile her way again.

Oh, shit.

I know that smile.

That smile is so damn dangerous.

That's his *I like a girl* smile.

And I need to shut down any more inappropriate thoughts of her, stat.

Chase's my guy. He's been there for me since we were kids. He was there when my dad spiraled into the bottle when I was in grade school, when Dad came home drunk and mean, then when he messed around with anyone in a skirt, till my mom—who felt terrifyingly dependent on him—finally kicked him out. Likewise, I was there for Chase when he was in college and his dad—his hero, his idol—died after a long illness.

There's no way I'm ever letting a girl come between us again. Once was enough and it damn near killed me.

As much as it pains me, I don't even look at Trina when we reach the bar and get out of the limo.

And it's painful because I'm desperate to stare at her smackable ass.

But I don't. Instead, I pull Chase aside for a few seconds and tell him my plan for the night.

"Hell yes," he says.

Glad we're in agreement on that. I just wish we weren't in such obvious unspoken agreement over how delicious our VIP guest clearly is to both of us.

And I know we're going to have to deal with that problem very, very soon.

5

TELL US EVERYTHING

Trina

Look, Ryker's still an asshole.

And Chase's definitely still a playboy charmer.

But Chase also seems like a legit good guy.

And Ryker's not quite the jerk I'd thought he was three hours ago. Or twenty minutes ago in the limo either.

My reassessment is partly because I've just learned he's got a soft spot under that gruff exterior. A desire to make things right.

And so does Chase.

But partly because I think I've seen Ryker before. I'm not positive, but if memory serves, a certain burly, bearded, inked guy likes to buy stacks and stacks of game books and crossword puzzles every few weeks at An Open Book.

When I mentioned my store, I swear he perked up.

That led me to cycle back through the memory banks of where I'd seen him before, and yup. Figured it out quickly. He's a loyal customer.

But then he shut down the book talk, so maybe his book buying fetish is a secret.

It's safe with me.

Once we reach the doors of Sticks and Stones, he turns to me, stopping before we go inside and guiding me to the left so we're chatting just outside the closed coffee shop next door.

"Here's the deal. Chase and I just talked about it, and you've got an endless supply of revenge selfies at your service tonight. Even a revenge video if you want to shoot us playing pool or whatever. Anything to make that good-for-nothing shitcake suffer."

"Aww, you really feel bad for forgetting my name earlier," I say, patting his arm through his white dress shirt.

Oops. Rookie mistake. That rock of a muscle feels real nice.

"I didn't forget it," he grumbles, but he doesn't elaborate, and I decide to let it go since, seriously. These guys are going above and beyond in the *getting even* department.

"Thank you, Ryker," I say genuinely, meeting his dark blue gaze. "I appreciate your zeal for payback."

"I'm not an Avenger for nothing," he says.

I look to Chase on the other side of me. "And thank you. It's more than I could have asked for."

"Happy to do it," he says. "I'm just glad we're spending the evening with you instead of him."

The funny thing is...so am I. I'm having a better time than I'd imagined, and I'm about to head inside when Ryker clears his throat. "But that's not all. Chase had an idea for what to do with the gifts you got for him. The jerseys and pucks."

Well, bring it on boys. "My ears are wide open," I say, turning to the golden guy.

"Why don't I get the Sea Dogs jersey signed by the whole team and Ryker will get the Avengers one signed by his team. Then we can set up an auction and donate the proceeds to a cause you like? Like rescue dogs or something?" Chase suggests, and I'm launching myself at him before he can finish.

"Revenge for charity! I love it!"

He wraps his arms around me, one that has me *almost* drawing another yummy inhale of him. But I don't want to overstep and go all pervy on him, so I keep the hug nice and chaste, then give Ryker one too. "You're not such a big bad wolf after all," I say.

He grumbles something I can't understand before I let go.

Don't want to push the grumpster, so I go inside.

We head to the counter, and I stare up at the list of games on a chalkboard. Shuffleboard, Ping-Pong, pool, darts and cornhole. Chase steps closer, bumping his shoulder to mine. I don't know if that was on purpose, but I like the feel of him so close to me. "So, what'll it be, Miss Book Babe?"

I blink, surprised. "Did you just give me a pet name?"

Chase's grin is all kinds of cocky. "You gave us nick-names. Only fair. And it seems fitting," he says.

"Was Miss Bookalicious taken, Weston?" Ryker asks his friend dryly.

Before they can get into a bidding war over it, I cut in with, "What if I want to pick my own nickname?"

Ryker shakes his head. "Nope. Rules of nicknames. You picked ours. We get to pick yours."

"But you can't agree on one for me!"

"I haven't even gone yet."

"Go. Now," I say, sweeping out a hand to give Ryker the floor.

He doesn't give in to my demand right away. He takes a deep breath, then, with a smirk, he declares, "Miss Inquisitive."

Damn. That's good. It's parallel with my names for them. With a huff, I narrow my eyes, a little annoyed he nailed it.

Ryker smirks. "That's what I thought."

"What's what you thought?"

"You like it," he says, and he's cocky too.

Chase flashes me a crooked grin. "Yeah, I think you do," he says, then steps a little closer, and takes his time saying in that smooth, deep voice, "Miss Inquisitive..." After a deliberate pause, he adds, his tone even swoonier, "The Book Babe."

I fight off a tremble. I feel almost surrounded by them.

Ryker lifts a brow. He noticed the shiver. Dammit. He turns to Chase. "A combo. Looks like we have a winner."

"And it fits," Chase says.

The name is bookish and kind of sexy, and I'm hoping that means he thinks I *am* sexy.

But wait. Which...*he* do I hope thinks I'm hot?

The trouble is I don't know. Is it both? But I didn't swipe those tickets hoping a couple of pro athletes would fight over me. And yet, here I am, enjoying the spotlight. Maybe even enjoying the twin focus on me. I can't blame the one glass of wine. Maybe I just like their attention after Jasper's attention strayed.

That has to be it.

That's all. No big deal. This is normal post-breakup stuff. I'm allowed to enjoy it, I'm sure.

I break from my thoughts as Chase gestures to the chalkboard. "Now, tell us which game you want to play first. As long as it's Ping-Pong."

Hmm. This is a tougher choice than I'd expect. Especially since Ryker clears his throat and says, "It's ladies choice. You said you might like both. You get to pick," he says, showing off that he remembers what I said earlier.

I tap my chin, considering Ping-Pong, Chase's favorite, and pool, Ryker's choice. Whichever one I pick will send a signal. Like I'm picking one guy over the other when both are helping me immensely. Before I can decide, Chase leans an elbow on the counter and meets my gaze. "Actually, I'm wrong. Pool is better for our plan."

That's not at all what I'd thought he'd say. "Why?"

"We want to make that asshole suffer, right? You said we're his favorite players. So let's make him really fucking jealous. Because pool is sexier," he says, and his smile is gone. It's replaced by a dark stare with those deep brown eyes that feel like they're...undressing me.

I shiver, enjoying the eye fucking. I even like the charm. I won't be fooled by it, but oh boy, do I ever like it, especially when he adds, "You said you wanted to learn how to play. We'll teach you."

I can picture the scene. Me stretching out against the pool table. Chase behind me, showing me how to line up a shot. Ryker coming around to the other side of me, adjusting my hips just so.

My chest flutters at the images racing through my brain. Images that are sexier than I'd expected them to be. Naughtier. Images of two men touching me at the same time.

The image makes no sense though. Who'd take the picture if they were both showing me how to play?

No idea, but maybe I don't care about the picture at all. I want to play pool with these two hockey hotties instead.

I don't let on though. They don't need to know that yet. "Let's rack 'em up," I say.

Ryker lifts his beer bottle and knocks some back, then sets it on a ledge next to the pool table.

With a serious stare, he regards the array of pool balls on green felt—most are mine—then tugs on his tie a little more.

Chase doesn't wear a tie.

I can't decide which look I like better—tie or no tie. "All right, you're gonna want to hit the purple ball," Ryker says decisively.

"Easy enough," I say dryly, because of course it's not. I haven't played much but I know pool is ridiculously hard. I'm determined to knock at least one ball in *not* by accident.

Which means I need a little help.

"You can do it," Chase says brightly, then comes around the table, moving next to me, his pool cue in one hand. "Let me show you." He nods across the table to his rival.

"Ryker, you want to take pics for her socials?"

Ryker nods and tilts his phone in the air. "On it."

"Then it's showtime." Setting down the stick, Chase unbuttons the cuffs of his shirt, taking his time rolling up his right sleeve, and revealing his strong forearm.

Then the other.

Mmm.

Wait, did I just purr?

I think I did.

Evidently, I'm learning all sorts of things about myself tonight. Namely, that I like thighs and forearms, as well as grumps and cocky charmers.

Speaking of, Chase moves behind me. He's not touching me. *Yet.* But his broad chest is mere inches from my back. His breath is dangerously close to my ear. His scent swirls past my nose.

He smells like the ocean, like I noticed before the game. It's a little stronger now though, probably from his post-game shower.

Ohh.

Hello, shower images.

My breath catches as I picture him under the stream of water.

Or is my breath catching from him moving a little closer? "First you need to line up the stick," he says in his smooth, deep voice that sends sparks down my spine.

I swallow, maybe to cover up the tingles. "Okay." I lift the pool cue in my right hand and slide it back, the end of it brushing over my left hand, splayed on the felt.

He inches closer, then wraps an arm around me. I'm caged in by this big man. I look down at our hands, Chase's coming around to adjust the cue. His hands are so much bigger than mine, and I'm flying ten steps ahead, picturing his hands on my arms, my waist, my legs.

I need to concentrate. Chase and Ryker aren't here to seduce me. They're here to help me get even.

A cause I hardly care about anymore.

I should try to care, so I lift my face, only to find Ryker's watching us from across the table, his eyes gleaming darkly. His camera's still pointed at Chase and me, but he doesn't look at the screen—it's like he can't stop staring at the action in front of him. Perhaps he's jealous. Or restrained. Maybe he's holding back.

But what? What's he holding back?

I don't know. I can barely focus even as Chase whispers more instructions in my ear. How to hold the stick, how to slide it back, how to hit the ball.

I can't think because he's so close to me, and Ryker is so intent on watching *us*, and my thoughts are racing wildly out of control. Maybe Ryker will come help too. Maybe he'll give me a tip. God, did all my feminism just fly out the door? Since suddenly I want two big men to teach me how to play a bar game, when dammit, I can learn on my own. I mean, there are books. *In my store.* And YouTube tutorials. And...

And...

And I still want them both to *show me* how to play.

Get it together, girl.

I yank back the cue, then slam it against the cue ball.

And it whacks the purple one with a loud and satisfying thwack, sending the ball speeding down the felt.

Right into the corner pocket.

Holy shit! I did it! "Hole in one!" I shout.

Both guys cheer, and I spin around and Chase is hugging me, and Ryker is right there too, offering a high five when I let go. I take it, then roll my eyes. "Gimme more than a high five," I say.

His jaw ticks, like he's debating it.

"C'mon, give Miss Inquisitive a hug. It won't hurt you," Chase goads.

Ryker stares at him like he wants to rip his head off, but then comes in for a hug and wraps his big, strong arms around me.

I draw a furtive inhale of Ryker. That forest scent makes me a little buzzy. A lot hot.

So does his beard. It whisks against my cheek. How would that beard feel in other places?

Like...between my thighs.

The answer comes astonishingly fast and in the form of an ache. *Good.* It would feel so good.

When he lets go, I slap on my best smile. "Should we keep playing?" I ask, and I hope my voice doesn't sound as husky as it does to my ears.

As revealing.

I bet these studs have women throwing themselves at them all the time. I don't want to be a groupie or a cliché.

I've got to stop fantasizing about the VIP experience I suddenly crave from the two of them devoted to me.

We finish out the game. News flash—I lose.

We play another game, and as we go, I try valiantly to return to the purpose of this night—making Jasper jealous.

I lift my beer, take a swallow, then set it down. "Jasper the dickless would lose his mind to be playing pool with the two of you."

Chase laughs. "Tell us more of the awful things your terrible ex did," he says. "This is your night."

"Yeah, let it all out," Ryker adds.

Well, there is one really terrible thing Jasper did. Besides *that*. Maybe it's the beer, maybe it's the company, and maybe it's my residual anger. Or maybe I just want to move the hell on for one night. "He was awful at sex."

You could hear a pin drop.

6

LICK SHOOT SUCK

Trina

Chase's jaw drops.

Ryker hisses.

"How the fuck does that happen?" Chase asks.

Um. I don't know. I honestly have no idea. "Not sure."

Ryker breathes fire. "How does he live with himself?"

"He should be ashamed," Chase adds, then gestures to a nearby booth. "We need something strong for this kind of horror story."

"Tequila time," Ryker remarks, then waves down a server and orders a round of shots.

When the server leaves, Ryker slides in the booth after me. It's circular, so he's on one side of me, Chase the other.

Shortly, the server brings three shots on a wooden board, complete with the accessories—salt and lime.

In tandem we lick, shoot, and suck.

My lungs burn and my mouth is on fire, but I'm filled with righteous energy. I'm ready to spill my own tea.

Chase breathes out hard, nodding resolutely. "All right. All the Stephen King I've listened to has prepared me for this moment." He stabs his finger against the wood of the table. "Right now. Bring on the horror story."

I don't usually kiss and tell. No one has ever asked, and I don't have a lot of ex-boyfriends. Just a couple others besides Jasper. I went out with a musician in college. Colin was cool and laid-back, and worked out as a sort of starter boyfriend. But after college, he moved to New York. Then, I met a sculptor on the apps and he was a lot of fun, and a lot of drama, so we burned out quickly.

Jasper came next and my family loved the outgoing guy with the dependable office job as a marketing manager. Jasper was great with my parents and wonderful with my older sister, practically wooing all of them with his *life plan* to settle down, have me move in, then get a house. I swear the night he met my parents they could see *more* diaper changing in their near future and were high on the imagined scent of baby powder in their dreams. After all, I'd been the flighty one, the wild teenager turned aimless adult who did impulsive things like adopt a three-legged dog when I happened to walk past a Little Friends adoption event in the park one random afternoon. "Can you even take care of a dog with four legs, let alone three?" Cassie had asked me when I brought Nacho home a year ago.

To prove her wrong, I enrolled him in dog agility classes, and we're entering our first competition in a month.

But Jasper was the real proof I was getting my shit together. There I was, with a stable guy, doing what my parents had done. What Cassie was doing. Hot mess no more, they'd figured.

"He's a good one. Be sure to keep him," Cassie told me the night she met him.

So, I moved in with Jasper when he asked me to. He was funny enough, and reliable enough, and he liked to cook with me. So what if he lost his mind when hockey came on TV, and so what if the sex was mediocre?

Jasper said I never relaxed in bed. That I just needed to let go and I'd finally enjoy myself.

Was he right? Maybe Ryker and Chase can answer that question for me. Tonight is for no bullshit. I draw a deep breath. Here goes nothing. "I mean, sex itself was fine," I begin, because it was good enough, I guess. It just wasn't exciting.

Ryker snorts. "Fine is for a plain bagel when there's no everything bagel available. Fine is a trip to the bank with no traffic. Fine is not for sex."

"Sex should be outstanding," Chase says, like he's making a speech before the whole damn land. "It should blow your brains out. It should make you forget your fucking name." Blow-your-brains-out sex sounds great in theory. But in reality? I just don't know. Maybe it's only for books. "So, what was the problem?"

He seems enrapt, deeply concerned by my sex woes. It's kind of sweet.

But I'm still a little embarrassed. Maybe the average sex *was* my fault. "I never had an orgasm through oral. Foreplay was kind of mid," I mutter.

What if Jasper was right? What if I was uptight between the sheets? I do think about sex a lot. "But I'm sure I just had unreasonable expectations," I say quickly, backpedaling. "I was expecting a parade. A marching band. Fireworks. The Fourth of July. Sheet-grabbing, toe-curling, scream-my-head-off sex. The whole nine yards," I say, and Chase's eyes are wide. A vein in Ryker's neck is pulsing. They both look...angry, but also aroused? I'm not sure. Maybe they're just shocked I've confessed it to two strangers. I backpedal, waving a hand, wishing I could unsay those words, wishing I could take back that tequila shot too. "I'm sure it was me. I shouldn't have expected so much. I probably read too many novels," I say, dismissing everything. I should never have said a word. This was a mistake. "I need to...check on my dog. We're staying with Aubrey and..." I say, needing a moment alone. "I'll be right back."

Chase stands, letting me scoot out, before either guy can say a word.

I race to the ladies' room, wishing I hadn't said *I want to be fucked good and hard and scream my head off* to two guys I don't even know at all.

Two guys I want.

7

ORGASM MATCHMAKERS

Chase

We have a problem.

We actually have two problems—the pact and the orgasm drought our new friend is suffering from.

But first things first.

The pact to never let a woman come between us again. The second Trina is out of earshot, I jerk my gaze to Ryker. "This is awful," I say, frowning.

"No shit."

"Like, the worst." I drag a hand through my hair. I'm having PTSD about our ex Abby all over again. I've had flashbacks ever since I realized Ryker was hot for Trina, which happened oh, say, the second we met her. Admittedly, it's been hard to keep the pact front and center every single second when she is so damn interesting, fun, and sexy.

But I've tried to rein in my inner flirt. Keep the

charmer in me locked up in a cage. Still, it's time to deal with the problem head-on. "This is like those logic problems from when we were kids," I say. "A train races through the forest and no one is around. How fast is it going when there are no survivors and they come across a doctor in the emergency room?"

Ryker blows out a long breath. "That is not how that logic problem goes. That's like ten logic problems mangled into one."

Now he gets it. "Yes. My point exactly. That's the situation we're facing. And we need to roll up our sleeves and solve it," I say. We've got to just lay it all on the table. My attraction to her, his attraction to her, then how the hell we can help a woman in need when neither one of us can clearly be the one to volunteer as her tribute.

This is a riddle of the highest order.

"Are you suggesting we flip a coin?"

I scoff. "She's not the passenger seat in a car. You don't call shotgun on a woman."

"Good. Because I thought you were saying that," he says, relaxing his shoulders a bit.

Then it hits me. "Wait. I thought we were both talking about the same thing. I was talking about the pact, and how awful it is that we can't help."

Ryker hesitates, then says, "I was talking about how awful it is that she's never had a good orgasm. I take the pact as a given."

"Me too."

A year ago, Ryker met a gal named Selena at a coffee shop during the off-season. He was doing a crossword puzzle, he told me later, and she came right over to him and asked if he needed help. He tossed out a hard clue as a challenge. Lo and behold, she got it. He asked her out immediately—a rarity for him—and she said yes. He didn't tell a soul at first, including me. But I was with my mom and little brothers on a vacation in Europe, so no big deal. While we were tromping through Prague and Paris, my soft-hearted friend fell fast and hard and soon I heard about it over text. When I returned a few weeks before training camp, I met a fabulous gal named Abby in the park where I was hosting a 5K race for charity. She chatted me up and asked me to go for a run the next day.

Hell yeah.

We had a blast working out together in the mornings, and then we had a blast working out in the bedroom.

One night, I took her out to dinner at a sidewalk café in Hayes Valley. I snapped a pic of us, posted it on social, then took her home with me for the night. Like I'd been doing while I was in town.

The next morning Ryker didn't show up for *our* gym sesh.

When I texted him asking what was up, he said *you fucking know*.

No, I did not.

But he would not even talk to me for days, till he finally exploded with *"You're fucking Selena."*

"What? No, her name is Abby," I said.

"Bullshit, that's Selena. I saw the pic on your feed,

and you knew I was in love with her. What the fuck is wrong with you?"

What was wrong with *her* was the question.

Turned out, she'd given us both fake names, along with a couple other guys, and was dating four dudes all at once.

When I confronted her, she laughed and said, "Men have been doing this for centuries. How does it feel?"

Like shit.

She smiled, waved, and told the story on a podcast, calling her social experiment *The Dating Experiment.*

That was real fun. Only saving grace is she didn't name names so it never got out that we were part of the duped.

But the worst part was how shitty I felt when it all went down—shitty in every way. I was so angry when Ryker was pissed at me for no reason. Then, when I learned what he thought I did, I was horrified.

Even worse? I thought I'd lost my best bud for a few days there. That sucked.

So we made a pact—don't let a woman come between our friendship again. We *don't* go to bars and call dibs on pretty girls. We *do* compare names and faces now. I don't want to get screwed over, and I don't want him to have the wool pulled over his eyes either.

Mostly, neither one of us wants the drama that comes from falling for someone else's woman.

Pass.

Besides, I'm dating, romancing, and married to hockey. That's the only way for me to live, especially since I promised my dad I'd look after Mom, Jackson,

Gavin, and Trevor. Romance can take a back seat till I retire. I won't let my father down. The man was my biggest champion growing up, and I won't break the promise I made him in his final days.

But since Ryker and I are talking about the pact now, I might as well say it again, so my buddy knows it. I look him in the eyes. "Look, I still feel bad about Abby," I say genuinely, since that mess was way harder for him than it was for me. Ryker was legit in love with the charlatan. I was just having fun.

Ryker shakes his head, exonerating me again. "We're good, man. I swear. And the best thing that happened to me was seeing that pic of the two of you."

I scrub a hand across my jaw and focus on this new complication. "And look, I knew you were hot for Trina. I've known since we met her earlier. If you want to go for her and see what happens, I get it. No shotgun calling, since it's up to her if she even likes your grumpy, ugly ass. But it won't ruin the pact, because, well we're talking about it. I'm happy to step back," I say.

Ryker scoffs. "What do you mean *you know*?"

I pull a face, like *c'mon, it's me.* "You forgot her name because you couldn't look away from her eyes."

Ryker huffs like a dragon. Busted. But quickly, he recovers, pointing at me. "Pot. Kettle."

"What?" I ask, cocking my head. "I've been playing it cool all night."

"Giving her the nickname Miss Book Babe? Patting her shoulder? Smiling like you're trying to win a toothpaste contest?"

I laugh. "I'm just entertaining her."

"Liar," he mutters, but there's a smirk on his stony face.

"Fine," I relent, smiling too. "She's fantastic and gorgeous. But I feel terrible about her situation. We *have* to help her. There has to be something we can do. Hypothetical lessons? Vibrator shopping?" I suggest, but those are fails. I think on it for another several seconds till an idea flashes before me. "What if we try to help her find a good dude? Someone who's not a selfish prick?"

"So you want us to be her matchmakers?" He sounds intensely skeptical.

"Maybe," I offer, desperate to do something. "Is it the worst idea? I hate to see a woman suffer in bed. We could be like...orgasm matchmakers."

A throat clears. "Or...I have another idea."

Trina's back.

8

AN EVERYTHING BAGEL

Trina

You can do this.

  You are a badass, book-devouring babe.

  Ask for what you want.

But Chase goes first, snapping his gaze to me, a guilty look in his brown eyes. "Hey there," he says tentatively, but I think what he really means is *how much did you hear?*

The answer? *Enough.* I heard enough.

I went to the bathroom to get a moment alone, and yes, to check on my dog. One quick text to Aubrey and I learned *Nacho's doing great, now go fuck them both and report back in the morning.*

Okaaay.

That answered my next question—what should I do about this...ache? This out-of-nowhere desire to slide one hand through Chase's hair, and run the other along Ryker's bristly jaw? This wish to be sandwiched between them?

Maybe I *have* read too many books. There's no way a night like I'm fantasizing about could happen in real life.

But then I rewind to the moment when I turned the corner and heard Chase say he knew Ryker was into me, and then when Chase admitted the same to Ryker.

Yes, I've heard enough to do this.

Maybe nights like that do happen if you take a chance. Maybe nights like that happen to impulsive people. To women who adopt three-legged dogs, apply for jobs at bookstores when their only prior experience is running an online book club, and who steal ex's VIP tickets.

I never thought I'd want two guys to throw me on a bed. But now I can't get these wild ideas out of my mind.

Do it.

My throat is dry with nerves so I motion that I want to sit down. Chase pops up, and I slide into the booth next to Ryker once more. I take a quick sip of my water. Chase returns in seconds, and once I'm there between them, the air is charged. The energy is crackling. *You're the impulsive one.* "So about my idea," I say, my heart beating so fast.

Chase swallows visibly.

Ryker breathes out hard. "What's your idea?" he rasps, sex in his voice.

You held up a sign at the game. Hold up your own damn sign. Fly your flag, girl.

Deep breath. "I do think you should be my orgasm matchmakers," I blurt out, somehow getting that out without dying of embarrassment.

"Elaborate," Ryker says, surprising me by speaking first. There's fire in his eyes though. Perhaps that's stoking him.

Me too.

I look to the golden-haired guy, then the bearded one, emboldened by my twin desires for them. "What if...the two of you showed me what it's like to have an everything bagel instead of a plain one?"

Then, so there isn't any confusion, I set my right hand on Ryker's big thigh, then my left hand on Chase's.

Ryker inhales a sharp breath. Chase lets out a low moan.

Then I add, "Both of you."

There's silence for several long seconds. A heady, buzzy silence. Chase covers my hand with his. That has to be a good sign. But he doesn't squeeze my fingers, or thread them together. Instead, he turns his face to me, his eyes serious. "The thing is...Samuels and I made a deal that we won't let a woman come between us," he says.

Oh shit. Oh no.

What was I thinking, putting myself out there like this? *Real bright, Trina. Go to a sports game for the first time and proposition two athletes. They probably get kinky sex offers like this all the time.*

"And we're sticking to it," Ryker says, sealing my fate

as a complete and utter idiot. Has anyone ever misread a situation worse than I did?

They think I'm a puck bunny. I *am* a puck bunny.

Like I've been burned, I rip my hands off them, feeling stupider than I did when Jasper made up the world's worst lies about his infidelity. Because this moment is all my fault. I could have prevented this awful feeling by, oh gee, I don't know, not asking a completely ridiculous question of two guys who are literally required to entertain me tonight as part of a press event.

They didn't take me out by choice.

They had to.

I botched this big time. I need to apologize. Then, ideally, grow wings and fly far, far away and snuggle with my dog on the couch and never people again.

I lower my gaze, clutch my phone, grab my purse, and get ready to make a quick escape.

"No big deal," I say, forcing out a laugh as I'm staring at my hands, and I get the strange sensation they're mouthing something to each other over my head. Guy code, or whatever. Still, I need to go. "I was just having fun. Sorry I said it. It's nothing. Didn't even mean it."

Ryker cuts in. "Whoa."

"Whoa what?"

He doesn't look at me though. He looks at Chase, and a sliver of a smile forms. "The way I see it, this is one of those logic problems with a very easy answer, Weston."

Chase trades a smile of his own. "What do you know? I was thinking the same thing, Samuels."

What are they talking about? I look to one, then the other, trying to read them.

Chase's grin widens as he mirrors me now, sliding a hand down my thigh, making my skin hotter. I hold my breath, daring to let dirty hope rise again. "Sharing wouldn't break that pact, would it, Samuels?"

Their friendship is so important that they prioritize it with a pact. That's admirable, and sexy too.

"But sharing's okay?" I ask, on the edge of my seat.

"The way I see it, sharing is caring," Ryker says, and I go up in flames.

"I mean, you'd definitely be *coming* between us," Chase says, his voice loaded with heat.

"You good with that, Trina?" Ryker asks, brushing his fingers down my arm, to my wrist, over the top of my palm.

"I've never done anything like this before, but I'm very, very good with it," I say breathily.

What are they doing to me? I feel like I'm vibrating. I'm a tuning fork between them. I wait for them to make the next move.

And they do.

Right here in the booth, Chase leans in and dusts a kiss to my hair. Ryker brushes his beard across my cheek.

"Come between us," Chase says, all silky smooth.

"Very, very soon," Ryker adds, in that gravelly tone.

I'm melting by the time they pay the bill, and so ready to have an everything bagel.

9

THE SHARING LOOPHOLE

Ryker

There are pacts and then there are provisos. Loopholes, if you will. This sharing loophole is the best mother-fucking proviso of all time.

As Trina hangs back to text her friend, Chase and I pay the bill at the counter. No need to beat around the bush, so while I'm waiting for the attendant to return with my credit card, I pull Chase aside to ask the blunt question. "Since she's never done this before, you got an idea of how you want this to go?"

Even though we're open in the post-Abby era about who we're seeing, we've never done a chapter-and-verse rundown of our past experiences, nor do I want to. That shit is personal. He hasn't needed to know I've had a few three-ways. I've always been the third party though—the guy invited into an existing couple for one night, usually to blow a woman's mind for her birthday or something. Worked for me since they didn't involve entanglements.

And in those cases, I took the cues from the two of them, since they'd often have mapped out how they wanted me to play with her.

That worked for me too. I don't want to be the center of attention—not before or after a hockey game, and not in the bedroom either. But I do want the woman I'm with to feel spectacular.

"I'm thinking," Chase answers, then he's quiet for a minute, staring off into the distance. Even though we don't play on the same team now, we have in the past. That's the look he gets in his eyes before he takes the lead on the ice or in the locker room.

After he blows out a breath, he turns back to me, confident, certain. "I have a few ideas about how this can play out, depending on what she wants. Overall, the way I see it in my head, it's gotta be like scoring in hockey. Sometimes you get the assist, and sometimes you score the goal. We'll just trade off."

"And blow her brains out for the win," I say with a decisive nod.

"Twice."

I scoff. "Don't set the bar so low, Weston. She needs more Os than there are dudes."

"Good point. Let's do it," he says, and we trade a few more ideas for the rest of the night.

Like in hockey, you need a game plan for a three-way, and also ground rules.

And we need to know what she wants and doesn't want.

Once we're in the limo, I don't take the sideway bench again. I sit next to her so she can be between us, right where she clearly wants to be. "We should set the GRs," I say, diving right into the business of pleasure.

Trina nods a few times, her eyes wide, maybe with a mix of excitement and trepidation. Both are hot. I can't wait to make her forget her worries and just let go in bed.

But the driver's lowering the partition. "Excuse me for interrupting. Where did you want me to take you now?"

Oh, right. A destination would be helpful. Trina said she was staying with a friend. "I'm having my floors done tomorrow, so I had to move a bunch of furniture around. My place is out," I say, since I hate messes. Don't want to bring a woman home to see one. That's just rude.

Chase gives the guy the address to his place in Pacific Heights, then raises the partition and tilts his head, looking Trina's way. "Ground rules. Ladies first."

Trina parts her shiny lips—she's reapplied her gloss —but she's uncharacteristically quiet. I don't think it's from a lack of things to say. Based on how wide her green eyes are, I suspect her brain is popping with filthy images.

"Well, I guess the first is...are you two into touching each other?" There's no agenda in her question—just curiosity.

And it's a good question. But easy to answer. "Nope," I say, at the same time that Chase answers with a "No. That cool with you?"

It's not accusatory. He's just feeling her out.

"Totally cool," she says, her tone light. "I mean, if you'd wanted to do that, it'd be fine. But I'm okay being the…"

"Center of attention," I supply.

She dips her face. "Yes."

"You will be," Chase says confidently. "Tonight is all about you. Every dirty fantasy. We'll give it to you. Isn't that right, Samuels?"

I tuck a finger under her chin, making her meet my eyes. "Don't be shy. Say what you want. Makes me hard hearing it."

"Yeah, it's fucking hot when you tell us what you want us to do," Chase adds, and when Trina shudders, I can already tell she loves being surrounded by us, bodies and words.

She turns to me, looking up from behind those sexy glasses, then reaches a hand to stroke my beard. Fuck yes, her hand feels good. I let out a low moan.

"This beard turns me on," she says in a whisper, seeming kind of awestruck.

And I have a damn good feeling what she wants me to do with it. "You want to feel it on your thighs?" I ask, then whisk my jawline against her face for a hot second. "When I spread your legs apart and devour you?"

Her breath catches. And she gives a desperate "yes" then switches her attention to Chase and looks down at his hand, clasping her fingers through his. "Your hands turn me on," she adds, sounding a little mesmerized.

She wriggles her hips back and forth, her left one

against me, her right one against him. "Feeling both of you really gets me going," she says.

"Someone wants to be surrounded by men," I observe.

"I do," she says.

Jesus, she is a filthy delight. And I am on fire in here.

I'm so damn ready to lean in and taste that pretty little mouth. To catch her moans and sighs on my tongue while getting her all worked up with my hands, *and* his hands, roaming over her lush curves.

But she sets a hand on my chest, the other on Chase's. "I don't know that I'm ready for a full man-wich though," she says.

I snort-laugh.

Chase cracks up too.

Trina lifts her chin faux demurely. "From what I've read, you kind of need to work up to it. Also, I've never—"

She stops, like her words are stuck.

Chase, such a helpful dude, finishes the thought. "Had a dick up your ass at the same time a cock's buried in your sweet, wet pussy?" His straightforward tone is the same one he used when telling the driver where to go, and it's borderline hilarious hearing dirty words said like *take a left, then a right.*

"Well, Mister Filthy," she says, bestowing a new nickname. "Just like we didn't play Ping-Pong tonight, I've never played double ding-dong. Or taken a—" She stops, her lips quirking up, her sexy gaze drifting to my straining erection, then to his obvious hard-on. "A fire-hose up the ass."

I drop another kiss on her cheek. "Good job using those fancy words," I say dryly.

Chase runs the back of his knuckles along her cheek, and says, "There's a whole list of items you can order off the Two Dudes Menu besides a double dicking. Let me handle the list."

"Like you're giving me the chef's special," she says.

That works for me too—Chase directing the scene.

But what works even better is when Trina pants out a feathery, "Can you guys just kiss me now? I'm dying here."

When Chase looks my way, his smile disappears. He's all business. "Kiss her, good and slow, and get her wet."

Yeah, I had a feeling he'd give the orders I want. For me to go first. Trina turns her face to me, her lips parted. She licks them, and I cup her cheek, stroking my thumb firmly along her jaw, teasing her, making her sigh.

A few hours ago, I slid into this car, annoyed. Cursing the rest of the night. I hated wanting her so much.

Now, with her heart and her charm and her beautiful boldness, I'm amped up in a whole new way. I brush my lips against hers, and when she makes a sound of surprise, I deepen the kiss. I run my tongue along the plumpness of her shiny bottom lip, teasing it with gentle bites.

She moans with each one. With a soft exhale, she

parts her lips farther and as she does, a little gasp radiates from the back of her throat. The sound rolls down my body, sparking flames everywhere. She's so delicate under me, so soft and pliant as I get to know her lips.

As I take my time exploring her mouth, I sense rather than see Chase's hand. He's running his fingers down the side of her neck. She shudders, and that's even sexier. The kiss grows hotter as I mirror him, letting go of her face, dragging my hand down her throat, over her chest, teasing at her full tits.

She gasps into my mouth as I reach the top of her breasts. I open my eyes, and wow. She's kiss-drunk, those green eyes sparkling with longing.

"Work her over, Samuels," Chase tells me, talking over Trina, and she arches her back.

She fucking likes it when we talk *about* her. So do I. So does my buddy. But I like to do my own thing too. I don't entirely follow his orders. Before I return to her tempting mouth, I rub my beard against her cheek, drawing out gasps and shivers.

"Mmm. I just can't decide how I'm going to eat you. If I'm going to spread you out on the bed and bury my face between your legs." A drag of my scruff. "Or push you against the wall and get down on my knees." A rub of my chin against her cheek.

"Draping one leg over your shoulder," Chase adds, getting into the seductive rhythm of the image I'm painting.

"Or get on my back and tell you to sit on my face," I muse with one more brush of my stubble against her.

With a plaintive moan, she leans her head back,

stretching her neck. "Kiss me," she demands in the sexiest, neediest whisper ever.

Chase takes over, kissing her swollen lips while I slide a hand over the fabric of her jersey, cupping one breast firmly. Chase kneads the other.

And our girl? She's squirming in the seat. As she gets lost in his kiss, I slide a hand between her legs. She presses into my palm, urgently and hungrily, clearly wanting more of what we're giving her.

We're going to overwhelm her with pleasure tonight.

I tease at the button on her jeans as he kisses her till they're both panting for breath. As I undo one button and rub my rough fingers along her soft flesh, Trina finally pulls away from him. Her eyes are bright. "When we get to Chase's place," she begins, as she catches her breath.

"Yeah, baby?" he asks.

A look at me. A look at him. A breath. "Don't tell me what's coming. Just surprise me."

Yeah, I don't hate this fan event anymore.

10

SECRET UP MY SLEEVES

Trina

When the door shuts to Chase's spacious home on a picturesque block of California Street, I don't know what to expect from this night with them. And that thrills me. I'm on edge, my cells crackling with electricity.

Quickly, shoes vanish, socks disappear, and we all drop jackets on a chair by the door. Chase guides me through the wide open living room, with floor-to-ceiling windows that look out over San Francisco.

Sex with a view. Yes, please.

But is that on the menu? Are they starting on the couch? What will they do to me there? My pulse soars in excitement.

"Put her up against the wall. Kiss her neck. Take off those jeans. I'll play some tunes," Chase says carelessly to Ryker.

I shudder. The way Chase has it all mapped out, and tosses his directions so casually half makes me wonder if he's done this before. But mostly I don't care if he has. All I care about now is them and me.

Those ten minutes in the limo were the hottest of my life. I can't imagine—truly I can't—how it could get better.

But I think it will and I am here for it.

The lights are low, shadowing exposed brick walls. "Take off your glasses. Get your hands against the wall," Ryker tells me.

I slide off my red frames and put them on a table. I can see well enough without them. When I glance at him, I can tell his blue eyes radiate dirty deeds. I want what he has to give so I spin around, following his orders.

Advancing closer, he crowds me against the brick wall. Clasping my wrists, he slides my arms up along the brick, kissing my neck as he pins me effortlessly.

I'm at his mercy, and he wraps one strong hand around both my wrists. Do I have a kink for being bound?

Girl, you're about to be screwed senseless by two men. You have more kinks than you ever knew.

And I want these hockey stars to unlock them all for me.

Dropping my head, I savor every second of bliss. "Mmm," I murmur as Ryker lays kiss after hungry kiss on the back of my neck.

Music starts from somewhere, a low pulsing bass as Ryker gets down on his knees, reaches his big hands around me and unbuttons, then peels down my jeans.

My heart climbs into my throat. He taps my right ankle. I lift it, and he removes the jeans from one leg, then the other one.

I'm wearing only Chase's jersey and a pair of sky-blue boy shorts with daisy flowers on them—undies that are one hundred percent useless now.

They're soaked.

Feet pad across the wood floor as Ryker rises, roaming a big hand over the fabric covering one cheek. Then the other.

"What do you think of her ass? Fucking perfect for smacking, right?" Chase asks, like he's appraising me. Gone is the sweet, charming guy with the congenial smile for the press.

After dark, he's all alpha, in command of me and, also, his friend. That surprises me. I'd have expected the broody, grumpy guy to want to call the shots. But Ryker seems content to let Chase play conductor. Maybe that's their thing? Is this how they run their three-ways?

Nope. Stop. Doesn't matter if they're threesome pros. In fact, it's probably better if they are.

I home in on the moment, on my body.

Ryker squeezes my flesh, then says to his friend, "Pretty sure you'll love smacking this ass. But best I take these off first."

The way they talk about me makes me feel like their naughty plaything. And their tone—almost like I'm not here—makes heat flare in my belly.

"Good idea," Chase says, his voice louder now. He's a foot away, and when he reaches me, he sweeps my hair off the back of my neck and kisses me there—an open-mouthed caress while Ryker peels off my panties. I step out of them, and I'm half-naked but all exposed.

Ryker grabs one cheek, manhandling me roughly, and Chase the other, gripping firmly. Their bodies flank me on either side. "Bet you're aching between your thighs," Chase says, almost like a taunt, like he savors holding my pleasure in the palm of his hand. He kisses my earlobe, flicking his tongue along it. "Are you, baby? All hot and greedy?"

My knees buckle. And I grow wetter. "I am."

"Bet that sweet pussy is so nice and slick," he adds and squeezes my ass harder, then bites my shoulder.

"Oh god," I say, yelping from the nip, but also moaning from it.

Chase raises a big hand. "You said you liked my hands. What do you want me to do with them?"

"Spank me," I say, surprising myself at the strength of my desire.

With a devilish grin, he says, "I thought so."

He smacks my ass and I cry out a "god yes" as pain and pleasure surge through me.

"Turns you the fuck on, doesn't it?" Ryker asks.

My pussy grows wetter in answer, then a bead of arousal slides down my inner thigh. I feel daring with these two, free to voice my wants. "Check," I rasp out, my throat drier than the desert, my pussy hotter than the equator.

I'm shaking with desire. Chase kisses a long trail

down the side of my neck. "Aww, you're so hot for us you're getting all demanding. Fucking sexy the way she needs us, isn't it, Ryker?"

"So hot, how horny she is," his friend seconds.

I wriggle my ass for them, shameless. "I want you both. I need you both," I say, my voice sounding like it's coming from some other version of me. The me who propositions two guys for a three-way, who goes to their home, who asks for filthy, beautiful things.

Chase nuzzles his smooth face against my neck, his hands roaming down my side. "Patience, baby. Just need something first," he rasps out, then adopts his Dom voice again. "Ryker, check her cunt for me. Tell me how wet she is."

Ryker slides his fingers over my ass cheek, and between my thighs, stroking me at last.

It's such sweet relief, and yet I need so much more. "Please," I pant, helpless to the lust surging through me.

"Like she's been turned on the whole damn night," Ryker says, confirming, and that sounds about accurate.

His thick fingers climb higher, heading straight to my clit, which is pulsing for him. For them. At last, Ryker strokes and I nearly howl from the pleasure. How is this already better than anything else that has ever happened to me? Is it because it's double? But it feels like ten times what I've felt when I'm alone with my high-speed toys.

"She's ready for you," Ryker says, talking about me like I'm a car and they're going to trade turns at the wheel.

Well, yeah.

Ryker grabs my wrists and spins me around, so I'm facing him.

No idea what's happening. No clue at all.

Until...

Ryker slams his mouth to mine while Chase yanks my ass against his covered hard-on, and maneuvers a hand over my hip, down, and right between my legs.

"Yes. You're so slick," he praises in my ear, as Ryker kisses me and Chase strokes my pussy. "Wrap your arms around him."

I comply, threading my fingers through Ryker's thick, soft strands.

While Ryker kisses me hard, Chase drops sensual kisses to my neck, all while he strokes my wetness, sliding, rubbing, flicking my center.

I'm bursting with pleasure everywhere, my pulse skyrocketing, my skin tingling, everything aching.

This is a parade. An anthem. An epic finale to a symphony. Chase is rubbing my needy clit while Ryker devours my mouth. It's all too much, the deluge of wild sensations.

I moan into Ryker's mouth as I rock into Chase's hand. "That's right. Give it to us. Come on my hand," Chase urges in a dark, dirty voice that has me rocking faster into his fingers, doing his bidding.

I'm close, so damn close. There's no part of me that doesn't want to come right now.

Ryker's kisses overpower me with their intensity while Chase's fingers fly, and pleasure coils low in my belly, then pulses.

A warning of bliss.

"Yes, I can feel how much you want it," Chase rasps out, pushing me on.

One more stroke, one more caress on my neck, one more kiss of my lips, and I let go of Ryker's mouth, gasping, "I'm coming."

My knees buckle and Chase catches me, then hauls me up as I shake from the aftereffects. While I'm still moaning, he brings his fingers to his mouth and sucks them, one by one. "Mmm. Need more of your sweetness really fucking soon," he says, like he's high on the taste of me. When he's done, he tenderly strokes my hair away from my face. "You did so well, *sweetness*," he says, and I like that nickname too.

"That's better than Miss Inquisitive," I say.

"Yeah, it's perfect for you, *sweetness*," Ryker adds, petting my hair too.

"I bet someday you could take both of us," Chase says, and Ryker growls his *yes*.

"Think you'd like that too?" Ryker rasps out, asking me.

This is only one night. That's not on the menu this evening. Still, I say, "I want that. Someday."

"I know you do." Chase presses a gentle kiss to my bruised lips, then lets go and lifts me up.

Oh! He tosses me on his shoulder. Well, that's fun, being handled like I weigh nothing.

"Wait. My glasses," I say, mildly worried.

"Got 'em," Ryker barks out, and cuts across the living room while Chase stalks down the hall, fireman carrying me. I'm shivering the whole way, barely aware of my surroundings—just Chase's soothing voice. "How did that feel? You deserved to come so badly," he says and his tone is soft, an aftercare type of voice I've heard about. Maybe dreamed about.

"Better than Maverick," I say, still woozy.

"Who's Maverick?" he asks as he turns into his bedroom, flicks on a light, and then gently lays me on a huge bed with a dark blue cover.

"My favorite vibrator," I say.

"You named your vibrator." He sounds delighted.

"Well, when you have a half dozen you need to tell them apart..." I say, trailing off seductively, because I don't want to talk anymore.

Chase is undoing a button on his shirt as Ryker enters the room. I sit up on my knees, move to the edge of the bed. "Let me," I say, but it's plaintive. I'm pleading to undress him.

He comes closer, clasps my hands, and brings them to the front of his shirt. "Take it off," he instructs as Ryker sets my glasses down on the nightstand.

I get to work on stripping Chase, sliding off his dress shirt, and letting it fall to the floor. I bite the corner of my lips when I set eyes on his chest, carved and muscular everywhere. They aren't model muscles, shaped by protein shakes and long lifting sessions. They're cut from the job, and he's covered in bruises and small cuts. I run a finger over the freshest, bluest bruise, touching it reverently. "Looks new. Does this still hurt?"

He shakes his head. "Didn't hurt when I got it. Feels good right now."

I spread my hands over his pecs, exploring his hard body as Ryker watches the whole time, stares darkly with the most intense look in those eyes. Maybe Ryker is a voyeur? Would he want to watch Chase fuck me? Would he jerk off while Chase bent me over the bed and pounded into me?

My breath hitches. My heart races. I'm flooded with brand-new ideas.

"What filthy thought just crossed your mind?" Chase asks, but I'm not looking at him. I'm looking at the man whose midnight gaze has me caught in its crosshairs.

Without thinking twice, I answer: "If Ryker would ever want to jack off while you fucked me."

Who am I? Who is this woman saying these things to these two men?

Chase whistles, clearly loving my dirty mouth, and praising it by running a finger along my lips.

"Maybe," Ryker says, noncommittal.

Maybe someday. Quickly, he undoes his shirt, revealing ink I only saw hints of in the photos online. A series of finely drawn compasses cover his right arm, stretching up to his shoulder and spreading into a tribal tattoo that extends across his huge pecs.

He's even more banged up than Chase, with bruises and cuts across his strong body. A scar, several inches in length, runs down the side of his abs.

I run a finger over it, reverently. "Hockey fight?"

He nods. "Blade cut me. You should see the other guy."

That's hot, the kind of adrenaline that must power

him on the ice. I never thought I'd find it sexy, only brutal. But tracing the scar, I'm finding his caveman side far too appealing.

"Come closer," I say, breathy.

He moves, standing next to Chase, so I can admire them both.

I spread my right hand across Ryker's chest, exploring his ink more thoroughly, then the dark chest hair covering his pecs while my left hand visits Chase's happy trail.

I shudder, but it's not simply from being ludicrously turned on.

It's from the power storming through me. A power I didn't know I possessed to turn two men on at once. They're both breathing hard, chests rising and falling, dicks straining, eyes darkening. They're both so wildly aroused.

"Can I?" I ask, my gaze straying to Ryker's bulge, then Chase's.

With a *that's sweet* grin, Chase shakes his head. "You haven't come enough tonight for that. If you want to play with our cocks, you're gonna need to earn it with a couple more orgasms." His tone turns stern as his hands move to his belt and he undoes it. "Take off your shirt, scoot back on the bed, and spread those beautiful legs for him."

The rest of our clothes disappear, and when Ryker's long, thick cock swings free, he grabs it, strokes it, and moves up on the bed too. "Let me see how wet you are for me," he says in his gruff voice.

Suddenly shy, I barely part my legs. What if I can't

relax? What if Jasper was right? What if this is why he strayed?

Ryker growls, admonishing me. "Nope. Nice and wide. I want to see everything," he says.

But even as I let my knees fall apart, I look the other way, still unsure of myself.

Ryker sighs, but he doesn't sound annoyed. More... thoughtful. He presses a kiss to my inner thigh. "Been dying to eat you out. Taste you dripping on my tongue. Feel you come on my beard," he says, so crass, and so clever, since those filthy words do the trick.

I relax, spreading my legs.

"Yeah. That's right," he says, then he looks up, locking his eyes with his friend. "Weston, you better play with her tits while I eat her out. Blow her brains out so she doesn't have to think," he instructs, and way to read me.

Way to solve me.

"I'm there," Chase says, climbing onto the bed in his naked glory, his dick nice and thick and pointing at me. "Move, sweetness. Gonna get behind you."

I sit up, letting him slide behind me so he's against the headboard, and I'm in his arms. "Lie back on me," he instructs.

I obey, settling into the big, strong canvas of his chest, feeling his hard dick against my back.

From between my thighs, Ryker says, "Good. Now put your hands on your thighs and show me your pussy."

With a shudder, I push my thighs apart more, feeling vulnerable and wildly daring at the same time.

"Turn her on while I eat her," Ryker says to Chase.

"Chef's special," Chase says, as his hands roam around to my chest. He squeezes my tits while his leaking cock thumps against my spine, and Ryker's beard brushes against my inner thigh.

It's a lot. A good *a lot*. I'm overwhelmed once again. Ryker hasn't even kissed my pussy and I'm already moaning, writhing.

He rubs that scruff along my legs, then stares at my center. "Need to taste you," he says, in a carnal groan.

"I barely got enough of her on my fingers. Tell me," Chase rasps out, his tone desperate. "Tell me how she tastes."

Ryker buries his face between my thighs and French kisses my pussy.

I scream in pleasure as the fireworks show begins.

This won't take long.

This won't take long at all.

Not as Ryker laps me up, stopping only to give his opinion on the main item on the menu. "She tastes like all my fantasies," he says before he returns to lapping, licking, sucking.

This is like nothing I've experienced.

This is nothing I've even dared imagine.

This is better than anything I've read.

Chase's fingers pinch my nipples while Ryker keeps me spread open with his hands, his lush mouth devouring my wetness, his talented tongue devoted to my aching clit.

I moan and thrash. Beg and arch. I rock up against Ryker, and I wriggle against Chase.

I'm melting into the men, sweat sliding down my breasts, desire taking hold of me.

My brain goes offline.

All I can do is feel as Ryker eats me with such passion I'm lost to the pleasure. I'm lost to myself. Lost to the orgasm that slams madly into me, sending a hot, sharp rush of ecstasy blasting through my core. "Yes, yes, yes," I call out, coming on his face as I'm devoured and adored all at once.

* * *

A few minutes later I'm still in bed with them, each man on one side of me. They're stroking me, kissing me softly.

What is this world I stepped into when I stole those tickets? "This is the real VIP treatment," I say with a heady smile.

"And you fucking deserve it," Chase adds.

But they deserve pleasure too. When I take a tour of Chase's body, my gaze lingering on his thick cock, hard as steel, then on Ryker's shaft in his fist as he lazily strokes, I frown.

"This isn't acceptable," I say with a pout.

"What's not?" Chase asks, all sleepy sexy.

"I'm going to take care of you both," I announce, determined.

"Yeah?" Chase sounds doubtful.

I don't feel doubtful though. I feel confident. Like I've got a secret up my sleeve. And I sure do. I stretch out my arms, smiling wickedly. "I earned it, didn't I?"

"You sure did," Ryker confirms. "How do you want us?"

"At the same time."

Ryker furrows his brow.

Chase laughs skeptically.

I get on my knees between them. With both guys lying down, I take a cock in each fist. And I show them just how well I can use both hands. I stroke and jerk till Ryker spills into one palm, Chase coming hard in the other.

Being ambidextrous has its advantages. Guess that was a double dicking in its own special way.

11

MY PANCAKE ERA

Trina

A rooster crows a gentle cock-a-doodle-doo. But that barnyard boy's about to get a serving of my attitude real fast.

I fumble around on the weirdly comfortable couch, slapping the coffee table in Aubrey's living room for my phone as I squint, trying to block out the bright morning rays streaking through the windows.

Where's my little dog warmer? Nacho always sleeps under the blankets with me. But maybe he's waiting at the door to do his business.

In the distance, a pair of voices float by. Something about batter.

Ohh.

Those are man voices. Right. I'm not in Kansas anymore. I'm in Sex Wonderland, and this is a nice big bed to wake up in. I blink away the last cobwebs of sleep and confusion.

"Cock-a-doodle-doo!"

I cringe, grabbing the phone, then silencing the rude but necessary alarm, along with the last of my disoriented thoughts. Fully awake and aware now, I sit up, shove my glasses on my face, then check the time. Eight-thirty on Saturday. I need to be at work at ten when we open the store. Plenty of time to do the walk of shame.

My gut churns, a little embarrassed. I haven't done one in a long time.

"That's not how you do it," Chase declares from a room far away, perhaps the kitchen.

"Yes, it is," Ryker insists.

"You have to whisk it *more*."

"Whisk it *less*."

They're arguing over pancakes? They're already back in their normal routine. I almost feel like last night didn't happen.

Maybe I should act like it didn't as I slink off? That seems easiest.

I stretch, looking around. Chase's bedroom is the size of a small country. This bed is its own city. I haven't slept this well in...I don't even know. The only thing missing is Nacho, and my heart aches a little for my guy. But I'll see him soon, and my life will snap back to normal. The dog, the bookstore, my online book club, occasional yoga in the park.

Last night will just be a distant, dirty memory.

That's fine. It's totally fine. It's not like I expected anything to come of my sleepover in sex paradise. And I'm not looking for anything. I'm only two weeks post breakup with Jasper. No one wants a girl on the rebound either.

I should find my clothes, wash my face, brush my teeth, and get out of here. Let them return to their regular lives too. Phone in hand, I pad to the en suite bathroom and freshen up, squeezing some toothpaste onto my finger.

When I'm done, I leave, and hunt around Bedroom-Landia for my shirt. I think I left it somewhere in the northwest territory. Ah, there it is—many feet away. I head over and grab a small pile of blue fabric from the floor.

I pull it on, grateful it goes to the top of my thighs since I have no panties in here. It's going to be seriously gross to pull last night's on anyway when I leave Chase's home. Maybe I should just go commando? Except, denim up the vajayjay might be worse.

I'll deal with that later. For now, time to bolt. I pad out, stomach dipping with nerves.

This is going to be awkward. The *thanks for last night* moment. The *good luck with your hockey games, those Os were real fun, and it's time for me to call a Lyft of Shame.*

Quietly, I walk down the hall, peering at my phone as I go.

Oh! There's an email from one of the apartments I applied to. A studio! It's available next week—nine days from now. I can't wait to tell Aubrey. Also, there's another email from Jasper, begging me to let him fill in for me at the Hockey Hotties calendar kickoff portion of the VIP experience.

With an eye roll, I delete it, but it also serves as a wonderful reminder to upload the pool pics from last night to my social feed.

Me and my new hockey besties, I write, then I post the pic and the caption.

"Suck on that, Jaspie," I say under my breath as I close the screen.

"We should start the coffee," Ryker barks.

"There's time," Chase says calmly.

"Hardly. It loses its flavor after you grind it," Ryker warns, and they're interacting like it's normal to argue about how to make coffee the morning after they double pleasure a woman.

But maybe it *is* normal? Maybe they do this often. I didn't ask. I didn't want to know in the heat of the moment. Maybe I'm one of many women they perform this service for.

Need an O? Call The Hockey Guys! For whenever you need a double team to take care of your peach problems!

Come to think of it, that's a hell of a service. Maybe if I were more ambitious, I could start it. Become a madame and run the Hockey Double Team. On the other hand, I could just mention it to my book club, and someone would post a vid demanding *someone write this now.*

But in the real world, no one wants a hookup overstaying their welcome.

Which means, I need to fly so they don't think for a second that the recently jilted girl who stole her cheating ex's tickets is going to latch onto them like a barnacle.

Anti-barnacle mode activated, I enter the open-concept living room. But my breath catches annoyingly when I see them. They're both shirtless. Chase is wearing gray sweatpants that hang low on his hips, his V-cut in full view and even more drool-worthy in the morning light. Ryker's wearing his dark blue slacks from last night, but that's all. His tattoos snake along his massive right arm and across his huge pecs, and I can't catch a break with my hormones. They're doing a little jig at the sight of the two men.

Plus, to make matters hotter, they're making pancakes.

That's just unfairly sexy.

"Allow me to remind you," Chase says as he grabs a skillet from a gorgeous wall-mounted pot rack that makes my mouth water, "the three commandments of pancakes are—one, don't overmix. Two, let the batter rest. And three, always use butter."

Ryker scoffs, and without seeing his face, I know he's rolling his eyes. "You forgot the fourth amendment. It was added to the covenant of breakfast last year and it's this—use real syrup."

"Thou shalt drown thy pancakes," I call out from several feet away, light and breezy, like I'm not totally wanting another night with them.

But what if it sounds like I'm angling for breakfast?

The guys turn their gazes to me. Ryker's unreadable, but Chase's lips tip up in a grin. "Hey, sweetness," he says, using the nickname he gave me last night all while looking and sounding like sunshine. Stubble lines his jaw. It's coming in golden brown, and I want to run my thumb across it.

Except I should go. They want me to go.

"Did you sleep okay?" Chase asks, all thoughtful and caring.

"I did. It was great," I say, then shift my gaze quickly to Ryker. Is he going to ask how I'm doing too?

For a second, his blue eyes look almost soulful. Vulnerable, like they're searching mine. Trying to read me.

But that's ridiculous. He's been arguing about how to make coffee and pancakes, not about me. I will not be clingy, so before he can even say a word, I add, "Anyway, last night was super fun. Thanks so much. I have to go. So, have fun with your breakfast," I say, breezily, making it crystal clear I'm *not* trying to crash their morning plans. They're probably going to make pancakes and then bench press small cars or something.

That soulful look in Ryker's eyes vanishes so fast I'm sure I imagined it, especially when he grumbles, "Your alarm is awful."

I flinch. Well. The grump has officially returned. Gone is the flirty side he broke out last night, but it's weirdly reassuring, Ryker's return to form. It'll make it even easier for me to go. "Yes, it is. But I don't wake up easily without it, and it worked and woke me up, and I should *clearly* take off."

Chase tilts his head, seeming confused. "What?"

"Leave. That thing where people say goodbye and go," I say, trying to make light of my pending exit. "I just need to find the rest of my clothes."

Ryker points. Like, aggressively points. "Living room."

I bristle. Well, that's clear. He wants me gone, and he doesn't even live here. He's one of those guys who's a beast in the bedroom, and a beast in life too.

No thanks.

Chase smacks Ryker's arm. "Asshole."

"She said she wanted to go. I'm fucking helping," Ryker says defensively, then clears his throat and turns to me. "Your jeans are on the coffee table." Then he looks back to Chase. "That better?"

"Did you wake up on the wrong side of the bed this morning?" Chase asks.

Ryker cracks his neck so loudly I wince on behalf of his bones. "Yes. I did. There were three of us in the bed, jackass."

And you wrapped your arm around my waist and spooned me, you beast.

"Aww, poor baby. Go see the trainer," Chase says, and clearly I am not needed in their bro banter.

I power walk to the living room, beelining for the coffee table. Huh. My clothes are neatly folded. And warm, I discover when I grab them.

A second later, there's a hand on my arm. Chase turns me around, his deep brown eyes exploring mine, like he's reading the room before he speaks. "Don't go yet. We're making you breakfast."

That does not track. "You are?"

"Stay. Let us feed you, at least."

"I don't think Ryker wants me to stay."

Chase smiles and whispers in my ear, "Let me tell you a secret. He woke up early to wash and dry your jeans and undies. I discovered him in the laundry room, hunting around for dryer sheets, and then he asked if I had flour and eggs and all that food stuff."

Is that my heart fluttering? Yeah, I think it is. Dryer sheets *and* pancakes.

"I like pancakes," I say, loud enough for Ryker to hear.

"Everyone likes pancakes," Ryker grumbles, but I can translate his pissy mood now, and his words mean *I thought you were leaving when I wanted you to stay for breakfast.*

I return to the kitchen, nudging Ryker's side. "Yes, everyone does, even the big bad wolf."

The wolf harrumphs, but then says, "Do you like coffee?"

"As long as it hasn't lost its flavor," I say, with a mischievous grin.

"Course it hasn't," he says.

Because you started it right on time for me.

I don't say that though. He knows what he did this morning, and so do I now, and I feel fifty million times better than I did when I thought they might have wanted to kick me out right away. Plus, these pancakes smell so good. I offer to help, and Chase lets me, so I show off my cooking skills. When the first batch is almost done, I say, "Want to see my party trick? I can flip a pancake five feet in the air."

"Show us," Ryker demands.

I slide a pancake onto the spatula, and flip it toward the ceiling, catching it a few seconds later. I take a bow.

Chase whistles. "And I thought jerking off two dudes at once was your party trick."

A laugh bursts from me. "I guess I have two party tricks now."

"But keep the first one just between us," Ryker says, without cracking a grin as he comes behind me, then slides a possessive hand up my back, curling it around my neck. Like he's sending me a message. He doesn't want any other men to share me.

I shiver from his touch. From the ownership in it. Then from the way he drags his fingers against my skin, pressing hard and firm. Like he's marking me as theirs.

But the thing is—I don't know if they want to share me again either.

And honestly, why would they? I'm just the jilted book nerd who poured out her bedroom troubles to a couple superstar athletes, and they're the competitive guys who wanted to prove they could fix me between the sheets. They won that contest, and now it's time for a victory breakfast.

That. Is. All.

And I'm here for sweet revenge on my philandering ex. I make a mental note to post the pool playing video later today so Jasper the Wonderless can cry in his oat milk over that one too.

* * *

When I finish a small stack of batter-y goodness dripping in decadent syrup, I say, "These are the best. And I'd know. I'm in my pancake era."

"My whole life is my pancake era," Chase says.

Ryker leans back in his chair. "Didn't you say the same thing about your chocolate chip cookie era? And your waffle—"

"Hey now," Chase chides.

"Don't forget your acai bowl phase," Ryker adds. "And there's also your daily devotion to coffee at Doctor Insomnia's."

"I like my rituals," Chase says, raising his chin.

"And Doctor Insomnia's coffee is life-giving. I will attest to that," I say, then push back in my chair so I can clean up.

But Chase sets a hand on my arm. "What are you up to today, sweetness?"

My chest warms. It'd be far too easy to get used to him calling me that. "Well, I got good news this morning. I found an apartment."

He offers a hand to high-five as I tell him about my email. "So after work, I need to sign the paperwork before Aubrey's landlord finds out she has a dog in her place, and then I only have nine days left of hiding my pup from him." I cross my fingers.

Chase's jaw falls open. "You have to hide the dog?"

I frown. "We sort of have to smuggle him in and out. But Nacho's quiet and doesn't bark much. He's a very good boy—well, except for his taste for undies. And he's at doggie daycare now anyway. Aubrey dropped him—"

"Stay with me," Chase says, like he's brooking no argument. "Both of you. For the next week."

I stare at him, bug-eyed, I'm sure. "My dog and me?"

He sweeps out a hand to indicate this space. He has a lot of it. "This is a three-bedroom and there's only one of me. I have a guest room. The designer set it up," he says as Ryker takes a sip of his coffee. I bet he drinks it extra scalding. With salt added to strengthen his ire.

But I focus on the guy making the kindest offer. "Chase," I reply, since I truly don't know what else to say. It's so generous. "I can't."

"Why not?" Chase asks, a little demanding. Or really, a lot.

"I just...that's too nice," I say.

"He is nice. He means it," Ryker says, like he's protective of his friend, and holy hell, that's...sexy too. Like when he offered to fuck up Jasper. Like when he said my trick was between us.

"I know," I say.

"He wants to help you, Trina," Ryker adds, making Chase's case.

With a *guilty as charged* smile, Chase just shrugs. "You should not have to hide Nacho away. Also, I love dogs. And my landlord"—he stops to point at himself—"is very dog friendly."

"I got that feeling," I tease, since Chase asked me to show him photos of my little guy last night. That was no hardship.

"I'm dying to get a dog someday," he adds. "Did you

know I spearheaded the Hockey Hotties calendar? It raises money for dog rescue. We have the kickoff event in a couple weeks, and pretty sure you're going to that?"

Butterflies flap in my chest, since thinking of that event—the final piece of the VIP experience—feels presumptuous after last night. But then again, Chase seems hellbent on being the world's most chill host, so I say yes.

"Excellent. And a bunch of my teammates are doing it—Erik, my goalie, who's marrying my cousin next weekend. Ledger, who's been on the team forever, and is the most sarcastic dude I know. Ryker will try to back out of it, but you can help me work him over, Trina," Chase says, making a pitch even though I'm already sold.

"Ryker, do it," I say, batting my lashes in an over the top fashion.

Ryker crosses his arms.

"Anyway," Chase continues, "I want to adopt a dog someday and teach him to surf. Well, when I retire. Does Nacho like to swim? We could take him to Crissy Field," he says, lighting up like a kid on his birthday. "Or a dog park."

Wait till I blow his mind. "He does dog agility," I say, like it's a secret confession.

Chase's jaw drops. "Shut the fuck up."

I hold up a hand as if taking an oath. "I solemnly swear he's most excellent at pole weaving and the seesaw."

Chase lets out a salacious groan. "You're killing me, sweetness."

He's killing me with kindness. "You really don't mind?" I ask just to be sure.

Ryker groans with exasperation. "Could he be any more clear, Trina?"

"Be my roomie for the next week. Till you can move into your new place," Chase says insistently, putting on his bedroom tone, like he's going all alpha on me again, then he looks to the guy across from him. "And you should stay here too."

Ryker pulls a face. "And why's that?"

"You're having your floors done, you said. You were going to get a hotel room. Just stay here. I have three bedrooms."

Was this planned? Are they trying to seduce me again?

Please let them seduce me again. Like, say, tonight.

Ryker's brow knits, and he legit seems as shocked as I was. I don't think this offer was planned. It's not designed to get me in bed.

"You spend enough time in hotels. We're both in town this week, and we both have road trips at the end of next week. After Erik's wedding."

"Aww, you know my schedule," Ryker says.

"Yes, because I pay attention to my job. Anyway, come hang with Trina and Nacho and me," Chase says, like that's that and there's nothing more to be said.

Meanwhile, I have questions.

Like, are we doing the sex thing again? Are we going to use three separate bedrooms? Where will we sleep?

Ryker sighs deeply, looking a little lost in thought. "I

am a bit tired of hotels," he finally admits. But then he looks to me, his gaze vulnerable like it was for those few seconds when he first laid eyes on me in the kitchen this morning. "You cool with that?"

Is this the gentleman side of the beast asking me? "Sure. I mean, you did wash my clothes and all. Wait. Does that mean you'll do my laundry for the week? Because I always wanted a laundry valet."

I swear he breathes fire as his answer. And I stoke it.

"But you have to separate the lights from the darks, Ryker," I say, wagging a finger. "Oh, can you do my delicates too? In cold water, please."

Dragging a hand through his thick, dark hair, he mutters, "Why did I do something nice?"

"Also, I'd really like blueberries with my pancakes tomorrow morning. Thanks so much."

Ryker rolls his eyes from here to the other side of the world. As Chase laughs he wiggles his fingers at me. "Gimme your phone."

I take it from the back pocket of my jeans, and we exchange numbers, then I do the same with the wolf man.

I check the time, wincing. I want to help clean but... "I should go," I say, apologetically.

"I'll take care of cleaning. I don't have practice till this afternoon."

"Is there a game tonight?"

Chase shakes his head. "Nope. Ryker doesn't have one either."

Which means they'll both be here and we'll do chores? Play Monopoly? No idea.

Chase walks me to the door, and before I can leave, he says gently, "Hey. No expectations tonight. Or for the week. I just want to give you a place to stay. Don't feel at all like there are any strings."

Too bad. I'd like the strings. I'd maybe like ties too. Like being tied to his giant bed. But I also am not in the right headspace to get involved, so it's for the best that we have zero commitments.

"Of course."

"But I do have one expectation," Ryker calls out from the kitchen.

"What's that?" I ask, intrigued.

He doesn't tell me. He shows me when he strides across the floor, hauls me into his big embrace, and kisses me deeply, thoroughly, tasting of coffee and pancakes and him.

It's a dizzying kiss, and my stomach is flipping, and my skin is tingling, and I feel knocked off-kilter in the best of ways.

When he lets go, there's no time to catch my breath since he nips on my earlobe. "Mmm. Last night, you smelled like strawberries. Now, you smell like *us*," he rumbles, and my knees weaken, then I ache when he rasps out, "Smell her, Weston."

Chase swoops in and drags his nose along my neck, and it's too early for me to be this turned on again, and yet I am. "Yessss," Chase murmurs, then brushes tender lips to mine.

It's a dust of a kiss that sends a ribbon of pleasure unfurling inside me.

I'm overwhelmed with their kisses and their words once again.

I leave, with two new roomies for the next week, and no idea what will happen when I return tonight.

12

A HOUSEWARMING PRESENT

Trina

Jaw agape, my sister clutches her pregnant belly, like her basketball baby is going to fall out from the shock of my choices. "You can't be serious?"

We're standing outside Aubrey's apartment building in the Outer Sunset, a chill whipping past us that evening. Nacho lifts his snout in the direction of the breeze, sniffing the air, his little tan nose working overtime.

"Yes, I'm serious, but it's only a week," I say. Okay, it's nine days, but who's counting? I sling my backpack up on my shoulder as I curse *this* timing.

I almost avoided my sister. I was out the door when Cassie ambushed me with a succulent ten minutes ago, arriving at the building unannounced while Aubrey was taking a call from a client begging for a balayage appointment. "Surprise! Just a little housewarming present for you and Aubs," Cassie said when she showed up.

Code for *I'm spying on you to see if you've shacked up with a drug lord at your bestie's place.*

That's Cassie—she thinks she's the helper but she's actually the challenger. She's willful and controlling, and I'm sure it's because deep down, she doesn't ever want anyone to overpower her, so she overpowers everybody.

Or maybe she just really thinks I'm a loser.

Cassie points to my pooch to make her argument. "You're going to take your darling dog," she says, and wow, she's trying hard if she's calling my pup a darling. "And let him live with someone you don't even know?"

Well, I know Chase biblically. Oops. I meant...them.

"I know him," I say, deliberately choosing to focus on one man only. Cassie doesn't need to know there's another super-hot hockey star bed surfing there too.

If my sister thinks I'm a hot mess for rooming with a new guy for a week, imagine what she'd think if she knew I hooked up with not one, but two guys.

I file that under things she will never know.

"How do you *know* him?" she asks, continuing her rant. "You hate hockey."

"No, I don't," I insist.

She gives me *the look*. The *I'm your older sister and I know better* look. "Trina, you despise sports. You actually wrote down a life goal to never go to a sporting event," she points out.

"Because you asked me for my life plan when you

took me out for ice cream a few months ago!" I point out. "I put it on there as a joke."

"And you never wanted to go when Matthew and I invited you to see the Renegades. He has season tickets, you know."

I know, I know. I hear about them every time I see her. Her husband is the team dentist for the Renegades football team, and I've had the audacity—her word—to turn down their offer of tickets. Gee, I wonder if it's the football I don't like or the judgment.

"Well, I like hockey now," I say defensively, and that's sort of true. I like some aspects of it. Like the fancy food and the suits.

"But..." she says, flapping her hands, building up a head of steam and sputtering so much that Nacho cocks his head, staring at her with concern, then whimpering.

I bend down to stroke him reassuringly. "She's fine, honey."

Then Cassie blurts out, "But he could be a serial killer."

I laugh, scooping up my dog in my arms. Nacho rewards my love with a face lick. "He plays professional hockey. They probably vet for that."

"You don't know for sure. Just stay with me," she says, gentling her tone. "We can have sister time before the baby comes." She holds her belly again, like she's using it as a lure for me. *Come to baby land. We can discuss whether I'm the size of a pumpkin or a honeydew.* "I want to bond with you. Help you be the best aunt you can be."

Because that should be my life goal?

I know my sister means well, but it's time to play my trump card. "Cass, I appreciate the offer. Truly, I do. But he lives really close to An Open Book, and I'm working a ton over the next several days," I say. I don't add that I took an extra shift to earn some money for the security deposit at the new place. She'd probably sister-nap me and force me to live with her rent-free, which would have its perks when it came to my bank account, but that'd be about it. "And it's going to be super easy for me to stay there till I move into the studio next week," I say. Cassie lives across the bridge in Marin County, thirty minutes from my store.

"But I come into the city a lot for work," she says, and damn, my sister is tenacious. "Like tonight. I was here seeing a client. I could drive you to work," she says in a sing-song voice.

"Cassie, I will be a badass aunt for your little bambino, but I'm going to live with Chase Weston for a week, and I promise he won't lay a hand on me to murder me. You have my word."

He might however lay a hand on me to, say, spank me. Pinch me. Bite me.

A girl can dream of unlocking more kinks.

Cassie sighs heavily, clearly frustrated she's losing this battle. "At least let me drive you to his place."

Before I can say thanks but no thanks, the front door swings open and Aubrey shouts, "I'm ready to take you to The Pound—"

I mime slicing my throat as Cassie peers at Aubrey. My bestie gulps guiltily, shutting the fuck up.

"To the pound what?" Cassie's tone drips with suspicion.

I jump in before this conversation crashes harder. "The Poundcake Factory," I supply, since there just aren't that many compound words starting with pound.

Cassie arches a well-groomed eyebrow. "The Poundcake Factory? What exactly is that?"

Think fast. "It's...a new pop-up shop in Hayes Valley. It sells pound cakes. Hence the name," I say, improvising as fast as I possibly can.

Aubrey smiles too big as she adds, "We saw it on social and got an invite."

Cassie crosses her arms. "I like pound cake. I haven't had any in ages. I'll go."

Uh-oh. Didn't see that coming. Think faster. "Oh, I just remembered," I say, snapping my fingers. "There's a live jazz band playing too."

Cassie shudders. She abhors jazz music. I've seen her walk out of restaurants that play jazz. "Okay, can you get me a slice of pound cake and bring it to me when we have dinner with Mom and Dad this week?"

I'm going to do everything I can to find a pound cake in this city. "I promise."

I give her a hug, thank her for the plant, then say goodbye. I breathe a sigh of relief when she drives off, and I can finally slide into Aubrey's tiny car with Nacho in my lap.

"The Poundcake Factory?" Aubrey asks as she puts the car in drive.

"Well, if you weren't calling it The Pound Palace I wouldn't have had to make that up."

"No. If you didn't bang them I wouldn't have needed to call it The Pound Palace."

"I didn't bang them," I point out.

"But you will. Or really, you better. Say, tonight?" Her voice rises with hope.

At a light, I turn to her, uncertainty racing through me. "I honestly don't know if they want to again."

She rolls her eyes. "He invited you to stay with him."

"But he didn't say it was to bang him. Or them."

"Because that would have seemed transactional. But trust me, he's wanting to make another transaction," she says with a naughty little purr in her voice, then she hits the gas and cruises through the city. "You're going to be a legend among women soon. You're going to be the patron saint of Double Teams. I bet women are going to build a shrine to you at your bookstore. You should tell the book club."

"I'm not going to tell the book club about my escapade."

"Then just tell me. Like, did you spend the entire day googling different positions for three-ways?" she asks salaciously as we hit a light.

Laughing, I roll my eyes.

"I'll take your silence as a yes."

I smile. "Not the entire day. Just during my break. I want to be prepared."

"If you want to be prepared, I can help you out with that. Here's a little something I picked up for you." Aubrey reaches a hand into the back seat, fishing around, then grabs something, and tosses it onto my lap.

A bottle of lube.

This is much better than a plant.

But I still have the cake problem to solve, so I start a group chat with the guys and ask: ***Do you happen to know any place nearby that sells pound cake?***

Well, they're competitive. Maybe they'll get on my new pound cake problem as fast as they handled the O drought issue.

13

A VISIT FROM THE DRAGON

Chase

I've traveled around the world. Played pro hockey in Budapest, Vienna, Toronto, New York, and Rio de Janeiro.

At twenty-seven, I've had a big life in five years in the NHL. But this, right here, is one of the coolest things I've ever seen. Trina's pup is tearing up a seesaw, then racing down the other side, and the little guy is doing it while missing one of his back legs.

"Mind blown," I say, cheering on Nacho under the glow of outdoor lights in the evening.

Trina too. Because look at her go. She's guiding him through the agility course at a nearby dog park I scoped out in advance. It's a busy park, with families pushing strollers and joggers tearing up the path even as dusk settles in. When Trina and Nacho arrived at my place a little while ago, I hustled them right out of there to take the little guy here for a treat.

Bonus? It's a perfect distraction from my incessant thoughts of her all day. From texts from my cousin, Lisette, too, telling me about every single friend she wants to set me up with at her wedding. It's like the singles table is her personal buffet of options for me, and I've run out of evasive emoticons to reply with. Last time she set me up with someone, it petered out after a few dates, but Lisette kept asking me over and over what went wrong. The answer? I don't have room for romance in my life.

Most of all, though, the dog park is a distraction from all my thoughts about the possibilities of tonight.

I home in on the man of the hour. So does a jogger from many feet away, craning his neck to watch the small dog soar over a little jump. He lands gracefully, then Trina points at the weave poles a few feet ahead. "Weave, Nacho," she says, eyes only on him.

That little tripod waggles his butt back and forth in a black and tan blur all the way to the end of the weave poles before he darts through a tunnel at Mach speed.

She runs along the side, chestnut hair flying, platform sneakers slapping the dirt, then waits for him at the end, arms thrust high in the air. "Good boy!"

Barking enthusiastically, he jumps up and down on one freaking back leg, eager for her praise.

Trina scoops him up and slathers him in kisses.

"That is officially the coolest thing I've ever seen," I say as I trot over to the pair.

"And my sister said I could never do it," Trina says proudly, a little defiantly.

"Let me guess. Big sister?"

"Yup," Trina says, then reaches into a pocket of her jeans and hands Nacho a dog treat. He chows down while a serious-looking dog trainer type pushes open the faraway gate, escorting a pair of Border Collies into the park. "It's peanut butter. His favorite," she adds.

"Mine too," I say.

"Aww. Want a dog biscuit, Chase? You'll have to jump through a hoop though," she teases.

Ah, that's an opening to the big thing on my mind, and I shouldn't take it, but impulsively, I answer with, "We already cleared the orgasm hoop."

I'm testing the waters probably sooner than I should, even though the other part of the *us* isn't here. Ryker said he had to run some errands.

"With flying colors," Trina says, then tilts her face, looking at me with curious green eyes, maybe waiting for me to say more.

I want to. God, how I want to. But I've got to play it safe, since I don't know what Ryker wants. This morning, he took off ten minutes after Trina, saying he needed to let the contractors into his home. I haven't seen him all day, so I don't have a stinking clue if he's been thinking nonstop about Trina too.

Just like I have.

Trouble is, I don't want to have the "I can't stop thinking about getting you naked again" talk with *her* without talking to *him* first. Pact and all. What if he's not thinking about her the same way? Maybe she's out of his system, and then where does that leave me? Confused. I'm not normally confused after one-night stands.

This isn't a one-night stand you dumbass. She's now living with you.

But what the hell *is* this?

My only choice for now is to skate around the problem, focusing on the dog in her arms. I scratch him under the chin and he leans forward and swipes his tongue across my face.

I grin like a fool. "That's it. It's official. He marked me, and I'm going to have to be his dog babysitter for the rest of time."

With a laugh, Trina sets her hand on my cheek, wiping off the remnants of dog kiss. I let out a low rumble, meeting her gaze for a few delicious seconds that make me want to haul her over my shoulder once more.

A shuddery breath seems to ghost across her lips, then she shakes it off. "I'm glad you like your temporary roommate," Trina says, petting Nacho too. The little dude pants harder. "I think he's tired though."

I glance toward the gate. "Can I walk him on the way back?" I ask, sounding like an eager kid. And I kind of am.

"Sure. What's the deal with you and dogs? You're kind of obsessed. Like more than I am," she says as we leave the park and she hands me his leash.

I sure am, and there's one reason for it. I take the leash, keeping a tight grip on my new buddy, who takes the lead on the sidewalk. "My dad was a veterinarian.

He loved all animals, but especially dogs, so we always had them growing up. But our last dog passed away shortly before my dad did."

Trina looks my way with gentle eyes. "I'm sorry about your dad, Chase," she says, sympathy flooding her tone. "That must have been so hard on you. And on your mom."

"Yeah, it was," I say, downplaying that terrible year, the damage to my heart, the way I changed. The way I *had* to change. "And after, she decided not to get another dog. She was too busy with my little brothers and raising them solo."

"A dog would've just been more work for her, she probably figured, and she was probably grieving still, adjusting to a new life she never expected," Trina says thoughtfully, understanding my family just like that.

Maybe that's why it's easy for me to keep talking when I don't usually get into the nitty-gritty. "When I was younger, my dad and I would go on long walks together in the evening with Bandit, and I'd tell him about school and the team and practices, and well, just life and stuff while Bandit trotted ahead of us, sniffing everything. I liked those times."

"I can tell. That's a nice memory," she says with obvious affection as we stroll past a thrift store with boxy army jackets in the window.

I let the fond memories roll past me for another few seconds, then say, "He was a cool one. Part Border Collie, part cheetah. Fastest dog ever. Dad loved him too and he kept us busy."

"Sounds like you two had a lot of fun with him and

got to spend some good times together *because* of him," she says as we turn onto California Street while twilight wraps its arms around the city.

"Yeah. We did. Someday, it'd be nice to have another Bandit, or a Nacho," I say, wistful, then I shake that off too. "But it's hard to have a dog since I'm on the road so much. That's why I still try to volunteer as much as I can. It's important to me, and it was to my dad too," I say, and wow. Do I sound like I'm tooting my own horn or what? I shift my focus to her. "Why does your sister think you can't handle a dog?"

Trina sighs, a little resigned. "She thinks I can't handle anything. Like, say, life. But maybe she's not wrong. I mean, I've lived in three places in the last month. My douchey ex's, my bestie's couch, and now with a guy I met...um, last night," she says with a wince. "She might be right."

Nope. No way. Not gonna let her doubt herself. "Your ex was a world-class asshole. He never deserved you, and you got the hell out the second you learned the truth. That takes guts. Hell, it takes serious ovaries, and you have them, Trina," I say, giving her a pep talk she didn't ask for but that I feel compelled to give. "And you take care of this awesome dog and look out for him and hold down a cool job. All while dealing with the aftermath of a shitty breakup. That's a lot."

And so is a breakup, so I add, "It's not easy dealing with the end of a relationship. My ex was a piece of work too, and sometimes you just need to take it easy and not expect too much of yourself. Know what I mean?"

She takes a beat, then nods. "Thanks for saying that. Cassie got on my case earlier this evening, so I think I needed to hear something nice."

"If you ever need a pep talk, I'm your guy. It takes time to get over someone—even the jerks. I mean, I wasn't in love with my ex. Romance wasn't my jam to start with, but still, the whole experience soured me on romance even more," I admit.

She shoots me a sad smile. "You and me both."

We knock fists in relationship solidarity, but that's not the solidarity I truly want.

I'm dying to know what she thinks about another night, but I've already decided to wait for Ryker. Instead, I jump over to an easier convo—the auction for the jerseys and gear Trina bought for her ex. I had the jersey signed by my teammates today, and Ryker did the same with his jacket, so we made plans to auction them off online this week, then give the money to her favorite rescue—the place where she got Nacho from.

When we reach my home, I unlock the door and head inside. Ryker's stretched out on the couch, phone in hand, brow furrowed, earbuds in.

And he looks...freshly showered.

Damn, he really wants to impress her. Plus, holy shit, do I smell hummus and olives and baba ganoush and falafels and lemon herb chicken?

"Did you get food?" I ask once he takes out the earbuds.

Ryker nods. "I picked up takeout on my way back. Didn't know what you liked, Trina, so I got a little of everything."

Well, how about that. "Look at you, showing me up with my guest," I tease, but is there a tiny bit of irritation coming through in my tone?

Maybe there is.

"You offered her a place to stay. I just got dinner," he says lightly. Then he adds, "And I found a bakery still open that served pound cake. It's in the fridge."

With an excited gasp, Trina's eyes grow wide, and she's staring at Ryker like he's hung the moon.

Out of nowhere, a dragon thrashes around in my chest.

I breathe out hard, but my lungs feel like they're sucking in a hot plume of fire. And I don't know what to do about it, so I grumble out, "Need to return a call real quick."

I head to my bedroom and shut the door.

Or really, I slam it.

14

A SECRET NERD

Ryker

After Trina toes off her shoes, she makes her way over to the couch with her dog by her side, and I watch her every move, cataloging her. She wears little flare jeans that show off some ankle, then a crop top that reveals a sliver of belly, and a short sweatshirt.

It's a fantastic tease, and I want to peel all those clothes off her. But it's the way she looks at me from behind those red glasses that makes my heart thump faster.

"Pound cake. Seriously. You're my hero," she says.

My chest warms. "Just wanted to help. No big deal," I say, evenly. Not gonna let on how much I like those words—*you're my hero*.

She joins me on the couch, patting the cushion. Nacho jumps up, then snuggles next to her. "Chase said he could sit on the furniture," she explains.

"I wasn't going to rat out Nacho. I'm also not surprised one bit that Chase gave him couch privileges," I say, then reach across her to pet the dog's head. I'm not a huge animal person but Trina clearly is.

"What are you listening to?" she asks, glancing down at my phone.

I'm glad I closed the text thread with my sister, Katie. She was firing off her usual litany of little sister questions I won't answer like—*you should ask out the girl from the VIP night! I could tell you liked her in the picture.* I swear, Katie thinks she knows everything about me.

"Wait, let me guess," Trina continues. "Is it *Seven Tips To Be As Scary As Possible When You're Really A Softie Underneath*?"

I'm not sure I want to tell her. Sharing things leads to people knowing you, which leads to them using you. Case in point—Selena. "No, it just comes naturally to me," I say, evading the question. Just like I've been avoiding Josh's email from earlier today. I don't feel like dealing with my agent's latest request of his grumpy client.

Pound cake and dinner were much easier problems to solve.

Trina nods to my phone. "Fine. Don't tell me you like *A Word Play A Day*."

Dammit. The screen locked on the podcast. "It's not bad," I say, noncommittally, but better the podcast than my agent's email.

"Whiskey comes from *aqua vitae*, meaning 'life water.' C'mon. That's way more than *not bad*. That's cool," she says.

I fight off a grin. "Suppose it is," I say as Trina studies my face.

"Don't worry. Your secret is safe with me. I won't let on you're a..." She stops to lean in closer, her face dangerously near to mine, so near I want to smother it in kisses. "A secret nerd."

I scoff. "Please."

"Takes one to know one," she says.

"You're a nerd?"

"I work at a bookstore. I read a book a night. There's nothing else I can be but a book nerd."

I'm seriously impressed with her page-flipping skills. "A book a night. I'm jealous."

"See? I knew you were on my team."

I narrow my eyes, huffing. It's easier this way. But she's relentless, so I bend, teasing her too. "Maybe I am, but you weren't reading a book last night, *sweetness*."

She dips her face, that shy vibe returning. "I was otherwise occupied."

I'd like to occupy her tonight too. If she wants that. If Chase wants that. Speaking of, where the fuck is my buddy? I'd really like to eat dinner and then introduce him to the joys of eating Trina. He is seriously missing out.

That is—if she wants us again. Because I do. *Badly*. Knew the second I wrapped my arms around her in bed last night that I wanted another night like that. That I wanted to take her to new heights. To make her scream in bliss, to edge her, to break her brain with pleasure.

And I'm getting horny, in addition to being hungry,

but we really need to lay down some new ground rules. Stat.

Trouble is, that's a conversation three people need to have, not two. So, I nod to the kitchen counter and the bag of food. "Did you know baba ganoush means... pampered daddy?"

Her lips part in obvious delight. "I did not know that at all. But I am going to work that into daily conversation starting tomorrow," she says, then tilts her head, studying me. "You know, Ryker. Your other secret is safe with me too."

What does she mean? Like last night? "Not sure what you're getting at."

"I've seen you come around the bookstore," she says quietly.

Oh. I hadn't thought of that. I drag a hand down my face. "You have?"

"Yes. Your eyes lit up last night when I mentioned where I worked."

"Well, it's a cool store," I say.

"I'm glad you think that. And I got the impression you don't like to talk about it. In public."

She's not wrong. "Why would I?"

She nods, then knits her brow. The furrow tells me she's trying to figure me out. "You buy a lot of books, and it just made me think *I bet he donates them.*"

Damn she is good. "Fine. I buy them and donate most of them to the library. They make sure the books go to kids in need. Kids at homeless shelters, in the hospital, and so on."

"And why was that hard to say?"

With a groan, I slump back into the couch cushions. "Because the team wants me to *work on my image online.* And I know they'd be all over that, but if I shared it with them it'd just feel...gross. Like I was patting myself on the back."

"Because nobody knows you actually do laundry and make pancakes and donate books?"

"And nobody should. I don't even know why it matters to the public."

"Because you're a public figure," she says, shrugging, like *it is what it is.*

"I just want to play hockey. And support my family. I don't want to have to tell everyone what I'm doing off the ice too."

"But people look up to hockey players. They look up to athletes. That's just reality. You can't change that," she says evenly, and she makes good points. So I open up a little more.

"That's why I was doing the VIP event with Chase last night. To play nice with my rival and show the fans what a nice guy I am." I adopt a saccharine grin.

"If they only knew how very, very nice to fans you are," she jokes.

"Yeah, let's keep that between us," I deadpan, then return to Josh's email. He said last night's photo op was great and the team wants me to please do more *positive press.* "Anyway, it's just annoying that I'm supposed to broadcast this stuff. What the fuck am I supposed to say? *Had dinner with Mom last night. I'm such a good son.* Or *went down to the library to give them some books. I'm so nice,*" I say, imitating a self-congratulatory post.

She seems to think for a minute. "Well, I could help you. I'm posting things for the store all the time. You could do it in such a way that isn't patting yourself on the back. And honestly, you might not even have to say that much. With the books, just take a picture and tag the org, or I could do it for you," she says with such genuine enthusiasm it's hard for even a guy like me to grumble.

"Yeah?"

"I like social media. Do you want me to help you?"

I hate taking help. But the way she asks, so sweet, so real, there's no way I can turn her down.

Especially since I need the assistance. "Yes," I say roughly, then I clear my throat and give her the answer she deserves. "Thank you."

"Anytime," she says, then her eyes twinkle. "In fact, we can start right away. I have some ideas."

Trina never seems to stop thinking. Her brain is always in motion. She tells me some of her ideas, and they're easy enough. A stop at the bookstore. A pic at the library. Something family centric.

"Sure. I'm in."

"Can you do Tuesday? To bring the books to the library?"

"Consider it done," I say.

"Good," she says, then pats my thigh, and I'm about to take her hand in mine, but then I catch myself.

Nope.

If I take her hand, I will drag her close for a hot kiss, and then I will want to tear off her clothes.

Where the fuck is my friend? I can't wait a second longer. I jump up. "Be right back."

I stalk down the hall and bang on his door, which swings open at my touch. "You done with your call? If not, I'm gonna eat," I say.

He's staring out the window, like he's lost in thought.

"Where is my buddy and why has his evil emo twin replaced him?"

Chase turns around. His jaw is tight. His eyes are cold. What's worse is when he says, "Shut the door. We need to talk."

15

THE T WORD

Chase

I pace around my room, dragging a hand through my hair, trying to get a grip on this stranglehold of jealousy that came out of nowhere and pummeled me to the ground. "We said we won't let a woman come between us," I say, but that only scratches the surface of this storm of unexpected emotions battering my chest.

"Right," Ryker says carefully, like I'm a rabid animal he must approach with caution.

"But I didn't expect...*this*," I say, irritation thick in my tone. I hate feeling this way. Annoyed and out of control.

"What's *this*?" he asks, stepping farther into the room, more out of earshot.

"This little twist," I say, then wince at how I sound. Pissy and caught up. I haven't even known Trina for a day, and I can't believe I feel this way, but I do. "I was jealous you got her dinner and the pound cake."

Ryker barks out a laugh, but then it dies quickly when he studies my face. "Shit. You're serious."

"Dead serious." And that's the issue. "I was jealous you solved a problem for her."

"Need I remind you that you offered her a place to stay," he says, waving his hand around my room. "That's a bigger problem to solve than a cake."

Fine, yes, I helped her with her landlord issue. But I still haven't peeled back the real problem. "But see, I want to do things for her—"

I can't get out the last word.

When I don't finish, Ryker must decide to change tactics since he approaches me, his demeanor calm, maybe reassuring. "Look, it's cool with me if we do different things for her. You took her to the dog park. I'm not the kind of guy who's gonna baby talk over her dog."

"I don't do that," I spit out.

Ryker rolls his eyes. "You do. And I'm not going to be the one who asks *how did you sleep*. But look, she needed a pound cake. That's my wheelhouse, man. Finding things. So I did that for her. Just like you gave her a place to stay."

He's right. I know he's right. We don't have to compete with errands or gifts. We don't have to fight over her. I don't need to be jealous if we want the same thing.

Just say it, man.

"But what's really getting at you?" Ryker presses,

folding his arms across his chest. "Because I don't think it's the pact. This doesn't feel like the Abby"—Ryker stops to fake cough—"Selena...deal."

That's the thing. On paper, there are some similarities. We want the same woman. But in reality, the situations are vastly different. We had no idea we were into the same woman before. Now, everyone's been on the same page since the start.

"It doesn't feel that way to me either. Since, well, we met Trina together," I say, the words stumbling out awkwardly. "Everything's in the open."

"It sure is," Ryker says with a little smirk. "Swinging dicks and all."

Jackass. He's so much cooler about this than I am. But that's how he's been most of his life. Steady as a rock. He had to be for his mom and sisters. But I've had to do the same too. So I let out a deep breath, prepared to say the hard thing.

But he says it for me.

"Are you afraid she doesn't want to sleep together again?" Ryker asks.

Boom. There it is. He said it. The T word—*together.*

I drop my head against the cold window then admit the stark truth. "Yes. I can't stop thinking about the way she melted under *our* touch," I say, but I have to face this head-on so I turn around and draw a soldiering breath. This is new terrain, talking about sex this openly, even with my buddy. Yes, last night we talked about a game plan for a hot night. But we were powered by the adrenaline and swagger of what seemed like a one-time opportunity.

Now, I want another night with her. Maybe even a whole week. But I also want Ryker to have her too. The way she fell apart when we pleasured her together was addictive. "I want to share her again. If she wants to. Do you?"

Ryker just smiles, like *took you long enough*. "I sure do."

We leave together, men on a mission.

16

BOSS BABE

Trina

Well, this is weird. My stomach is rumbling, and I'm twiddling my thumbs on the couch. Okay, not twiddling. I'm flipping pages on my Kindle, gobbling up the first chapter of a new Hazel Valentine romance, and wondering how long two guys can talk.

But it feels like twiddling, because I'm waiting, and I'm trying, I swear I'm trying, *not* to assume they're talking about me.

But it's been nearly twelve hours since they've touched me, since they both kissed me at the door like they'd go mad without me. Not even a brush of a hand or a bump of a shoulder.

Are they trying to decide how to let me down gently?

Whatever, dudes. I'll be fine. I sigh, petting Nacho.

"At least you make sense to me," I say, grateful for this stinker. "Men, not so much."

He offers me a chin for rubbing, and I comply.

But I'm tired of waiting. When the door creaks open at last, I set down my Kindle, pop up from the couch, and smooth a hand over my shirt.

The second they turn the corner into the living room, I start to talk, but Ryker's faster. "We want you, Trina. We want to share you. Tonight, and for the rest of the week."

I tremble everywhere, my breath hitching, and my words drying up as they advance toward me, Chase taking over. "I didn't offer you a place to stay to seduce you. I legit wanted to give you and your pooch a home for as long as you need. I know you're not interested in anything more, and that's cool with me. But I've never done something like last night before, and I just can't get you out of my head. We have to have you again."

We.

I burn from the excitement racing through my body. From the acknowledgement of his first time too.

"I can't stop thinking about the way you fell apart when we touched you," Ryker adds in a bare husk of a voice. "Getting to eat you while he turned you on everywhere was the hottest thing I've ever done. I've never wanted a repeat of a three-way till now, and I'm absolutely dying for another time with you."

Twin confessions, each different, each electric in its own way. I kind of love that Ryker's done this before, but never more than once. I feel even more wanted, and it's heady.

Addictive for sure.

"Playing with your pussy while he kissed you made me so fucking hard," Chase adds.

Is this my life? They want me that badly? Together? My veins are flowing with liquid desire.

I lick my lips. Shudder out a breath. "Good. Because I wrote out a long list today of things I want us to do. All the ways you can have me...while I have the two of you."

They groan like animals.

Ryker closes the distance between us and scoops me up into his big arms. "Show us that list. Now."

I tell Nacho to stay on the couch like a good boy, then I look up at the bearded beast. "How about we *do* the first item?" I suggest with a coy smile.

He crushes his lips to mine. And I moan into his sexy mouth as he carries me to the bedroom with Chase muttering, "Fuck food. We're going to fuck you instead."

Yes, fuck food indeed.

* * *

Things I *didn't* Google today—positions for threesomes.

Incognito mode notwithstanding, I wasn't going to take a chance of someone walking up behind me at the store and seeing vids of two guys double-banging a woman.

But things I *did* look up on the shelves of An Open Book? Threesome scenes in sexy novels. Bennies of working in a bookstore. After a few quick skims of some choice chapters, I found that the sandwich method is only one of many options.

I'm down for that but first I want the D. With a side of D.

And tonight I want to boss them around a bit.

So once the guys strip off all their clothes, I take off my glasses and point to the bed.

"Lie down," I say, and I don't at all sound like a lady Domme, nor do I feel like one, *but* I'm positively giddy watching two ripped men lying down on a king-size bed, big dicks pointing at me.

Me.

They're naked and I'm still in my bra and panties, and I like the power play as I settle between them, one knee between Ryker's thighs, the other between Chase's.

"What's it gonna be, sweetness?" Chase asks in the deep, swoony tone that sends hot sparks down my spine.

I'm feeling a little saucy, so I give him a "How about you let me show you like I said?" as I slide a hand through the coarse hair on Ryker's muscular thigh.

Ryker lets out a satisfied sigh.

I do the same to Chase, and the controlling man murmurs, "Dying to know what you're up to."

"You really are bossy. If you let me be in charge for ten seconds you might get this," I say as I reward Ryker for listening well by stroking his shaft.

Ryker glances at Chase. "Just shut up. It's worth—"

His words die on his tongue when I lick the tip of his cock.

"I'll fucking listen," Chase says, watching hopefully like a dog waiting for a treat while I draw the head of Ryker's dick between my lips, wriggling my hips as I happily taste him for the first time. As I fist the base of his dick, I run my fingers up Chase's leg, rewarding him at last. I slide my hand higher, up along the inside of his thigh, and he groans all while I draw Ryker deeper.

"Mmm. Your mouth. Your fucking perfect mouth," Ryker murmurs, curling one hand around my head, holding me in place.

I flick my tongue along his length while I cup Chase's balls. Chase lets out a throaty *yessss*, then threads strong fingers through my hair.

Ohh.

That's really nice. Chase's pushing my hair from my face so he can watch me suck his best friend's dick.

Maybe I'll put on a show.

I lock eyes with Chase. His glimmer.

As Ryker relaxes into the moment, I lavish wicked attention on his dick, flicking my tongue along the head, then sucking it like a lollipop while Chase watches with dark eyes and parted lips and strong hands keeping my hair from obscuring the blow job view.

I can't leave Chase hanging though. I take mercy on Mister Bossy's throbbing cock, stroking once, all the way up, then squeezing the tip right as I suck Ryker's dick far into my throat.

"God, yes," Ryker groans, gripping my hair tighter, turning me on even more with his rough touch. "You need to feel her mouth. It's fucking paradise."

Well, he makes a good point.

In an instant, I switch men. As I grip Ryker's dick, I suck on the head of Chase's, lapping up a bead of arousal that's just waiting for me.

Chase utters a moan of surprise, then Ryker wraps his hand around my hand, showing me how he likes it, and I nearly combust. My cells are on fire. I'm sucking Chase's dick and jerking off Ryker's with him, and every inch of my body is electrified.

"Look at you, sweetness," Chase says, staring savagely at me devouring his cock. I try to imagine how I look to him—lips stretched wide with his dick while my hand is wrapped around another man's thick shaft. My hair frames my face, and he sweeps it back so he can stare at my blow job lips. "Just look at you. You're so fucking worked up you're rocking your hips."

He's right. I'm fucking air as I give their dicks the attention they deserve.

Taking care of two men is winding me up. I'm hot all over. And wet beyond words between my thighs.

Ryker wraps his hand tighter over mine, and I respond by shuttling faster while drawing Chase to the back of my throat.

They both groan in tandem, and the deep harmony of their vocal pleasure is such a rush.

I could come from servicing them.

But Chase pushes up to his elbows, slowing my momentum. "That's enough," he hisses, then clasps my face, stopping me immediately. "Now it's my turn to call the shots."

His tone is so authoritative that I sit up, listening.

He's up and moving, prowling around me. "Thoughts of you tortured me all day long. When I was on the ice, and in the weight room, then seeing the trainer, I was imagining how you'd taste. I need to eat you till you're coming hard on my mouth."

His stern order sends a wild thrill through me, especially when he finishes it with, "And why don't you suck Ryker's cock while I eat you? But tease him. Toy with him—just like you teased me. I can't have your mouth full of cock while I go down on you. I need to hear all the sounds you make when I eat that sweet, sweet pussy."

With a shiver, I smile as I unhook my bra. "Sounds good to me."

"And you better tease her right back," Chase tells Ryker.

"With so much fucking pleasure," Ryker answers.

I strip off my undies, but just so I don't tempt the beast in the other room, I set them on top of the bureau, out of Nacho's reach.

Then, I get on my back and I spread my legs for one man and lick my lips for the other. I'm not feeling shy tonight.

I'm feeling bold and beautiful under their gaze.

17

OPEN WIDE

Chase

She is heaven. Warm and slick, salty and sweet.

And loud.

Trina is so damn noisy that I'm humping the bed as I devour her. I swear I could come from going down on this goddess. She's muttering *oh god* with every lick I bestow on her and with every kiss she gives Ryker's dick.

Too bad I'm going to have to shut her up any second. But first I need more of her. I wrap my arms tightly around her fantastic ass, drawing the wet paradise of her pussy even closer to my hungry mouth, then I lap her up, licking and flicking that little diamond of pleasure.

She tastes so sinful and she's so outrageously wet. I break for a second, because I've got to tell her.

Except. Wait. No, she likes it better when I tell *him*.

She's twisted her face toward the side of the bed. Ryker's standing there, teasing her lips with the blunt head of his cock.

"She's fucking delicious, isn't she?" I say to him, and she rocks against me, seeking more of my mouth.

His tone is feral. "Her pussy is like dessert," he says, while stroking her face.

Trina answers with an arch of her back then tugs him closer by the base of his dick, pushing him into her mouth.

"She's such a greedy girl," I add, French kissing her pussy for a few delirious seconds as she moans.

"Pretty sure she's greedy for my cock right now," Ryker says, offering more to her, feeding her another inch of his dick, but that's all he'll allow.

And yeah. She's ready. She's fucking ready for what I want to do to her.

Before the three of us started this evening, we asked her a few key questions about how far she wants to go tonight in bed, and she told us exactly what she's interested in. I don't plan on pushing her past her limits, but I do want to give her a rocket blast of pleasure.

I suck on her clit, then let go. "Fuck her mouth, Ryker. Fuck that sweet mouth but don't forget—she comes first. And once she does...be a gentleman and give her a minute."

Trina's eyes flicker with wicked want as she manages a strangled *please*. Well, she can't quite talk right now with his dick in her mouth.

With a cocky grin, Ryker runs his thumb over her

top lip. "I won't shoot till our girl does. Now, eat her good, Chase."

"I plan to." I go down on her like crazy, starving for her pleasure, eating her till she's writhing and panting, then till she's so lost from the bliss, she drops his dick from her mouth at last.

"Oh god, yes, yes, yes," she cries out as I haul her closer, burying my face in her pussy while giving Ryker a stop-sign hand.

Trina shudders everywhere, coming ridiculously hard on my face, her hands grabbing at my hair, her body convulsing.

When she's clearly reached that overly sensitive point, I let go, swipe a hand over my face, then look to my friend, who's stroking his eager dick. "Favor, Ryker," I say casually, like it's nothing.

"Yeah, man?" he asks on a lazy upstroke, taking the same attitude.

"Want to know why I said to give her a minute?" I ask as I rise and move around the bed to the nightstand.

Trina's watching me with sex-drunk but curious eyes.

"Got a feeling," Ryker says.

"I want to know too," Trina puts in, all rusty with desire.

I open the drawer, grab a condom, and frisbee it across the bed to my buddy. He catches it easily.

"Suit up and fuck her. But tell me how it feels. I need a play-by-play while she sucks my dick and takes yours."

Trina swallows visibly, her eyes widening. She's still splayed on the bed, flushed and sexy. "Can he bend me over the bed, please?"

Her eager tone is impossible to deny.

I lean over her, cup her cheek, and kiss her deeply. "Yes. You deserve a good, hard pounding, baby. Get up and lift your ass for him."

Ryker's already at the foot of the bed, sheathing his cock, while Trina scrambles off, slides in front of him, and presses her hands to the mattress, lifting her lovely ass. She cranes her neck behind her and shoots him a nervous but excited look—a look that makes me even harder.

"You want this cock badly, don't you?" he rasps out, running a hand down her back as he notches his dick against her heat.

"I do. Dying to feel you," she says to him, then turns to me. "And you."

"You're doing so good," I tell her since our girl deserves all the praise. "She's working so hard tonight, and she needs more orgasms," I say to Ryker, then narrow my eyes. "Now give her another. And do it fucking soon."

Ryker pushes in. With a sharp gasp, Trina shudders, her face so blissed out. Then, she looks even better when I get on the bed, kneel in front of her, and offer her my cock. "Open wide."

18

LIFE KINK

Trina

Before I met these guys, I never knew I wanted two men at once. Now I can't imagine wanting anything else in bed with such ferocity. Such intensity. I'm driven mad with lust. I'm hot and sweaty and wet and bursting.

"She's so fucking tight, man. The way her pussy is gripping me is insane," Ryker says with a carnal moan.

Sharp pulses of pleasure jolt my body as Ryker pounds me mercilessly. He punctuates each deep thrust with a stroke of his fingers over my clit, frying my cells.

I want to scream in pleasure, but my mouth is full. Chase's holding my face in his big hands while fucking my mouth.

"I can't fucking wait to get inside her. But how did you last with this mouth?" He slides out, giving me a break for one hot second.

A second where my legs shake and my brain scrambles from their conversation about me.

"Because I like the sound she makes when she comes more," Ryker says, and pleasure twists in my belly, a low, delicious pull that signals a storm is coming soon.

"I'm close," I say on a whimper.

Chase growls. "Me too. She sounds so fucking hot when she comes," he says, then serves me his dick again, and I take it, lapping up his thick shaft. "Need to hear that sound real soon. Can you get her there, man?"

I'm nearly there from their words, and I can't answer with my own, but I just nod desperately so they know I'm right there with them on the edge, then I maneuver a hand between my thighs, over Ryker's, rubbing my clit with him.

He strokes and fucks, and soon, the pleasure is barreling through me, and I'm tipping over the edge, shattering in a million ecstatic pieces. There's no room in me for anything but pure erotic bliss. It surges from my center to the ends of me.

"Let us hear you, baby," Chase urges, easing out. "Be as loud as you want."

I'm crying out instantly from the climax, while Ryker slams deeply into me, chasing his own.

He's close as well. I can tell by his pants. By the hard, heavy grunts. Chase is too, stroking his dick by my face. I want to finish him off with my mouth, but all at once, my brain pops with an image.

"Come on me. At the same time," I demand.

Chase roars. "You heard her," he says to his partner in pleasing me.

In no time, Ryker pulls out, while Chase flips me to my back effortlessly. Ryker must remove the condom in a flurry, since he's bare now, bending over me, jerking his dick on my stomach till he comes with a howl, ropes of white streaking across my stomach.

"Yes, fucking yes," Chase says, and the sight must send him over the cliff too, since he's painting my tits with his come.

The sight is so dirty, so sexy that I shove a hand between my thighs, flicking my clit furiously while rubbing their come into my tits with my other hand. Seconds later, I'm launching myself into a third orgasm from my own fingers.

As I come loudly, they're sandwiching me while kissing my face, my hair, my cheeks. They're adoring me with their mouths and their tender touches as I pant and moan. Then, they both curl against me, holding me post-orgasm till I come down from this high.

Only I don't think I ever will.

* * *

Sex is messy when you're doing it with one person. But two? This shower is extra necessary.

I'm standing under the rainfall shower in Chase's city of a bathroom, finally clean of the evidence of my double dose of spunk but savoring the hot water.

Oh, and I'm savoring Ryker's hands on me. His attention makes me feel soft and special.

After a speed demon shower before I got in, Chase left to take Nacho for a pee break. That's something Jasper never did—walk my dog—so I'm feeling a little soft and squishy for Chase too.

Ryker stands behind me, roaming his soapy hands down my back, spreading my strawberry bodywash over my skin. When he finishes my back, he spins me around and washes my arms, then my belly one more time. When he's done, he meets my gaze, a concerned look in his dark eyes. "How are you feeling?"

I blink as the steam enrobes us, trying to get a read on him, but his face is stoic again. "Um, good? Should I not be good?"

He drops a kiss to my forehead, lingering there. "Just making sure. It was a lot for you," he says softly.

Ohh.

Wow. That's another thing I'm not used to either. A guy checking in with me post-sex. Asking thoughtful questions. My skin warms up, and I don't think it's from the heat of the shower.

"Turns out I like...*a lot*," I say, a little vulnerable as I make that admission.

He tucks a finger under my chin. His midnight blue eyes capture mine with a steadiness that unnerves me since I don't know what it means. Especially since he's so quiet as he studies me, head tilted, thumb stroking my chin. Then, at last, he speaks. "Me too."

My heart beats so fast, understanding his silence now. I swallow, trying to figure out what to say next. But maybe this is one of those times when words don't matter.

I just let out a heady breath and say, "I'm still hungry. Are you?"

With a smile, he says, "Famished."

* * *

Dried off and lotioned up, I pull on an An Open Book T-shirt, with the words *I like big books and I cannot lie* on it. Then I grab a pair of sleep shorts from my bag in my room, along with my glasses, and pad out to the kitchen where I'm greeted by twenty pounds of love, charging me.

I bend down and Nacho leaps into my lap, tail wagging madly. "Was I gone forever?" I ask him.

With a happy whimper, he licks my face, giving me his yes. "Well, now I'm back, little guy," I say, then kiss his snout and return him to the couch. Immediately, he burrows his nose into the corner sofa pillow like it's his new girlfriend. He's actually rubbing his face against it. "Well, someone is in insta-love," I remark as I head to the island counter to join the guys, where they've set down the takeout food.

Chase hands me a glass of white wine. "Thank you," I say, drawing a satisfied breath.

This is the life. Mediterranean food. A late-night hang with two fantastic guys. My favorite critter nearby.

But when I take a swallow, I nearly spit up the sauvignon. So much for good behavior. The perfect pup has turned full perv again. Nacho has shoved the couch pillow between his legs and is humping it.

Mortified, I set down the glass, pop up from the stool, and rush over to him. "Nacho! No! Stop now!"

That only motivates him more. He pumps faster. Rocking those doggy hips wham-bam-thank-you-ma'am style. This is so embarrassing. My dog is getting it on with our host's pillow, and I can only imagine how he's going to defile it any second. I do *not* want to clean that up. I will die.

"Go, Nacho!" Chase shouts.

"That's it, boy! Bring it home," Ryker catcalls.

"Don't encourage him," I beg.

My face flushes beet red as I grab my randy beast, but he clutches the pillow tightly, and I have to wrestle it from his libidinous paws. "We are guests," I say, admonishing him when I finally free the pillow from his grasp.

But the horndog is still humping air. "You were supposed to be a model canine," I chide as the guys cheer him on.

Not fair.

Nacho pumps a few more times, determined to mate with a cushion.

Then, one more time for those in the back.

But, like a wind-up toy winding down, Nacho gives a final half-cocked thrust before he runs out of steam. Thoroughly shamed, I set him on the geometric area rug in front of the couch. "Stay here. On the floor. And don't embarrass me a second time," I say, and Nacho curls up like he did nothing disgusting.

What a short memory.

Chase snorts from the counter.

Next to him, Ryker laughs. "Good luck with that. Your dog likes to eat undies and fuck. Chances are high he'll embarrass you again."

I cover my face. "I can't believe he did that," I say as I return to the counter, shooting Nacho a steely glare before I join the guys.

"Really? You can't?" Ryker asks with a lift of his brow.

Chase pours some wine. "I mean, after everything you've told us about him."

"Seems like this tracks for Nacho," Ryker adds.

"But hey, at least he didn't...*finish*."

I sigh. "Yes, there is that small victory."

Chase pats the chair. "Eat. Drink. Then, you need to get some sleep."

"Yeah, you have to work tomorrow," Ryker says, gruff but caring too. "You need your rest."

Wow. Is this aftercare? For my newly unlocked threesome kink? If so, sign me up. But, in all fairness, I'm pretty sure being told to eat yummy food and go to bed early is, in fact, one of my pre-existing kinks.

It's a life kink, if you will.

I sit down and we eat. This should feel strange, a post-sex meal with two guys. I've only ever done post-sex fooding with one guy, of course.

But the three of us seem to slide into these moments naturally, like we did this morning with the pancakes. Still, as I scoop up some hummus onto a pita, I'm brimming with curiosity I just can't keep to myself.

After I take a bite, I say, "So, I'm dying to know something, Chase."

"Hit me up," he says, putting his fork down before he takes a bite of the herb chicken.

"You've never done this before. This whole—" I flap a hand in the direction of the bedroom, suddenly shy again.

After what I just did, how can I be shy? Maybe it's because talking about sex is its own kind of intimacy. It's one thing to strip naked physically. It's entirely another to do it emotionally, with words.

I try again, owning my awkward as much as I own my pleasure. "This whole...three-way."

"Devil's three-way," Ryker adds dryly.

I sit primly. "I prefer manwich," I say, then laugh with them.

From my dog's dirty deeds to nicknames for threesomes, I don't miss my ex one bit.

Wow.

I really don't.

I sit up straighter on that realization. I don't miss Jasper. Also, I *can* relax in bed. I *can* let go. I just needed to be with the right guy. Or, really, the right guys.

"My ex was wrong," I say, almost like I've come out of a trance.

"About literally everything," Ryker mutters. "Except liking hockey."

"Facts," Chase says.

I shake my head adamantly. "Yes, but he was wrong about me too. He said I couldn't relax in bed. That I was all up in my head."

"That guy never deserved you for a single second," Ryker bites out.

Chase narrows his eyes, his tone turning dark and protective. "I swear if I ever see that guy…"

I kinda want to see them run into Jasper, but only because I like the protective sides of Ryker and Chase. I take a deep breath, and it feels cleansing, like I'm letting go of the last remnants of Jasper, the last pieces of doubt. I don't feel like Jasper has as much power over me even as he did last night. I haven't even bothered to check my socials to see if he's commented on any of the photos I put up.

Maybe those revenge pics helped.

But more likely, maybe a couple nights of great sex did the trick. It's like I'm leaving behind the revenge era, and moving into the…well, the devil's three-way era.

Speaking of…

I take another bite of my hummus-covered pita, and when I've got some food in me, I return to the topic that intrigues me most. "If you've never done this before, how are you so good at…the whole directing thing?" I ask Chase, eager to know.

The golden guy leans back in his stool and wipes a napkin across the corner of his mouth, letting a slow smile spread.

But he's not the one who answers my question. Ryker clears his throat. "He's not team captain for nothing."

I turn to Ryker, intrigued. "But you're not on his team?"

"Not now, but we played together when we were younger."

"So you know his leadership style?" I ask.

"Yep. On the ice, off the ice, Chase always has a plan."

I shift my gaze to Chase. "So, you're naturally that way in bed too?"

Chase scratches his jaw, then gives a quick nod, owning his bossy side, but his leadership side too. "I suppose so. And Ryker here just gets the job done. That's his style. No fanfare. Just delivering one thousand percent."

I hardly know Ryker and yet I know that describes him perfectly. Makes me think I was wrong last night in my assessment that his personality style is the challenger. He's more the loyalist, since he's a defender, which is what he does on the ice.

"When did you two play hockey together?" I ask, then snag an olive and pop it in my mouth.

Chase watches the olive slide past my lips with avid interest before he says, "We were on the same team in high school and middle school."

"And grade school," Ryker puts in, then adds with a cheeky grin, "Shocking, isn't it, that we met on the ice."

Immediately, my brain supplies an image of an outgoing boy and a more reserved one connecting through sport. "I'm picturing the two of you at a rink skating awkwardly, passing a puck back and forth, then saying, *Did we just become best friends?*"

Chase laughs. "Close, but not quite."

"Fine, what did I get wrong?"

Ryker leans closer, brushes a strand of still damp hair from my forehead. "We didn't skate awkwardly, sweetness. Not once."

They're so cocky, and I love it.

* * *

After dinner, I try to insist on cleaning up alone since Ryker bought dinner and Chase gave me a home, but they insist they won't let me do chores solo. They help me, and once the kitchen is clean, we all head down the hall.

Will we go to separate rooms?

But as quickly as that thought arrives, it disappears since Chase nods to his big room—our sex room. "You're sleeping with *us*, Trina."

Well, it *is* an order, so I follow *them* and slide into the big bed. Ryker's right behind me. But even though I'm dead tired, and so damn worn out, there's one thing we have to discuss.

The ground rules going forward.

My stomach swirls with nerves, but we've already vaulted past last night's ground rules, just like we bypassed separate bedrooms. This will be awkward no matter what, so when Chase dims the lights, I dive in.

"So, we're doing this for..." I flash back to the start of the evening and to Chase's words. "The next week while I'm here?"

That came out a little strangled, but at least I said it. There.

Ryker turns to me, his expression thoughtful. "That work for you?"

For a brief moment, I picture nights with them beyond next week. But that won't happen. That's not on the table for them, and truly, it'd be foolish of me to imagine anything past the next week. Even if I've moved past my ex, that doesn't mean I need to move *to* a couple new guys.

I gulp, then nod.

Chase slides in on the other side of the bed, kissing my shoulder. "I know you're not looking for anything more. No pressure then from anyone."

"We'll just have fun as we work through your list," Ryker adds.

That'll take some time. We're all busy, and I checked out their hockey schedules today. With them being on different teams, and with my shifts at the store —since sometimes I work nights—we won't always be around at the same time.

"We were very productive tonight. We crossed off one, two, and three," I say with a sly grin.

Chase lifts a brow, cycling back to the start of our sex seminar, I suspect. "One was double BJs," he says, like he's counting off.

In no time, Ryker jumps in, "Two was pussy worship and dick devotion at the same time."

"And three was fucking and fellating," Chase concludes, but then taps his chin. "But now I really need to know something—was rubbing our come all over your sweet tits while you played with your pussy on your list? Because that's some very specific smut."

"And I am here for any sort of improv work in bed," Ryker adds.

I just smile. "I went off script for that one."

But speaking of my list, there is another ground rule that'd be good to establish. Only this is a tougher one to broach. It might cause jealousies, and I don't want to divide them. I do want to be on the up and up. Still, I feel wobbly and uncertain as I say, "So, um, I hate to bring this up, but what happens if, well, if I'm say, in the shower with Ryker, and well—"

Chase narrows his eyes, his voice like a hiss. "This your way of telling me you blew him in the shower?"

"No! I didn't. I didn't even think about it."

"Gee, thanks," Ryker deadpans.

Shoot. I've made this worse. "I didn't mean that in a bad way—"

"I'm kidding." Chase grins and sets a reassuring hand on my shoulder. "It's all good. I swear."

I breathe a sigh of relief. "You had me going."

He kisses my cheek. "If you'd have asked me a couple hours ago, I wouldn't have known what to say. I was trying to figure out what I wanted, but Ryker and I talked beforehand," Chase continues earnestly, just putting himself out there for me. "We like sharing you, but it'd be selfish as fuck if I said you two can't touch if I'm not home or in the same room, know what I mean? Or vice versa to be honest. Now, do I want to shower *with* the two of you? Like, get up in the morning and shower?" He shrugs, but it's a *that'd be a no* shrug. "I probably don't. But if I'm sound asleep and you feel like sucking the chrome off his bumper, have at it."

"Or if you need an O for the road before work, I'll take care of it," Ryker offers.

I snuggle into the pillows. I want to wrap myself up in these fantastic ground rules. "I guess that makes you orgasm makers," I say.

"Better than orgasm matchmakers," Chase says, and the guys knock fists across me.

"Way more fun," Ryker seconds.

This has been fun. Wildly fun.

But it's also been intense. Incredible. Surprising. Eye-opening. And also, just...good.

These guys make me feel so good about myself.

I didn't feel that way at the end with Jasper. I definitely didn't feel good when I found my darling puking up panty parts. And I've felt like a loser the last few weeks, ditched by a guy who took me for granted and only cared about his precious hockey tickets.

But looking back, I don't think I felt so great when I was *with* Jasper either. I stayed with him because he was good enough, or so I thought. But mostly I stayed because my family liked him.

I stayed longer than I should have.

This time, I won't overstay my welcome.

But I do want them to enjoy my company when I'm not naked as much as they do when I'm dressed for D. So I home in on the thing they like best. "Why do you like hockey so much? Since it's so fast-paced? I noticed that last night. It's wild to watch. There's always something going on, even though I had no clue what was happening. But the whole time, I was thinking *they're flying.*"

Chase rolls to his side and props his head in his hand, eyes twinkling. "That's why it's the best. It's relentless. You're always moving. Always going," he says, pure enthusiasm in his voice.

"But...what the hell is going on? I just...never liked it because," I say, a little guilty for disliking their livelihood, then it hits me. I never liked hockey because I never understood it. "Because everything was happening all at once and I couldn't figure it out."

"Want to know the basics?" Ryker asks, his voice brighter than I've ever heard it sound, a sort of youthful wonder to it.

If Jasper had asked, I'd have rolled my eyes and said no way. I never wanted to understand hockey when I was with him, since he operated on a *hockey before you* level. But these guys live and breathe the sport for a living, for their families, for the pure love of the game, and I want to understand *them*.

"Sure, but I'm a total newbie."

My two guys give me a lesson, showing me videos on their phones, explaining the basics from face-off to goal, blue lines to red lines, and penalties to power plays.

Ryker finishes with, "So that's hockey."

"Basically, it's exhilarating," I say, summing it up.

"You got it," Ryker says.

"And you have to be fearless."

"Exactly," Chase adds.

I let out a contemplative sigh, connecting all the dots of what they just told me. "You play on ice, but you need to be fueled by fire. That's the hockey vibe."

Chase laughs, then it turns into a yawn. "That's all you need to know, Trina. Hockey is a vibe."

"Hockey is life," Ryker adds.

Wait. *Wait.* I think I understand hockey now. I park my hands behind my head, letting a smile take over. "I'm pretty sure I had a hat trick tonight," I say, pausing as they both lock eyes, waiting for me. "Of Os."

They both look stupidly happy as they say *yes, yes you did.*

I settle deeper under the covers, my eyes fluttering closed when I hear a whine.

A sad, plaintive cry.

"My darling," I say, sitting up at the sound of Nacho. He's stretching up on the side of the bed, pawing at the cover.

I look at Chase hopefully. "Um...can he?"

"He better," Chase says, then scoops up my pup and hands him to me. Instantly, my dog settles under the covers, curling up right against my chest.

"Wait," Chase says. "He sleeps between your tits?"

I glance down at my main squeeze. I'm so used to his sleeping preferences I hardly think about them. "Yeah, he claimed this spot a while ago."

"Fucking alpha dog," Ryker grumbles then turns the other way with a huff.

When I wake up briefly in the middle of the night, Ryker's nose is buried in my hair, and Chase's hand is on my thigh.

A devil's sleeping three-way and one dirty dog.

19

A GIFT FROM THE HOCKEY GUYS

Trina

In the morning, I get ready for work quietly so I don't wake the sleeping athletes. It's game day—well, night—for both of them, and I want them to have their rest. I tiptoe to the kitchen.

I'm as fast as can be as I whip up pancakes and slice strawberries, then leave them on a plate, along with instructions for heating up the stack on a pink sheet of paper I ripped off from a notebook in my purse.

Don't fight over the pancakes, guys. I made enough for both of you. Now, go work out hard and play harder tonight. And don't forget, strawberries make everything better.

PS: I'm thinking #4 on the list sounds good. Maybe soon?

.   .   .

Then, I tell them what number four is.

I head to the door with Nacho leashed up and ready to rumble at doggie daycare, but before I reach it, a voice still gravelly with sleep calls out gruffly to me, "Where are you sneaking off to with that cutie?"

My heart thumps from the affectionate term for my dog. I swivel around. Chase's a snack and a half. His hair is beyond disheveled, all golden brown and messy in the morning light. His stubble's a day thicker. He must not have shaved yesterday. He scratches his jaw as he strides across the hardwood floors, all backlit from the windows, looking like scrumptious morning sin as he comes up to me at the door, then bends and scratches Nacho's head.

"Well, I was leaving for work a little early so I could take him to doggy daycare," I say. "I have an author coming in for a signing this morning, so I figured it'd be easier if Nacho went to Throw Me A Bone."

Slowly Chase rises, cocking his head, one brow arched. Clearly that doesn't compute for him. "Um, no."

"No...what?"

"No, you're not taking him to doggy daycare." He's as commanding as he is in bed, and the tone is dangerous for me to hear first thing in the morning. I'll be ordering new panties before sundown.

But I focus on the conversation, not my reaction to his voice.

"Why?" I ask, letting the word stretch out because I'm really not getting his meaning.

He points his thumb at his bare chest. "*I'm* doggy daycare. I want to help with your dog. I'm free for the next several hours," he says with a lopsided grin. "Coach stopped morning skate this season, so I don't have to head to the arena until the early afternoon. So if that works out for you, I'd really like to spend the morning with Nacho. If you must know, we made plans already."

We.

He's talking about my dog the same way I do.

Dear god. My heart is thundering stupidly fast. Yes, it's just an offer to take care of my dog, but it's also the way to my bruised heart. "Sure," I say, with a smile. "I'd really appreciate that. But what are your plans?"

He closes the remaining distance. "Don't you worry about that," he says, then curls a hand around my head and presses a stubbly kiss to my cheek.

Mmm. That tone of voice is definitely doing its thing. "Since I don't have to rush to doggy daycare now, I suppose I can say thank you properly," I say, lifting my chin and meeting his naughty gaze.

The man reads me instantly, since his eyes darken, and he erases his grin, replacing it with a stern expression. "Get down on your knees like a good girl."

I obey, then part my lips seductively, opening for him, waiting. He takes out his cock, then pushes my hair from my face and slides a thumb along my jawline. "I almost hate to mess up your lipstick. But I'm going to do it anyway."

Once I draw him into my mouth, he continues to lavish me with praise and dirty words. "That's right. That's a proper thank you."

I take him deeper and he fucks my mouth merci-lessly, till his groans get longer, telling me he's close.

I steal a glance at my dog, and the perv is staring up at Chase like he's tapping an annoyed paw and saying *can you move it along.*

But that's better than trying to hump Chase's leg while I finish him. I give a deep suck, then Chase floods my throat with a strangled grunt.

And I spoke too soon.

My randy dog has wrapped his arms around Chase's calf and is doing the doggy dance. I swat my dog away as Chase eases out of my mouth with a laugh.

I jerk my gaze to the dog. "Couch. Now. Go sit."

Like he wasn't the paragon of perv, Nacho trots away, tail wagging.

Once my pooch is curled up on the couch, Chase looks down at me with a sexy smirk. "Your multitasking with simultaneous dog training and BJ finishing deserves a reward."

"A peanut butter biscuit?"

"Better," he says, then hauls me up, spins me around, and pushes me against the door. He yanks up my sundress, tugs down my panties, and squeezes my ass.

"I bet more spanking is on your list after the other night," he says huskily.

I shiver. "It is."

He kneads my right cheek, soft, gentle, a little tanta-lizing, before he lifts a hand and smacks.

I gasp. Then I moan when he rubs his palm over me tenderly again, smoothing out the sting. He does the same to my other cheek, and when he raises his hand again, I tense but with delicious anticipation. His palm comes down harder this time. I moan again.

"Remember when you said you just had unreasonable expectations in bed?" he whispers in my ear. "The night we met you?"

"Yes."

He brushes his lips across my ear. "You should have unreasonable expectations. So we can exceed every single one of them."

God. *Yes.* "News flash. You are. Oh, and I learned I like spanking."

Yup. That's another kink I'll toss into my big box of bedroom quirks. I'm gonna need a bigger boat for my fantasies.

"Good," he says, then squeezes my ass again. "Mmm. This ass. I want to play with it, Trina."

He hasn't even seen my note yet, but he's clearly eager for number four. Me too, since the only way I'll be able to climb the double dick mountain is with a little booty action beforehand. Hence, number four—butt play.

"You should then. *Soon*," I say, encouraging him.

"The things we'll do to you next time," he says, and I love that *we*. Love that he talks dirty to me about *their* plans for me as he plays with my clit while smacking my ass, then pinching my nipples till I'm melting and breaking apart before work.

I'm still gasping for air when he brushes a tender kiss to my lips. "Love your ground rules. Make sure to take care of my buddy sometime too," he says.

"You looking out for your friend's dick?"

"I'm thoughtful like that."

You know, he really is. And since he mentions Ryker, that reminds me. "There's something you can help me with for Ryker."

"Name it," Chase says.

I tell him what I need. "Can you send it sometime today?"

"I'm on it," he says, then I kiss him back, a buzzy, druggy kiss that's dangerous. It could lead to skipping work and lazing away the day. So I break it. I'm not such a hot mess that I'd miss work.

I am, however, a hot mess in other ways, so before I head to the store, I brush my teeth and change my panties.

* * *

That afternoon, I'm leaving the bookstore when Chase sends me a picture of Nacho sitting on a chair staring longingly at a latte—presumably—next to a guy who looks a lot like Chase.

> Chase: Took Nacho out for coffee with my little brother this morning. Travis tried to use your dog as a lady magnet, but I said nope. Travis has to learn to be charming on his own.

> Trina: Such a good big brother.
> Teaching him important life lessons.

Chase: You'll be pleased to know
Nacho didn't try to hump Travis's leg.
So...maybe that's progress for him?

Trina: Or perhaps your brother doesn't
have a humpable leg.

Chase: Fair point. My calf might just be
very fuckable. But I'm concerned your
dog might be trying to recruit a third
guy into our night-time crew, Trina. He
was pretty excited when the UPS driver
showed up to drop off a delivery of
protein powder right after you left.

Trina: Please say he didn't try to make
little leg babies with the delivery guy?

Chase: He's easing him in with tongue
first. He licked his leg rather than
mated with it.

Trina: So...we keep proving the
fuckable-ness of most legs.

Chase: You and your fancy words.

As I turn onto California Street, heading to my
temporary quarters, my phone pings again. This time,
though, it's Ryker. Well, this is like the double jackpot
text day. I open it, but there's no message. Just a link to a
Scrabble game. Bring it on. I hit accept. A minute later,
he's made the first move.

Latex.

Trina: Show off.

Ryker: That implies I only played that word to peacock in front of you.

Trina: You did.

Ryker: I play to win.

Trina: Well, Mister Competitive I've got...

I play the word...*moxie.*

Ryker: Yes, you do.

We vie a little more, then the group chat pings, the one I've so cleverly named The Hockey Guys At Your Service.

I open it as I reach Chase's block.

Ryker: Placing an online order. Do you need anything from the store?

Trina: Hardware store? Shoe store? Toy shop?

Ryker: Hardware store, Trina. I'm ordering from the hardware store.

Trina: Oh, I love tools. A lot.

Chase: She definitely doesn't need a hammer though.

Ryker: She has access to two already.

Trina: But can you order me some screws? It'll help me with some items on my to-do list.

Chase: Fixed your last text for you.

He sends back a screenshot that changes the last word to *screwing.*

Trina: Actually, please make it a nailing.

Ryker: That's a step above a screwing.

Chase: And right below a pounding. Pretty sure that's on your list.

Trina: Why, yes it is. Then ideally, some avocado sushi later.

Ryker: Order accepted for everything.

* * *

That night, while I'm lounging on Chase's couch with my main squeeze, and finishing a romance for this week's book club, there's a food delivery, but no chance for leg babies. Nacho stays on the sofa. I take the bags and thank the guy. Back inside, I unload some scrumptious groceries. Eggs and strawberries, blueberries and yummy bread, veggies and noodles. It's a feast. The best part though is when the doorbell rings a few minutes later and a delivery guy from Ding and Dine drops off fresh avocado sushi.

And a note.

From the hockey guys.

It's delicious, but the thought tastes even better. So good in fact that I turn on the last few minutes of some hockey. But when the game ends, one guy will likely come home tense and tight. The other exuberant.

* * *

Ryker is home first from his game, but I'm only half awake when he slides into bed.

"Saw you won," I say sleepily.

"We did."

"And you played well," I add.

He chuckles as he nuzzles my neck. "How do you even know?"

"Hey, I'm a fast learner," I say.

"Are you a hockey expert now like you're a lexiphile?"

I roll my eyes at the ridiculous word. "Like I said, you're such a show-off."

He drops a soft kiss to my shoulder. "You like word show-offs."

"Also, how do you even know the word for word lover?" Then I shake my head, answering the question myself. "One of your word podcasts."

"Yes," he says. "It's called...wait for it...Lexiphiles."

"Then impress me with some word thing you learned on the Lexiphiles podcast."

In a raspy voice, he whispers, "Lexiphiles rhymes with sexiphiles."

"Is that even a word?"

"I think the term for that is just *horndog.*"

I laugh, then it turns into a yawn.

"Go to sleep," he says softly.

It's sweet, the way he doesn't push for sex, just like it's sweet how he lowers his guard with me when the lights are down.

"I will, but how's Chase?" I ask, a little worried since his team lost. Will he want to fuck it out or does he shut down after a loss? I've only seen him after a win—the other night. Ryker's team lost that game on Friday, and he was moody. Then again, I think he was moody because he didn't want to entertain a VIP guest. Maybe they've been doing this long enough that they let the losses roll off them.

Ryker's quiet for a beat, then in a resigned voice, he says, "In a bit of a funk. I ran into him outside. He's going for a walk."

My brow knits. "Is that what he does when his team loses?"

"Sometimes. He just beats himself up so much."

"Does he need anything?"

Ryker shakes his head. "To stop beating himself up," he says with a heavy sigh.

I sigh too. "I hope he does."

"Me too."

20

GOOD MORNING TO ME

Trina

In the morning, I don't want to get out of bed. I'm having the most fantastic dream.

Like my body's made of liquid and desire as some dream guy kisses me. Here, there, everywhere.

Then, I moan, and huh.

That doesn't sound like a dream moan.

And it doesn't sound like it came from me either. It's a man's moan, and that man has a thick beard that's grazing the back of my neck.

My eyes flutter open. Chase's side of the bed is empty. He came in late but I don't know when. At some point in the middle of the night, I just realized he was here, a hand on my dog and me.

Maybe that was all Chase needed after his walk.

I'm guessing my dog's in the living room, licking his food bowl hopefully. Because here in bed, it's just Ryker and me. He's holding me and dusting a soft kiss to my shoulder.

But his breathing is even, regular.

Is he kissing my neck in his sleep? I think he is. That's somehow sexier than his waking neck kisses. His strong arm is roped around my waist, but his fingers are a little busy, gently stroking my stomach.

It feels so good.

And maybe it was dream me who got turned on but wide awake me is aroused too. I stretch against him, hoping he wakes soon.

Then, his steady breathing halts, his body jerks, and he must reorient since he quickly wraps his arms tighter around me. "You smell good in the morning," he rumbles sleepily in my ear.

"So do you," I say, since Ryker's yummy when he's got that forest scent working, and when he smells like dirty dreams, like he does right now.

"But I bet you taste even better," he adds.

I snuggle closer. "Want to find out?"

He rubs his beard against me in a clear yes. "I'm starving. You better sit on my face now, and hold onto the headboard."

Yes, please!

A minute later, I'm wearing just my sleep cami, and I'm rocking against his warm, hungry mouth, his bristly beard scratching my thighs in the most delicious way.

I'm moaning and gasping, and he's growling and groaning as he grips my hips. He tugs me down against his face, devouring me. I don't know how he can breathe, but I don't think he cares. He's eating me out like he'd happily die this way.

I don't know who's louder—him or me. But I know this—his sounds send me over the edge as I hold on tight to the headboard.

When I finally come down from my morning high and flop to my stomach beside him, he drags a hand across his mouth, then strokes his cock a couple times.

I shake my head. "Nope, that's mine. I want it right on my chest."

"Get on your back and take it."

I comply, lifting up my tank, then pushing my breasts together for him. A minute later, he's straddling my chest, fucking the tunnel of my tits, then painting me with his come.

He collapses onto his back too, then hands me a tissue. We're both still panting and groaning when the door creaks open, and a few seconds later, Chase says, "Good girl. I see you took care of Ryker's dick this morning like I told you to."

Ryker flips him the bird. "I took care of her pussy, you jackass. Also, she didn't have to do any hard work just now. I was pretty much all about her today."

"Aren't you just a perfect book boyfriend then," Chase teases, and his mood seems the same as always —upbeat, outgoing. He must have stopped beating himself up about the loss.

"How do you know about book boyfriends?" I ask as I get out of bed, grabbing my glasses.

Chase lifts a playful brow. "There's this woman— let's call her our temporary roomie—who likes books.

Big, spicy, dirty books. So, maybe I did a little research."

Then, he demonstrates just how well he did his research when I reach the doorframe and he leans against the door. He rakes his eyes over me from head to toe, and nails—just fucking nails—the doorframe move.

I bite the corner of my lip.

Chase lets a rumble escape his throat, then says, "I fucking need you."

Need.

That word lights me up all over again. He does need to fuck it out. But first, he heads into the en suite bathroom, runs the tap, then returns with a washcloth. He hands it to Ryker, and my morning lover cleans up my chest as I take my glasses off. Then, like they planned this, Chase says to his friend, "Kiss her while I put that butterfly vibe on her."

What? There's a butterfly coming my way? Mondays just might not suck after all. "Nobody told me this was a vibrator party," I say, my voice full of glee.

"You mentioned you liked Maverick. Let's see how much you like the one we got for you yesterday," he says, then pulls a pretty pink contraption out of the nightstand.

"You little sneaks," I tease, but then the teasing fades when Chase straps the toy around my waist, positioning the butterfly right over my clit.

He hands Ryker the controls and tugs me to the end of the bed.

After he covers himself, he fucks me good and hard

while Ryker kneels behind me, working the controls as he bites my neck and kisses my ear.

It's official. All my circuits have overloaded, and I am bursting, buzzing, and blissed out everywhere. This was not on my list. Not at all. This is just a pure book boyfriend move.

Or really, a double one.

* * *

The next morning, I have just enough time to take my boy around a block or two before work, so I grab Nacho's leash and get my tripod ready. Ryker's at the gym for a workout, but Chase is lounging on the couch, listening to something on his phone, so I wave and motion to see if he wants to join me.

"Always," he says, tucking his earbuds away. "Scary birds circling the apocalyptic sky can wait."

"Elaborate," I say as we leave. "On the scary birds."

"Oh, just this horror story I'm listening to," he says as we reach the street.

"You meant it?" I ask, intrigued. "The night we met when you said you read horror stories."

He shrugs, downplaying it. "Well, I listen rather than read."

"Chase, it's the same. You're earhole reading instead of eyeball reading," I say.

"Sure. We'll call it that," he says evasively, and I bet he had a teacher somewhere along the line who said listening to a book was cheating. "Did someone tell you that listening doesn't count?"

"Probably, like it's TV, but whatever. School was never my thing. Not like it is for you and Ryker, obviously," he says, a little resigned. Like maybe he thinks I was a genius student? Or that I want that in a man?

"I was a good student," I admit as Nacho stops to sniff a tree. "But a little aimless once I graduated."

"You?" he asks, like he doesn't quite believe that.

"One hundred percent. I didn't know what I wanted to do after college. I flitted around from job to job. I did random things, like event planning, then social media for a winery. But nothing was very...interesting. Honestly, I mostly just wanted to get paid to read. I still haven't quite found that gig yet, but the bookstore comes close enough."

"Doesn't sound aimless to me," he says as the dog resumes his pace, trotting by my side.

"Tell that to my sister. And my parents."

"They don't like your job?"

"I think they just expect me to do something they understand. Be a teacher, or a nurse, or a librarian. Even *own* a bookstore. But running it? They don't know if it's my endgame or just a way station. And honestly, I don't know either."

"And I don't think you have to know. You're happy doing it, right?"

"It's fun. It works for me. That's sort of all I've figured out."

"Sometimes I think we try too hard to have all the answers," he says, sounding a little faraway for a few seconds, even distant as we round the block.

"But you have it figured out, don't you? Because, hello. Pro sports is not an easy job to get."

"It's not like I have *any* clue what I'd do if hockey didn't pan out. I mean, I have zero idea, Trina. So basically, I really need hockey to work out," he says in a playful whisper, but it masks a certain amount of desperation. *I think.*

I bump my shoulder to his. "News flash. *It is.*"

He smiles but then looks to the sky, like he's searching for something he can't quite find. Maybe looking for his father there? My heart lurches for him. I'm not sure he'll answer, but impulsively, I ask, "Is he part of what drives you? Your dad?"

Chase sighs, sort of contemplatively. "Yeah. He did such a great job taking care of us when I was a kid. My mom didn't work outside of the home. She raised us and helped him out, and when he was sick, he was worried about how she'd handle it all. My brothers were still young. He was so torn apart knowing he'd leave that task to her. All the responsibility," he says, with obvious emotion in his voice. He swallows roughly. "I promised him I'd look out for them too though. I try to do that. Every day. And I really hope I can."

That explains so much about him—his hockey-or-bust drive, but also his charm. It's like he needs both to deliver on this promise. "You are," I say, emphatically.

We're quiet for a stretch, just walking the dog as I absorb what Chase shared. But there's one piece of the Chase puzzle I don't quite get yet. Maybe his reading tastes are just a predilection, but I'm curious if there's more to it. "You don't strike me as a horror guy."

He laughs skeptically. "Yeah? Why's that?"

"Blood and gore and fear? It doesn't quite align."

"Course it does. I play hockey. We're all about blood and fear," he says, then flashes me his cocky grin—a grin that I'm beginning to recognize as his trademark. Then he sighs, like he's letting down his guard. "So," he says, scratching his jaw. "I was kind of...*flat* after my dad died. I felt...nothing. Which in theory sounds good for an athlete, but in reality is pretty bad. I was a little unmotivated. And that wasn't going to cut it. I couldn't afford to be unmotivated. Fortunately, I picked up a horror novel at the time, and the fear and the adrenaline in the story sort of jolted me. Made me...*feel again.*"

That actually tracks surprisingly well now that he says it. "I get that."

"And I got hooked. The stories kind of get my blood pumping. Keep me keyed up."

"I could send you some horror recs. Some new novels that are good in audio. Horror isn't my specialty, but I have to know the whole store."

His smile is magnetic. "That'd be cool."

Briefly, I wonder if it was the dog he craved when he asked me to move in for the week, or if it was the chance to talk about life and stuff while walking a dog.

21

MY DIGITAL STYLIST

Ryker

It's lunchtime and I'm not due at practice for two more hours. Gives me plenty of time to handle this task with Trina. Should be a quick and easy errand.

But as I walk up Fillmore Street toward An Open Book, I don't feel the same way I've felt the previous times I've headed into this bookshop. All those other times, I was stopping by alone to pick up books from the wish list at the library. This time, though, it almost feels like a date.

With her.

But that's a ridiculous feeling. We're not having a date in the middle of the day. This is just her lunch break on a Tuesday and she's helping me out. Still, as I pass a quirky gift shop a block away, I double back to check my reflection in the window, adjusting the cuffs of my Henley then running a hand over my beard. And maybe through my hair too.

There. I'm ready to see Trina.

I resume my pace, and I try to ignore the way my pulse speeds up as I near her store, because that's a dumb reaction to a fucking store.

Game day attitude on, I push open the door, swing my gaze around the endless shelves, teeming with stories and information and history and words that I just want to gobble up, till I find her. She's in the romance section, near the front of the store, and she's adjusting a sandwich board sign. It's for the Page Turners Book Club. There's a lipstick-mark design on the sign, and it says this week, they're meeting Friday at six. Trina tugs the board an inch or so, then pushes her red glasses up the bridge of her nose and studies it.

Damn, she's adorable.

I kind of just want to watch her in her element for a minute, but that seems stalkery. Especially when she peers toward the door, then spots me and shoots me a smile that makes me feel things I shouldn't be feeling.

Like, *possibility*. Such a dumb, dumb thing.

I try to shuck it off as she raises a finger, letting me know she'll be just a minute. I give a nod because it's not a big deal. This is just her helping me with a little project. An image makeover—that's all.

She heads behind the counter then calls me over, reaching under the counter and grabbing some books. "Here are the books you picked out. I pulled them for you."

"Oh. Thanks," I say. I sent her the list this morning, but I guess I figured we'd go around the store and grab them together, and now I'm hoping this doesn't shorten our not-date. But even if it does, it's fine. It's completely fine.

"And when I ring you up, I'm going to take a picture of you," she says, walking me through this whole image thing she mapped out the other night. "And you don't have to smile. Or look like you're posing. It's just a candid shot."

She makes it sound so easy, but my shoulders still tense. I roll them, trying to let go.

"You can do this," she says, encouragingly.

"Just don't make me look like a jackass," I mutter.

She tilts her head. "Ryker, I know you don't want to tell the world, but you really do want to help, and this is what your picture will do. It lets people know how they can help too."

Fine. She's right.

She breaks out her phone and shoots a picture of me buying the books. After she drops them all into a canvas bag then thrusts it to me, she hustles around the counter, telling a woman in a cardigan near the self-help section that she'll be back in a little bit.

That must be her boss since the woman says, "Take your time. And for the love of all that is holy, please check out the new taco truck and tell me if I should go there tonight."

"Tacos are always a good idea, Marisa," she says, then we head out.

"So, is that your book club Friday night?"

"It sure is. I started it online but brought it into the

store," she says, sounding proud of her accomplishment. "Are you angling to join us? I should warn you, we're discussing a super-spicy football romance this week."

I sneer. "Should have been hockey."

"We can't have all the books be about hockey."

"Why not?"

"Well, if every romance is about hockey, then where's the anticipation? Where's the tease?"

"Ah, I get it. The football romances are the foreplay, but the hockey romances come in and finish the job."

"Exactly. And we all need a good tease, don't we? I mean, you're kind of a tease," she says.

I lean a touch closer to her as we continue our stroll past a café with a chalkboard menu, listing more coffee drinks than should be legal. "So are you."

She shoots me a smile that feels private, even though we're in public. And I like it far too much. So I clear my throat and shift gears. "You'll take more pics at the library?"

"Yes, and I did a little something for you." There's a little wobble in her voice as she opens her phone.

"Okay. What is it?" I ask, guarded.

"I set up an account for you since you don't have any socials," she says, and shit is getting real, but she quickly assures me. "It's private right now. You can review it before we make it public. I grabbed some of the shots of you from the team's feed. And then I think we can just add to it here and there," she says, and her voice pitches up as she shows me the screen while we walk.

Warily, I check it out. There are a couple pictures from this season, from practices and games—standard media kit stuff. Then a picture from a game last year, a hard-fought one where we eked out a victory at the last minute. Another one of the team walking down a corridor of an arena in our suits. And damn. There's a shot of me playing in college. Trina did her research.

Then a couple more. A pic of my oldest sister, Ivy, and me at a fashion show Ivy dragged me to several months ago. She's been writing about fashion trends for a bunch of places, trying to make her mark in that world. The image is a selfie she snapped of the two of us in front of the runway. Finally, there is a picture of my mom and me from a few years ago. I'm hugging her after a game. "Where did you get that? And the one of Ivy and me?"

"The other morning I asked Chase to send me some," she says, and it comes out like a confession. "He reached out to your mom and he got these pictures. I thought because you're so close to your family, it'd be another cool thing to show on your feed. What do you think?"

She sounds so hopeful.

And I think my heart thumps annoyingly for her. She's been in my life for less than a week and she's already done something incredibly nice, but also something that feels...real. The woman figured me out in only a few days. "Thank you," I say, my throat a little tight with unexpected emotion.

"You're welcome." She sounds happy, and I like the sound of that. "Oh, also, she said to remind you that you're having lunch with her and Chase's mom next week, after you both return from your next away series." Trina gives a crisp nod. "Whew, hopefully I got that message right."

I smile. "You did. And it's on the schedule."

"You're close with her?" she asks as we walk. Her tone is curious, but not pushy. When I first met her, I suspected she was up to no good with all her questions. Now, I can hear her legit interest in people, and in me. Which I like too.

"My dad took off when I was in middle school, so it's my job to look after her and my sisters," I say, and that's more than I tell most people.

"That's why you didn't like Boner Boy," she says, and I jerk my gaze to her in question. "At Katie's prom. You really do worry about boys and your sisters," she says.

I sure do. "Yeah. I don't want them to get hurt."

"Did your dad hurt your mom?" she asks.

I tense at the mention of him. But I don't hold back this time. Trina's been so warm, so open, in bed and out of bed. I don't trust easily, but I trust her. "Not physically. But he insulted her when he was drinking. Put her down. Then, cheated on her. He wasn't a good guy, Trina," I say, my jaw ticking as I think of the man my mom finally freed herself from. "When she got rid of him, I made a vow to myself to always look out for them."

"Seems like you're doing a great job."

"I don't want her to have to make hard choices again. Like staying with someone who doesn't treat her right. She deserves a nice home on the water, endless spa days, and as many dinners with her friends as she wants. That is all."

"I love that you feel that way and that you look out for her like that," she says, with a tenderness that hooks into me.

"I try," I say.

We're quiet for a small stretch of the block then she says, "Thanks for sharing. I know you don't do that easily."

Yup. This woman just knows me. "I don't."

"But I'm glad you did with me," she says, then adds, "And I got the impression you were the protector type."

"That's not an Enneagram type and you know it," I say.

"Please. I know. But maybe it should be."

"Maybe you should consider *that* my personality type, Miss Inquisitive," I say, trying to lighten the mood.

"I will," she says with a playful lift of her chin, one that turns into her eyes straying to my right arm and the ink on it. "What does that all mean? All your compasses?"

She doesn't let up. She doesn't ever stop asking questions. But I've got to hold something back, so I whisper, "Ask me in bed."

"Adds that to my to-do list," she says, and mimes making a check mark.

When we reach the library, she takes one picture as I head inside. A little later, when I leave, she shows me the pics she took. "Hmm. I don't look like a jackass," I say.

"You look like a guy who's quietly posting things that matter to him," she confirms.

Putting these out there publicly doesn't do much for me. But if it helps others, it's worth it.

"I'm like your stylist," she says, then bumps her shoulder to mine. "Your digital stylist."

I roll my eyes but only to make light of my next request. A bigger ask. "Want to get tacos? I mean, your boss wants a review of them and all."

"Aww, is that your only reason for asking? You're looking out for my job?"

"Yes," I grumble.

But she knows it's a lie as much as I do.

We eat and then I walk her back to the bookstore. She stops outside, giving me a nervous but flirty smile as she glances from side to side, like she's making sure no one's around. "So," she begins and her nerves are the cutest thing ever. "Want to come in for a second?"

My skin heats up. "I do," I say immediately.

A minute later, she's guiding me to the back of the bookstore, then opening the door to the manager's office, and the second it closes, I take off her glasses, hook them on her shirt, and hold her face.

She lets out a soft breath.

My heart is pounding. I slant my mouth to hers and kiss her—a slow, sensual kiss. She has to go back to work. I can't send her out there with her lips all bruised and whisker burn covering her pretty skin. Everyone would know then, and there are no ground rules to cover that. But I want to have all her kisses. The passionate ones, the gentle ones, and the lingering ones, like this. It's a kiss that feels like a promise that we'll come together later.

When I pull away, she gazes up at me, then bites the corner of her lips. "Thank you," she says.

"Anytime," I say, then I open the door and walk away from her, wishing I could have kissed her one more time before I left.

* * *

When I head to the arena a little later, Oliver texts me. I click open the message from the Avengers' publicist.

> Oliver: It's a brand-new era! Ryker Samuels is on social and we love it.

I huff, but I know this is a good thing.

> Ryker: Glad you're happy.

Really, that's all that matters. I couldn't care less, but he cares, so there's that.

> Oliver: Even Bryce Tucker couldn't make this look bad.

My jaw tightens at the mention of the podcaster who dubbed me King of Grunts. But whatever. I've given him nothing to spin the wrong way, and I'm about to shut the message when Oliver sends another.

> Oliver: P.S. Is your friend dating the VIP guest? Saw a pic of them at the dog park. So cute!

I stop in my tracks, then click on the shot. There's nothing romantic in it, but my first thought is *no one better make any trouble for my buddy and our girl.*

My second is that I wish I were the one at the dog park.

And my third is—I need to get on the ice and block out all these annoying thoughts.

22

THE GIRLFRIEND ISSUE

Chase

I'm finishing up on the elliptical at the Sea Dogs gym that afternoon, getting in some light cardio next to Andrei, our top winger, when Erik marches in. Our goalie's got his game day *nothing fazes me attitude* on, and he's waggling his phone my way. Stalking across the gym, he multitasks like the badass he is, trading trash talk with Ledger, who's doing curls on a weight bench.

I can't hear what's coming out of Erik's mouth though, since I've got to finish up this chapter in a Stephen King-esque end-of-the-world tale. The narrator is sick. But not as sick as the world is in this horror story. As birds spiral out of the sky, ready to peck everyone to death I'm sure, Erik stops in front of my machine and motions to my earbuds.

So much for finding out if the birds are on a rampage or not.

I pop out my earbuds as I lower the speed on the machine. I'm almost done anyway. Andrei, never one to miss a moment, takes out his earbuds too as I say, "No, Erik, you can't play with your Switch till after the game, and only if you get a win."

Though we all need a win, to be honest.

Erik doesn't take the bait. Instead, he thrusts his phone at me. "Dude. Lisette said you're dating that girl who came to the game."

I flinch. What the hell? Then, I peer at the screen. Holy shit. That's a hot photo of Trina and me at the dog park the other night, along with Nacho hightailing it out of the tunnel.

Hot as in it sure looks like we're doing more than just *talking.* Someone—maybe a jogger, maybe a walker, maybe the dog trainer person—snapped a shot when Trina was touching my face post dog kiss. *Innocent dog kiss.*

But I'm gazing into her eyes like I'm planning to devour her. If a picture says a thousand words, this one says *I want to rail you tonight.*

Well, the camera doesn't lie.

But the caption takes a lot of liberties.

Sea Dogs team captain is romancing VIP guest and her pup.

The Internet is fast. How the hell do you get from VIP guest to dating like that? "That's presumptuous," I say, though in all fairness, Trina and I got from VIP suite to VIP guest in the bedroom in one night.

"And Lisette said she's been texting you about meeting some of her friends, but she's not sitting you at the singles table anymore. She wants you to bring your new girlfriend to the wedding," he says, and it's clear this is a demand delivered straight from the bossiest of bossy cousins in the world.

I'm not usually speechless but there's a first for everything because...*new girlfriend*? My cousin decided I have a girlfriend because the Internet said so? "She's not my girlfriend," I say, but that sounds weak as it comes out of my mouth.

I mean, *of course* she's not my girlfriend. But denying that she is feels a little shitty too.

Ledger curls the weight for another rep. "So, you take out a hot VIP guest one night and the next night you play with her dog, and you're *not* seeing her? What are you doing? Moonlighting as a dog walker, Weston?"

"Pucks and Pups is your new side hustle?" Andrei asks as he moves to a mat on the floor to stretch his hamstrings.

"That's a good name," I say, dodging the girlfriend issue.

Erik clears his throat. "Lisette said she wants to meet her since she's been trying to set you up forever, and she can't believe you did it on your own."

Jesus. "What am I? Anathema to the ladies?" I ask, and oh, shit, that's a Ryker word. A Trina word. Those nerds are rubbing off on me.

"My fiancée is sending me text after text. I gotta tell her something," Erik says, a little demanding, a little desperate. I hardly ever hear him that way.

Ah hell, I have to help a teammate out.

I hit end on the workout. "Gimme a second," I say. I can't rope Trina into this without her permission, and I definitely don't want to get roped into another Lisette setup.

I head out into the hall, still a little stunned at the situation stirred up by a photo. I take a deep breath then I hit dial, and as soon as she answers, I hear mild concern in her voice. "What's up? Everything okay with Nacho?"

"He's perfect," I say, quickly reassuring her. "I'm at training now, but before I left, he said he needed to take an afternoon nap to get ready for his date with a throw pillow tonight."

"Oh, good. Though I thought it was a carpet he was seeing."

"He's double teaming, evidently. First the pillow, then the carpet." I hesitate then dive in. "Anyway, I need your help with something," I say, wincing. I prefer to be the one helping than the one asking.

"Sure," she replies easily. "What is it?"

I scratch my jaw. "My cousin is getting married to my teammate, the goalie. This Sunday. And since you came to the game, and since my cousin saw some pic of us at the dog park—"

"There's a pic of us from the dog park on Saturday night? Who took it?" She doesn't sound alarmed yet. Just concerned, understandably so.

"Just some random person walking by. It's an innocent shot, but you know how the Internet is. They're sleuths, and it didn't take long to figure out that you were the VIP guest. And now, my cousin wants to know if you're my plus one," I say sheepishly.

Trina pauses for a moment before responding. "Is this a real date or a fake date?"

That is an excellent question. And I don't entirely know the answer. But I need an answer badly, so I finesse the situation with an, "Uh, both? Ryker is bringing his sister Ivy, so it won't just be us two."

"Does Ryker know?" she asks.

Am I supposed to ask Ryker's permission? What the hell are the ground rules for this? We didn't map out this little twist in our situationship planning convo because of course we didn't—I didn't see it coming. But my top priority is reassuring Trina. "I'll tell him later. He'll be cool," I say, then I explain the situation a little more to her, asking if she'd mind being my plus one for Erik's wedding so that Lisette won't bug me about setting me up on more dates. "I really don't want to be set up. I just want to focus on hockey."

That's my one and only goal. I made my dad a promise, and you don't renege on dying promises. You treat them solemnly. I've had a great run in the NHL so far, but it could all end any day. I've seen other careers cut short by injury. Or just by a player losing his edge. I won't lose my edge—not to romance, not to dating, not to anything.

"Hockey comes first," she says, knowing me well on this count already, then she laughs softly on the other end of the line before asking, "Can one of the fake date ground rules be I get a dance with each of you though?"

Damn, she really just goes with the flow of life. If hockey is a vibe, Trina sure is one too. Maybe Ryker will be as chill as she is. There's nothing to be pissed about anyway. She's just my plus one. "That can be arranged."

"Well, she better not set you up for the next week. One of the unspoken ground rules is no one else gets to have you or Ryker."

Her possessive streak is ridiculously hot. So hot I better not get caught up in it while I'm at work.

The arena is beautifully loud with the roar of the fans at game time. Powered by the noise of the hometown crowd, I step out onto the slick surface, ready for anything. The Los Angeles Timberwolves have been giving us a tough time this season. They're a fast team, playing aggressively and taking advantage of any weaknesses. That means I have to stay in the zone. Despite my earlier distraction, adrenaline rushes through me as I take my position at center for the face-off.

The ref drops the puck and I grab it right away, then pass it quickly to Ledger who's waiting behind me. He tears off toward the other end with two of their guys chasing him. He passes around one defender then another, finally sending it up to Andrei who shoots it toward their goal.

But their goalie is faster.

That's how the game goes early on, and only when

we skate off the ice at the end of the first period do I wonder if Trina is watching me.

I doubt it, but I sure hope she is.

Wanting that is a whole new feeling—one I dislike and like at the same damn time.

23

TOYS, TOYS, TOYS

Trina

"Where did you get this pound cake?" Cassie asks through a forkful of spongy dessert, which she's eating before dinner. "It's amazing."

"The Poundcake Factory," I say with a straight face. We're at Oak and Vine, our parents' favorite restaurant in the city, a cute little café in Hayes Valley.

"Oh, right near here, you said?" Cassie asks, like a dog with a bone, or perhaps a pillow.

"Cassie, is the baby still moving all the time?" I ask, wanting to shift gears far away from my imaginary dessert shop.

Cassie sets down the fork. "Yes, he or she does somersaults," she says, proudly rubbing her belly.

Mom turns to me, a hopeful look in her eyes. "Trina, don't you want to experience that someday?"

My father coughs into his hand, perhaps a suggestion for her to stop pressuring me, but it's hardly a firm warning since she waves a hand, dismissing him. "They're such wonderful things. Motherhood, pregnancy, family...I want you to have all that before it's too late."

"Yes, at twenty-five my clock is ticking," I say dryly, praying this dinner flashes by in a wink.

"Let's solve Trina's housing situation first, Mom," Cassie says with a laugh that's definitely at my expense.

"I have solved it," I snap, annoyed with her. "I have a place I'm moving into next week."

"And until then you're living with some guy you hardly know," Cassie adds, like she wants to get me in trouble. I clench my jaw. I didn't need Mom and Dad knowing about my unconventional living arrangements.

"Oh! Is it serious?" Mom asks, rustling around in her purse for something, then grabbing her phone. "Is it the guy in the pic that was with you and Nacho?"

My mom stalks me online? I better make sure I don't accidentally make out with both Ryker and Chase at the wedding. Though, can you accidentally make out with someone? No, make-outs are definitely intentional. I'll just have to keep my frisky mittens to myself at the wedding on Sunday.

"Does he treat you well?" Dad puts in before I can answer my mom.

Mom's eyes twinkle with, presumably, baby rattles and pacifiers. "When can we meet him, Trina?"

Never.

Cassie nods to the TV in the corner of the bar. "Right now. Well, virtually. He's on TV."

Who needs a voice when you have a big sister?

"Ooh, an actor?" Mom asks.

"Sweetheart, I think he plays sports," my dad says, nodding to the hockey game on the screen, and this dinner is worse than Nacho humping a pillow in front of my two guys.

A million times worse, because my parents have stamina that a three-legged Min Pin does not possess.

Weirdly, I'm dying to watch the TV, but I also want time to speed by, so I meet my sister's gaze and fall on the sword. "Tell me more about how big the baby is."

That earns me a small respite, but at the end of the meal, the conversation comes back to me.

"So, are you seeing this guy a lot? Outside of his home, I mean?" Mom asks, enthused.

One dog park visit and we're a thing? Well, maybe it'll get them off my back for a couple days. "I'm going to a wedding with him this weekend."

"Oh, how lovely," Mom says.

It'll be lovely, too, when he fucks me senseless with his best friend very, very soon.

When I finally escape the *we not-so-secretly hope you'll follow in Cassie's footsteps* dinner, I head to Chase's home. After I walk Nacho, I find myself drawn to the TV in the living room. Maybe I can catch the end of their games.

Such a weird thought for a sports hater like me. And yet, I've been antsy since last night to check out the action on the ice. But before I turn the TV on, I tilt my head, studying a pile of things on the living room table.

There's a new cuddler cup.

And a stuffed monkey toy for a dog.

As I peer closer, I stifle a laugh. In the middle of the dog bed is a hot pink vibrator promising "fantastic booty stimulation."

I pick up the little thing, turning it around with avid curiosity. I've never let anyone in through the backdoor, but I can't stop thinking about how it might feel to be overwhelmed by these two men at once. To feel them both inside me at the same time. I love when they crowd me, when they press their big, strong bodies against me.

It's a heady thought, taking both at the same time, but double penetration isn't number four. I'll need to work my way up to that kind of kink.

I'm about to put the vibrator back down when I spot a pastel-yellow card in the cuddler cup too. I flip it open.

Toys for both of you.
  Your roomies

My heart glows. I swear it shines in my chest. Chase said they got me the butterfly together the other day, and I try to picture the scene. Did they shop for me online? Did they do more shopping today? I doubt they went to a sex shop together in person, but did they go to a dog toy shop for my favorite critter?

With a smile I can't erase, and a blooming, giddy feeling in my chest, I flop down on the couch, holding the card. They're so good to me, and I'm determined to understand them more. To connect with them.

With my dog at my side, I flip back and forth on the TV between the Avengers game and the Sea Dogs game, rooting for both teams and both men.

Leaning close to the screen, I try to follow the action as Chase zips around the ice. He's a blur of speed and agility as he maneuvers through the other players, weaving in and out, dodging opponents and passing to his teammates.

Then, in a blink he jumps off the ice. Shifts, the guys told me the other night, and I don't entirely get why or how, but I'll figure it out. Soon, he's jumping back over the boards, and he's on the ice again.

The tension in me ratchets up as I watch. When he makes a shot that misses by mere inches, my heart aches for him.

When I switch to Ryker's game, I shout "yes" a mere minute later as he blocks a shot on goal. I can almost feel his intensity through the screen. His ferocity as he skates. One lesson doesn't make me an expert, but I can read people, and it sure seems like he's frustrating the hell out of his opponent.

As I watch, I feel like I understand both of them more deeply than before. Hockey isn't just a game for them. For Chase, it's his passion, his drive, and a way to fulfill a promise. For Ryker, I suspect it's part of his whole protector side. It's how he takes care of his mom and sisters since his father didn't.

It's not just a silly game with sticks and stuff. Hockey is to them what books are to me—part of my soul.

* * *

But the Sea Dogs lose while the Avengers win. Will Chase beat himself up again? Or will he need to fuck out the loss, like he did on Monday morning? I squirm a little at the thought of an anger bang. And on that note, a shower is always a good idea, so I take a quick one, and I've just pulled on a tank top and sleep shorts when a yawn pummels me.

Well, it *is* after ten.

That's prime reading hour, so I grab my little guy and slide into bed, then open my Kindle. I never finished the Hazel Valentine—nightly sex is putting a serious crimp in my reading style. I devour more of the tale, till my eyes flutter, and my thoughts scatter to bookstore meet-ups, and tacos, and toys, and wedding dates this weekend. They blur together for a long time until in the distance, I hear the faint sound of a door unlocking.

24

A RULE FOR A RULE

Ryker

Once the door's unlocked, I push it open. It smacks hard against the wall.

That feels satisfying. Not quite as satisfying as slamming an opponent into the boards, but this'll do for now since earlier today I found out that Chase has zero problem with public affection. Zero desire to ask me about it either.

I don't even give a fuck if he's in a funk about his team's loss. Too bad.

"Dude, don't take it out on my wall," Chase chides. He's right behind me since he was waiting in the garage when I arrived and parked my electric car right next to his.

Waiting to tell me he's now *dating* Trina. Or fake dating. Or what-the-fuck-ever it is.

How convenient.

I make a show of rubbing my fist against the wall, like I'm removing the nonexistent scratch. "All good."

"Dude, seriously." He stares at me like *what gives*. "Why are you being such a dick?"

But I'm not buying the *Ryker's a little bitch* line that he's selling. Nope. We had a deal. We had ground rules. They did not include deciding on his own that she's *his* girl. And she didn't even think about me either.

I point to my chest. "Me? *I'm* being a dick?"

He shuts the door quietly, then tips his forehead to the hall. "Lower your fucking voice."

This is rich. He's playing the *Trina is sleeping* card. "Want to take it outside?" I ask, puffing up my chest. We're not small guys, but I'm bigger, and I'm not afraid to use my size right now.

Or ever for that matter.

He holds up his forefinger. "It's *one* wedding date," he says defensively. "Oh, and she wants a dance with each of us. She asked about you, man. If you were cool with it too," he adds, and that's not helping. That's not fucking helping at all to know she was thinking of me. It makes me like her even more, and this is going to end badly for me. It just is. "So, I ask again, why is it such a big deal?"

"Gee. That's a good question." I scratch my head, like I'm lost in thought. "Maybe because, oh, I don't know, we didn't talk about it."

"And I said why in the garage. It all came up so quickly, and I had to make a decision."

My chest is a vise, and I can't stand this too-tight feeling, like something is strangling me. I can't stand *feeling*, period. I just wanted to enjoy the victory tonight. To spread Trina out on the bed and take her apart. To work through the sexiest list ever.

Four nights, and I already like her. This is so fucked up. What seemed like fun Friday night—hell, even the next few evenings and mornings—is a mess now. And the mess is inside me.

I stalk into the kitchen, hunting around for a scotch or something, but when I yank open the cupboard this feels all wrong. The glasses are his glasses; the bourbon is his liquor. Nothing is mine. I slam the door shut.

Chase follows me, then lifts his hands almost in surrender, his voice lowering too. "Look, man, someone took a pic of us. Someone else—someone I don't know —made a decision we were dating. My teammates took that and ran with it. You know how Erik is. He's relentless. So is Lisette."

Yeah, but I didn't kiss Trina in public today. Because of ground rules the three of us set up. And, more so, the ones we didn't set up. That's what pisses me off. I took them into consideration, but you didn't.

I press my lips together so I don't let that awful truth out. I'd be the schmuck in this temporary threesome.

Pass.

"Yeah, I know," I say, just to say something. So I don't seem like I'm silently stewing in my own...self-loathing.

But goddammit. I could have kissed her on the street. And then where would that have left him? We'd be two dudes messing around with the same girl, only this time everyone would know. There is no winning in this situation. Someone will always be the third wheel. I huff out a breath. "Look, this whole thing is just a bad idea," I say.

Because, evidently, I can't handle my own heart. It's me. I'm the problem.

But Chase isn't done. He's pacing, loosening his tie, jerking at the knot. "No. It's *not* a bad idea. It's just...I made assumptions and then I asked her. I should have checked with you too, but I didn't want to draw any more attention to her, or us, or whatever the hell this is," he says, gesturing wildly to the hall, then the kitchen. "Like, *hey, let me ask Ryker too because...that girl? That fantastic girl? Yeah, we're both spending the week with her. At my house. No big deal, right?*"

When he puts it like that...

Still, I cross my arms. I hate that I'm so annoyed. But mostly, I don't want him or her to know the truth. I've got to keep that locked up.

"And I know we have a pact and all," Chase adds.

The fucking pact. That's the thing. That's the heart of this. I'm the guy getting shafted again. "We made a pact for a reason. So this shit wouldn't happen," I say, even though I know on one level this situation isn't like Selena-slash-Abby, but hell, if it doesn't feel like I've been blindsided a second time.

"This isn't the same," he says, his tone softening at last as he downshifts to apologetic. "Look, we should have made ground rules for public stuff. *I* should have thought of ground rules for public situations. I didn't think to do that. That's on me, man. And I'm sorry."

Two words—*I'm sorry*—and it's impossible for me to stay mad at my friend.

Even though I was never mad at him. Not really. I was mad at myself.

I reach out my hand, *it's all good* style. "We're cool," I say, letting go of my irritation once and for all.

He smacks back, obviously relieved as he says, "Let's just make a new ground rule that we'll talk about stuff that we don't have a ground rule for."

"A ground rule for a ground rule. How very meta," I say dryly.

"And Ryker's back," Chase says with a grin, then comes in for a bro hug.

I clap his back when the sound of footsteps grows loud.

Too loud.

Too close.

Followed by the pad of paws.

And then one very angry-looking goddess. "Is that what you think? *We're cool?*"

25

A NEW PACT

Trina

It's one thing to talk about me while they're playing with me in bed. That's something they know I like. It's a bedroom kink they've unlocked.

But to do it behind my back?

I park my hands on my hips. Like a mob heavy, Nacho sits next to me and barks in my defense. My little enforcer.

"You're making plans for me *without me*?" I ask with narrowed eyes. Maybe I am overstepping as a guest. But so be it. If I cross a line, I'll stay with—ugh—Cassie.

That'd be better than two men thinking they can make decisions for me.

"I thought you were asleep," Chase says with a gulp.

"And that makes it okay?"

"We didn't want to bother you," Ryker adds quickly. That's unlike him, to give a snap, emotional answer.

But I don't care.

"Oh. By all means then, continue arguing about the ground rules for *this bad idea.* I'm not bothered at all."

Ryker groans, dragging a hand down his face. "I didn't mean that," he says, sounding devastated.

But is he devastated I heard them? Or devastated over what he said?

"What did you mean then?" I point to Ryker. "Because you said it was a bad idea." I wheel on Chase. "And you mentioned that damn pact. And yet no one asked me a thing about any of this," I say, with a fire fueled by my own irritation but stoked by this surge of emotions I've been feeling tonight. By this new over-flow of them for their kindness, their humor, their sexi-ness. Hell, I'm learning about hockey for them, and now they're talking about me behind my back, and it feels like it could be Jasper all over again.

Like everything is a lie.

Like I'm the one being tricked.

My lower lip quivers, and clearly I'm not just angry. I'm hurt.

"Sweetness," Chase says, advancing toward me.

I hold up a stop-sign hand. That pet name won't soften me.

"Don't," I say, sounding wobblier than I want to. "What the hell is this pact for real? That first night you said it was a pact that you wouldn't let a woman come between you? But is that the truth? Is it like a pact that you could both score me or something?"

My stomach roils at the awful thought. It's a whole

new way of being used. What if they made a pact they could both fuck me, then discard me after a week?

You idiot. They did.

I need to go. I turn around before anyone can answer, but Chase is lightning fast, grabbing my wrist, spinning me around.

"Oh god, no," he says, sounding awful, then sighing heavily.

Ryker comes closer too, cautiously, like they both think I'm a wounded animal. Maybe I am.

"Trina, we dated the same woman once and we didn't even know it," Chase says, blurting that out like it costs him something.

Wait. What? That's the pact? "You did? How does that even happen?"

Chase swallows roughly, looking almost embarrassed, but Ryker takes the question. "I was seeing her and then she went after Chase too. She was playing both of us," he says, like he's trying to keep his voice even, but I can tell that was hard for him to say.

"What do you mean exactly?"

"It was this whole thing," Chase says, wincing as he lets go of my wrist. "Like a social experiment. She wanted to do what men have been doing all along," he says, sketching air quotes. "And she engineered everything so she was dating four guys at the same time to see if she could actually pull it off. She specifically went after the two of us because she knew we were friends and wanted to drive a wedge, and she gave us different names," he says, and he sounds ashamed. Like he was made a fool. And he was.

"I hate her," I say, flipping from hurt to anger in a heartbeat. I despise that she hurt my two guys.

Chase's lips quirk up. "You're possessive."

"Well, I don't like that she fucked with you." At my feet Nacho barks in solidarity. "My dog doesn't either."

"We didn't either," Ryker says, sounding tougher now.

"So what happened with her?"

Ryker lets out a long exhale. "She talked about it on some podcast. I never listened but my sister did for us and told me. It sucked, but she never named names. Ivy said it was *her thing*. She's kind of a provocateur and she does these different social experiments, usually about dating. Claiming she's a model, and seeing how men respond. Or pretending she's rich. Or making herself look older to see how guys respond to older women versus younger women. She never uses names since it's not about the people—it's about what she pulls off. It's this whole thing. It's her shtick. So we all moved on."

My spine tingles. I want to throttle her. "If I ever see her..." But then I focus on the more important issue. *Them.* What happened to *them.* "So that's what the pact was about?"

"Yeah," Ryker says with a nod. "I was falling for her and it sucked. Then I thought Chase was fucking my girl, and that messed me up. I was just in a really bad place. When we found out what was actually happening we didn't want it to ever happen again, so we made a pact to be open about this stuff. Women, dating, and so on."

That makes so much more sense now. "I knew the

pact was about your friendship but the way you were talking tonight, it sounded different. Like it was about me," I say softly, letting out a long, relieved exhale.

Chase tilts his head, stroking my arm again. "In what way?"

I sigh, feeling like the foolish one now. "I don't know."

"Yes you do," Ryker presses, reaching for my other hand and threading his fingers through mine in a reassuring touch. "Be honest. That's all we have here."

Ugh. He's right. I look up, meeting both their gazes. "I thought it meant you made a pact to see if you could both...fuck me. Like I was a game."

Ryker squeezes my hand emphatically. "You are not a game."

"You're not some challenge we gave each other. You're not a bet," Chase adds, clearly determined to make me see that.

I feel stupid for thinking the pact was about me but comforted they don't see me as a prize to be won or traded. "Good," I say softly. "And I'm sorry you went through that. But I have to know something. Do you think this is the same thing?"

I sure hope they don't because it doesn't sound at all the same to me.

Chase jerks his head back and forth, adamantly. "No. Not at all. Neither one of us was together with her in the way *we* are. This thing with us?" He runs his fingers along my arm, then looks to Ryker and back to me. "It's totally different. And we've all been honest from the start. The photo today just threw me for a loop. I guess I'm fake dating you and he's not, and that's weird," he says, sounding so apologetic.

I hate that he was worked up.

I hate that Ryker was hurt.

And I hate, too, that we have to worry so much about what others might think.

But I try to picture my parents' reaction if I told them I was dating two men, and it's too uncomfortable an image. My mom would want to know who was putting a baby in me. My sister would kidnap me and steal me away to deprogram my latest manifestation of hot mess-ness. "It'd be weird if I was fake dating both of you," I admit, kind of sad, unexpectedly.

"That might be a little strange," Chase says with a helpless shrug, and that's the reality.

"My family would flip out," I say heavily.

What we have here works behind closed doors. I don't think it could ever work in public. But behind closed doors, I want to feel like we're all in this together. Even if it only lasts a few more nights. So I lift my chin and say, "I'm a part of this. Whatever this thing is. We're all part of it. Don't make rules about me without me."

Chase nods, obvious contrition in his gaze. "We won't."

Ryker comes closer. "I'm sorry. Forgive us."

I love the way he says *I* and *us* in the same vein. Like all those parts fit perfectly together. They seem to, for me.

I laugh and all my anger is gone. "You're forgiven. But now you can show me how sorry you are in bed."

Chase's eyes sparkle. "Anything you want."

I tug on Chase's loosened tie and Ryker's knotted one at the same time. I catch the scent of ocean and forest drifting off them respectively. "Have I mentioned how much I like this whole suit thing?"

Chase's lips quirk up in a lopsided grin. "You didn't have to."

Ryker's eyes lock with mine. "It was obvious the night we met you."

Well then. Way to know my kinks.

* * *

A few minutes later they're out of their suits, dressed only in boxer briefs, and they're sliding under the covers with me. Ryker strokes my hair and Chase holds my hand and my dog settles against my chest.

This isn't on my list.

But maybe it should be.

Because this position settles my fears completely. It soothes my heart and my mind.

I feel wanted in a whole new way because neither one of them asks me for sex tonight. Instead, they're giving me comfort. And that does something to my heart I wasn't expecting. It expands for both of them.

26

MORNING WOOD

Trina

My rooster alarm doesn't wake me up. It won't go off for another thirty minutes. But two roosters do. Seriously, how do men even sleep with these hard-ons?

There's a very ambitious one nudging my stomach. And, yup. Another stick poking my back, and that one's quite unyielding too.

But tongue wins. Nacho's licking my face, which is code for *get me the hell out now or I'll whizz on the bed*.

Quietly, I grab my dog and make like an inchworm down the bed so I don't wake the two sleeping beasts.

I pad out of the bedroom, tug on a sweatshirt and slides, and leash up my guy.

Fifteen minutes later, I'm back and brushing my teeth.

Well, you never know.

I check the time on my phone, and I don't have to

be at work for two more hours, so I plop Nacho in his brand-new bed, giving him a stuffed monkey to get busy with.

I return to the...sex chamber. I could use a little more cuddling time. And maybe I could use a little chance to share my fresh morning breath with my two favorite men.

But when I walk into Chase's room, I stop in my tracks. Huh. The bed is empty.

Darn.

I guess I'll...

Oh...

There's a hand on my back, gliding up my shirt.

Then, lips come down on the side of my neck, and I feel the brush of a beard.

I shiver.

"Come back to bed," Ryker says, in a sexy morning rumble that comes with minty breath.

"We want you to think about us all day today at work," Chase whispers in my other ear.

And hello fresh breath too. Now, I'm doubly turned on.

"If you insist," I say.

"We really fucking do," Ryker says.

"Besides," Chase adds, curving a hand over my butt, "if you want us both at the same time, you need to do four first."

I shiver but tense at the same time. Four is like the butt stuff starter pack. I *want* them both fucking me at the same time—that's lucky number six—but I've never so much as taken a finger where the sun doesn't shine, so I figured we better practice.

Hence, four. Butt play.

And some fingers and toys seem necessary since their roosters are announcing their intentions to break me in half. Both men are crowding me in the doorway, boxers still on but rock-hard erections pressed against me.

Ryker grabs my hair, tugs a handful to the side, and kisses my neck hard, all while rubbing that big cock against my hip.

Chase roams a hand over my breast, the other hand curving over my ass, his dick saying a demanding hello to my hip too.

I'm snug between them. Exactly where I want to be.

I sigh into their twin touches, this new kind of *everywhere* foreplay I've become addicted to in a few short days. I had no idea I'd like being flooded with pleasure so much. Crowded this intensely. On each side, they kiss my face, my ears, my jawline. Then, Chase grabs my chin and yanks me toward him, giving me a view of his attire.

Hello, tie.

How did I miss this? He's wearing that tie from last night, with only his boxer briefs.

I jerk my gaze to Ryker. He's dressed the same— boxer briefs and his tie. And I'm ten times more turned on. I tug on his neckwear, then Chase's. I might even purr.

"How about we do four and five?" Chase says.

I didn't see that combo coming but I gasp out a very enthusiastic yes. After all, five is all about trust.

* * *

These guys don't fuck around. Ryker's mouth is on my pussy in seconds, while Chase just started tying me to the headboard of his bed.

My bearded beast laps me up like I'm his breakfast, lunch, and dinner. In no time, I'm writhing against Ryker's face while Chase tugs on my wrists.

I'm on my elbows and my knees, and my ass is up in the air. Chase is tying my right wrist to one side of the bed, my left to the other, while Ryker's licking me. I am spread wide. "I don't know how I can stay like—"

I swallow my words when Ryker sucks on my clit ravenously.

Holy fuck.

Ryker's voracious in the morning. He spreads my cheeks apart, then buries his face in my pussy, rubbing that dangerously sexy beard against me till I'm moaning indecently loud.

"There. That should hold," Chase says evenly as he ties the last knot, like I'm not being eaten out like my kitty's a starving man's meal.

My thighs are shaking. My knees are buckling. And my arms are stretched wide across the bed.

What even is this position? Upside-down spread eagle?

Ryker's tongue goes deep in me, and my brain goes offline. "Oh god," I cry out.

Then, out of nowhere, there's a buzzing sound.

God, I'm so close already. What are they doing to me? I turn my face on the bed, my cheek smushed into the sheets, but all I can see is Chase moving away from the bed with something in his hand.

Then I don't really care where he's gone because Ryker's groaning and flicking, lapping and devouring, all while his powerful hands are spreading me open till I can't take the buildup of pleasure inside me.

It's too much.

Too powerful.

Too good.

I'm sweating and shouting, and then coming so fucking hard I don't know if these are words I'm making up or if I'm just babbling.

Everything blurs, and the world shatters into bright and beautiful colors. But there's no let-up.

Because the second Ryker eases away, Chase moves behind me on the bed, kneeling between my spread legs as he slides his fingers through my slickness.

"Are you going to finger—"

"Trust me, baby. Just trust me," he commands, standing between my spread thighs now.

And I let go as the answer comes. He's not fingering me. He's using my orgasm as lube.

For my ass.

He spreads my own arousal right there while Ryker grabs a toy from the nightstand.

How many toys did they get for me? Ah, who cares? When Ryker gets on the bed next to me, he roams a possessive hand down my back. "The way you taste in the morning drives me fucking crazy," he praises, then turns on a bullet vibrator.

My belly tightens with anticipation.

"Morning sex just hits different, doesn't it?" Chase asks as he rubs the hot pink vibrator against my ass.

"Are you going to fuck me with that this morning?" I ask, both nervous and aroused.

"Shhh. Sweetness," Chase says. "You like surprises, don't you?"

"I do," I say, but the words are slurry when he pushes it a little deeper, right as Ryker slides a big hand down my stomach, heading straight for my clit.

Holy fuck.

Ryker's playing my clit with a bullet vibe while Chase's introducing my ass to sex, and I can't do a thing but offer my aching center to them.

My wet, aching center and my newly eager ass.

Tied and bound, I raise my hips higher, seeking out the vibrator Chase is slowly, sensually working into me, then rocking down against the one Ryker's grazing across my overly sensitive clit.

I shiver, and a bead of sweat slides down my chest. This is intense.

"You're going to do so good when we fuck you together," Chase praises, then adds a little lube and pushes the vibrator another inch.

I draw a sharp breath.

"You okay, baby?" Ryker asks, meeting my gaze.

"I think so," I say, on a tight pant.

Everything's tight. My breath, my ass, my whole body. But everything's deliciously intense, too, as Chase pushes the toy a little deeper, and I let out a shameless moan, then an obscene one as Ryker turns up the heat on the vibrator.

Soon, I'm moaning, gasping, and rocking my body against two toys. Pleasure jolts my body, sharp and strong, till I'm desperately trying to claw at sheets to hold on because I'm lost.

I'm just lost to the pleasure.

I'm falling to pieces again, crying out from my second orgasm. When they turn off the toys and set them on a hand towel on the bed, I collapse onto the mattress. I'm still moaning and probably will be for days, but I want so much more.

"Chase, I need you to fuck me," I say, but it's more like a beg.

He lets out an appreciative groan. "I know you do, sweetness."

"I'll get her ready for you," Ryker says as he moves to the headboard, untying me, kissing my wrists when each one is free. He lifts me up and pushes my messy hair from my face. "Do me a favor?"

"Sure," I say, breathless.

"Ride him good and hard," he says, his deep blue eyes flaming with lust.

"Okay," I say, my voice feathery as I picture fucking Chase. But I have to know *why* Ryker wants me to fuck his friend like that. "Why?"

He smirks as he cups my cheek possessively. "Because I'm going to play with that perfect fucking ass while you fuck his cock."

That's it. I'm cooked. I am officially on fire.

We all move around the bed, getting in new positions, till Chase is on his back, and I straddle him, sinking onto his covered cock.

"Ah yes. Fucking yes," the man under me growls, grabbing my hips roughly. Thrusting powerfully. This is the first time he's seemed lost too—a little out of control as he pumps up into me like he's dying to come.

Well, he deserves to. I set my palms on his broad, sturdy chest while he roams his up my stomach on a path to my bouncing tits.

"Best view ever," he says, kneading my breasts as Ryker's hands come down on my ass.

He's kneeling right behind me, his hands covering my cheeks while I ride his friend.

Then Ryker lets go of one cheek, his hand traveling to my hair, gathering it in a fist and yanking it back, jerking me up.

He covers my mouth with his while he slides his thick shaft against my ass.

And I tremble everywhere.

"Yes, our girl loves that. She fucking loves being surrounded," Chase encourages his friend as Ryker thrusts his tongue in my mouth while Chase holds tight to my hips, fucking me deeper, filling me.

When Ryker lets go of my lips with a groan, he stares at me like he never wants to let go. "Kiss him now," he tells me in a feral command.

Oh, god. He hardly ever gives orders like that. It's so hot, and I have no choice but to obey.

I bend closer to Chase, my tits pressing to his chest, my hands sliding into his thick hair. I kiss my other lover as he pumps deeper, my hips meeting him thrust for thrust.

Then I feel cool liquid on my ass, and that buzzing again.

Before I know it, Ryker's sliding the toy back into me. Just an inch or so, testing me, stretching me.

"Oh god," I groan against Chase's mouth.

I can't think. I feel everything. Everywhere. And soon, as Ryker fucks my ass slow and steady, I can sense his hand behind me, working his shaft too as I sloppily kiss Chase.

Ryker's jerking his cock as he fucks my ass with a toy, and I can't focus anymore on this kiss. I can't focus on anything. I clutch Chase's shoulders as he drives deep into my pussy, then I feel a pull in my belly, a coil of pleasure.

In seconds, it bursts like fireworks, and I cry out, coming again as Chase shouts, "Fuck, baby yes, give it to us."

I do. I give it to them. All of my pleasure. All of my body. Everything, all at once, as Ryker grips my hip roughly, grunting as he spills hot come over my back.

Chase shudders, cursing, coming, and moaning my name. Not sweetness. Not baby.

But Trina this time.

And it feels different.

Because Ryker says it too, like my name is precious to both of them.

Yes, morning sex does just hit differently.

Trina

I need a nap, but there's no time for that so I'll settle for fuel. After I shower, I practically float into the kitchen on a waft of freshly brewed coffee, though the eggs and toast are luring me too.

I'm dressed for work in cute flare jeans, and a flower-print shirt. I lift my nose to draw a satisfying inhale, savoring the smell of the food and the sight of two shirtless men.

"Never cook with shirts on," I say.

"We'll start a band. The Shirtless Chefs," Chase says.

"Name's probably taken though. All the good ones are," Ryker says, plating some scrambled eggs.

I move between them, grabbing a mug, then Chase slaps my wrist. "We're serving you. Sit. Now."

I hold up my hands in surrender. "All right, all right.

But why?" I ask as I settle in at the counter. "I hardly did anything today."

He huffs, deliberately over the top. "You did the most work in bed," he says, and I scoff.

"I was tied up."

"It's a lot of work for the woman."

Ryker arches a brow as he grabs two slices of sourdough bread from the toaster. "Have you been studying the caloric output of various threesome positions?"

"No. I've been participating in a lab experiment, you jackass," Chase says, and their boyish insults make me smile. "And my conclusion is this—it's more work for the woman than the men. So the least we can do is feed you and take care of you."

I shrug happily. "Works for me. I like food."

And so does the beggar dog at my feet, who clearly wants me to drop a piece of my egg. I shoo Nacho back to his bed, then return to the stool. The guys come around to the island counter and sit on each side of me. Ryker drops a kiss to my cheek, then hums, sounding deliciously happy. It's the first time he's seemed fully relaxed outside of bed, like he's letting go of some of his hard shell.

Chase plants a kiss on my other cheek. "I like it better when we all get along," he says, and my heart goes a little fluttery.

Okay, a lot.

"Same here," Ryker says, and I know it costs them something to admit this. Their shared vulnerability makes me feel all soft for them, like I'm made of flutters as I savor their morning attention.

"We only have a few more days left. Let's make the most of them," Chase adds, and...the flutters die a hard death.

"We will," I say, trying to sound chipper, but likely failing. I don't want to think about Monday morning when I move out and they head off to their next series. Chase travels to New York, then Boston; Ryker to Seattle. They'll be far away, and I'll be moving into a studio.

Best to focus on the here and now. I pick up my fork and dig in with a "Yes, let's do that." Then I shift gears. "Is everything set up for the online auction?" I ask since Chase has organized all the details.

He grabs his phone, checks something, and shows me the screen with a ticking clock. I try not to think of *our* ticking clock. "Went live this morning as planned."

"Damn. Look at those bids already," Ryker says, peering at the screen too. "You're going to bring in a nice haul for Little Friends."

"I'm so excited about that," I say. The funny thing is we planned this as "revenge for charity" but now it just feels like a fun thing that belongs to us. It's *our* project, and Jasper has nothing to do with it.

As Ryker scrolls through the bids, an idea pops into my head. "What if we share it on your social feed?" I suggest, enthused. "It'll help with your agent's goals and your goals."

He gives a crooked grin. "Your brain is seriously sexy," he says, then takes out his phone, unlocks it, and hands it to me. A few seconds later, I'm posting about the auction on his news feed, then handing him back the phone.

Which reminds me, we have one more "moment" planned as part of his reputation makeover. "Don't forget we're seeing your grandma tomorrow at lunch."

"Dude. Say hi to Dorothy for me," Chase says, chiming in. "She cleaned up last time I played poker with her."

"She always does," Ryker says.

And more flutters come my way over how they talk about Ryker's grandma. Evidently, just having breakfast and normal conversation with them on a random Wednesday is a romantic risk. But a pounding makes me hungry so I tuck into the eggs again.

As we eat, Chase's phone buzzes. He picks it up. "Might be my mom."

"Aww, such a momma's boy," Ryker teases.

"Pot. Kettle," Chase taunts back, then his brow knits as he reads the screen. "Huh."

I snap my gaze to him. *Huh* doesn't sound good. "What is it?" I hope he's not checking out press reports after the last two losses. That can't be good for his stress levels.

But Chase quickly erases his frown as he looks Ryker's way. "It's just this Sea Dogs fan account. They picked up the pic of you at Trina's store yesterday and mentioned her."

"What the hell?" Ryker fumes.

For a second, fear flashes across my skin. Did they see me pulling Ryker into my office? Did I mess up everything we worked out last night when I did that? But the office is around the back hallway of the store and totally out of view. Still, nerves skate over my skin until Chase sets the phone down, showing it to us.

"Gianna sent it," he says, then gestures to the pic of Ryker buying books at the counter.

Whew. That's a relief. It's the pic *I* snapped.

"And they took it from *my* new social account," Ryker says, stewing.

Gosh, he's cute when he's mad about the world. I kind of love it because his ire gives me a purpose. "Yes, that's the point," I say gently. "We're putting it out there for that reason. We took this pic."

"I fucking know that," he grumbles. "That's not even the issue."

But before I can ask what the issue is, I read the caption.

Better not be sharing team secrets, Cap! The new GF of the Sea Dogs captain works at An Open Book, where crosstown rival Ryker Samuels shopped yesterday. Serious so quickly that she's hanging with friends again after meeting them both at the game the other night? Seems so.

I tense. Is Ryker going to feel like he's not an equal part of this *us* again?

"I don't like this," he says.

And I need to reassure him it'll be fine, so I set a hand on his rock-hard shoulder. "They don't need to know what it's really like with the three of us."

"It's better this way. Trina said her family would lose their shit if they knew she was with both of us," Chase says, jumping in too. "But I won't make a big show of her and me at the wedding, I swear. That'd be fucking rude to all of us."

A dark cloud drifts over me at the mention of my family. But I don't want to think of them right now. I want to make sure Ryker's not feeling like a third wheel, so I turn to him. "You're not just a friend. Just because I have a fake date with Chase doesn't make what we do any less real."

Ryker drags a hand down his beard, shaking his head. "Don't you two get it?"

I furrow my brow and look to Chase, who appears equally confused. "Um, no," Chase says.

Ryker gives him a stern stare. "I don't need you two to make me feel like I'm a part of *this*. We talked it out last night, the three of us. And we're good. I fucking trust you two. Both of you. But I don't trust *people*. And I don't want *people* jumping to conclusions. Or figuring out what we do at night or in the morning. They'd have a field day. Two rivals and the girl with the cheating ex," he says, then turns to me, and cups my cheek tenderly. "And I definitely don't want anyone talking shit about *you*."

And my heart trips over itself again. "They aren't."

Chase is quick to reassure him too. "And we won't let them. We won't give them anything to talk about. Besides, it's not like this is Page Six," he says, naming the gossip outlet. "If the Selena-slash-Abby thing didn't get out, this won't either."

He takes a pause, clearly devising a plan. "And listen, when the three of us are out together, we'll act like friends. *All of us*. That feels fair and right. And that's got to be a new pact, okay?"

"I agree," I say, then wait for Ryker's reaction.

But my broody guy is quiet again, unreadable again.

Chase, though, is not. He's clearly determined to steer this ship out of choppy waters. "Listen, I'm not going to be all touchy-feely with Trina in public in front of you. That'd be disrespectful to you, man," he says, and great, just great.

Now my insides are doing cartwheels over how much Chase cares about his friend. How he wants to do right by Ryker. My pulse surges.

And I swear, if I'm not careful, my feelings for both of them will snowball from crush to something deeper very, very soon.

"Thanks, man," Ryker says quietly, appreciatively.

Chase claps Ryker's shoulder. "While we're in this," he says, then draws a circle in the air, indicating the three of us, "we're *all* in this. There's no picking sides or playing favorites. I fucked up by not asking you yesterday, but I am seriously grateful for the save at the wedding. Lisette has been on my case, and I just can't go there and be introduced to all the women she wants to set me up with. And even if this thing ends the next day, no fucking way do I want to be introduced to someone while I'm with you," he says to me.

It's like a seesaw, the emotions inside me. I love that he's focused on me. But I hate that he's mentioning the end.

Ryker offers a fist for knocking. "Not your fault, buddy. It's the world's. People saw that pic of you and our girl, and they made assumptions. That's how this thing spiraled. We just need to look out for each other."

Chase knocks back. "We will." Then he beckons me with his other hand. "Bring it in, sweetness."

I set my fist on top of theirs. The three of us.

"This is our new pact," Chase says, like a declaration, and the serious tone makes the snowball...snowball.

28

FLIP FLOP

Trina

The next day is my favorite kind of day. A day off.

Normally I'm all about spending a no-work day in do-nothing mode where I devour a book, hang with Aubrey, and take Nacho to the dog park.

But my sister has a baby shower coming up soon and since I'm already the screwup in the family, I can't very well show up with a pack of diapers because that's all that's left on the registry. I'm certainly not going to be able to afford the thousand dollar stroller that's on her wish list.

Which means it's Target time before Ryker and I visit his grandmother for lunch and a pic. I'm in my guest room—AKA my clothing storage room—picking the perfect sweatshirt to go with my burgundy crop top when Chase strides into the bedroom. "You still going to Target? Need a ride?"

"Is it the overwhelming desire to spend more time with me or is it that no one can resist Target?"

"Don't ask me an impossible question if you don't want the answer."

"Fair enough," I say, and since Ryker's off at practice, I head to the garage with Chase and hop into his electric car. He's around this morning, has practice tomorrow, then a game on Saturday afternoon, while Ryker has a game Saturday night, with Sunday off for the wedding. Then there's Monday. When this is all over. And I don't want to think about Monday.

"You can put on music if you want," Chase offers as he slowly backs out of the steep drive.

"Whoa. Multiple orgasms. Feeding me. And now, DJ controls. You're going for the full book boyfriend trifecta," I say.

He scoffs. "With the amount of Os you've had it's more like quintet. Nope, make that sextet since I like the sound of that word."

"Me too, but why don't we play one of your scary books instead of music?"

As Chase shifts into drive, he shoots me a doubtful look. "Seriously?"

"I've never tried one but I feel like I could handle it. I'm tough."

"If you say so," he says, dubious. He hits play on his phone, and a deep, foreboding voice floods the car. "There was a creak in the empty tunnel, then a rattling cough. A chill swept over her. Taylor spun around, gripping her makeshift knife, before she stepped onto something soft, and wet. Oh god. The stench of the rotting corpse—"

I cover my ears, shrieking. "Stop it right now! I'm shaking!"

Chase barks out a laugh as he hits stop. "I warned you."

My pulse skyrockets. "Put on something pleasant."

"Why don't you pick something, sweetness?"

With my skin still crawling, I go to his app and look for a sample of a romance novel. Something escapist and sexy.

With shaky fingers, I find one from Hazel Valentine and Axel Huxley. *Ten Park Avenue.* I hit play. "Look, facts are facts. Women want three things: Batteries that don't die. A lover who knows when to shut up. And a dress with pockets."

"Yes," I say, joyful again. "Yes. Yes. Yes. This is a universal truth. There's actually a store on Fillmore called Better With Pockets."

Chase taps his temple. "Pockets. Noted."

When we reach Target, we head in together and I call up the registry on my phone. "Let me see what's in my price range." Then I roll my eyes, showing him the list as we pass the women's clothes and head to baby wear. "I am not buying her nipple cream."

Chase cringes. "Diaper rash cream is a gift no-go too."

"Exactly. Get that yourself. Same thing applies for pacifier wipes."

"Are those all on there?"

"Cassie is very thorough," I say with a nod.

"Show me the list."

We stop by a display of sapphire blue towels, and I hand him my phone. As he reads a new tale of horror, his deep brown eyes glaze over. "You know what? This is far too complicated. Just pick something that's not practical and it's my treat."

"You really don't have to get something for my sister."

"It's not for your sister. It's for you. I like doing things for you," he says.

My heart softens even more. "You're so sweet, especially since I'm dreading this shower," I say as we turn down the next aisle.

"I know. It makes me sad that your family doesn't quite understand you."

"Me too. I think I'm just used to it by now," I say with a shrug.

But what doesn't make me sad is getting to spend this little extra bit of time with Chase in a Target on a Thursday morning, especially when he says, "But I like to think I understand you."

My heart speeds up, beating at a rapid clip as I meet his gaze. "I think you do too," I say, then I whisper, "And I like it."

"Me too," he says, and we lock eyes for several heady seconds till he adds, "Dying to kiss you."

"Same," I say.

He leans in slightly but then pulls back. "Dammit. If Ryker can't kiss you in the store, I can't either," he says.

What is he doing to my heart? His loyalty to his friend is too appealing.

Once we're out in the car and away from crowds in a quiet part of the parking lot, he presses a kiss to my lips that I wish could last longer.

I wish so many things could last longer.

But still, I'm acutely aware that our time is running out. It feels like the middle of a vacation when the calendar inexorably flips. You pass the midway mark, and you just wish you could make the hours go on and on and on.

But you can't. Vacations always end. Just like this unconventional arrangement will in a few more days, no matter how hard my heart beats around my men.

* * *

Dorothy makes a wiggling gesture with her fingers. "Come to mama," she says to the pot of chips on the table in the community games room. We're at the condos where she lives just over the Golden Gate Bridge, and she's decimating Ryker and me in poker.

Ryker huffs. "I bet this deck is weighted or something."

"Or perhaps you're just not as good as I am," she says, matter-of-factly, sliding the chips next to her.

"I've won before. A few times," he says, all grumbly and Ryker-y.

"You cling to that, why don't you?" She winks at me as she shuffles the cards.

"You can't be good at everything, Ryker," I tease, jumping on the pile-on-Ryker train.

"I'm very good at cards," he says, insistent.

"Pfft," Dorothy says. "The universe doesn't give out gifts that freely to everyone. You've got to take your pick. Sports or games."

"She's right," I weigh in, totally on Grandma's side.

Dorothy shoots me a wise smile, her eyes crinkling at the corner. "Listen to your girlfriend. She knows what she's talking about."

Ryker's lips part, and I swear the correction is forming on his tongue. He's about to say I'm not his girlfriend. And really, I should say the same too. But I feel kind of like a jerk saying that. Or maybe I enjoy the sound of the word girlfriend too much.

"She's a friend," he says evenly, but perhaps like it costs him something.

Dorothy rolls her eyes. "You can call her a friend, but I can tell the truth."

"Grandma..."

"You're not fooling me," she chides, and I hide a smile.

"Grandma," he says again.

"Seriously? How many times are you going to *Grandma* me? You've spent this entire card game making eyes at her."

My stomach swoops. I dip my face, trying to hide my laughter, or maybe it's my hope. This silly hope that'll never see the light of day that I could be both their girlfriends. But that's crazy. That's not the real world.

"I already told you," he says, but it's a pointless argument.

She's decided. "I don't care what you told me. I can

see with my eyes. I can feel it," she says, tapping her chest. "Now, let's play another round."

She deals and when I take out my phone and snap another shot for his social media feed, I don't feel like his friend either.

I feel like I belong to both of these guys. The trouble is I don't know what to do about all these new feelings that don't have a home in the real world.

* * *

Ryker drives me back to Chase's place a little later. "Thanks again for coming. And the pics. And...being so cool with Grandma," he says as he crests Divisadero.

"Of course. I love her already."

"Pretty sure she feels the same about you," he says.

As he drives, I glance over at his hands on the wheel, then my eyes travel up his arm, checking out his ink once more.

He told me to ask him about them in bed, and I never did. But now seems as good a time as any. "So, why compasses? Is it for travel? Adventure? Something else?"

At the light at the top of the hill, he shoots me a smile that says my question was inevitable. "It's a reminder that if I get lost, I can find my way back."

"To what?"

"To wherever I'm supposed to be," he says, then holds my gaze for a long, weighty beat.

My heart flips for him, like it did for his best friend earlier today. And since we're in his car with tinted windows and the light is still red, I say to him what Chase said to me at the store. "Dying to kiss you."

Ryker curls a hand around my head and kisses me for a hot, heady second. That's all, and I want so much more.

* * *

Later, I'm alone at the dog park, urging Nacho through the triple hoops, then cheering him on when he nails all his skills.

"Who's the best boy in the world?" I call out, and he jumps—okay, it's more like pogo sticks—up and down.

I pick him up and give him a kiss on his snout, then glance around. Is someone going to take my picture? Ha. I'm not interesting without a famous athlete by my side.

Fine by me. I never wanted the spotlight, but as I leash up Nacho, and leave, I feel a pang in my chest. A wistfulness.

Next week, I won't come to this park. I'll be in my own tiny studio in the Outer Sunset, taking a bus to work across the city, and using any little extra dough on doggie daycare for this little love bomb.

I'll be back to my regular life.

Though I can't help wondering what it'd be like to come here to this park, not just with Chase but Ryker too? To laugh and play, like I did with Chase at Target, and Ryker with his grandmother? Then to kiss?

My heart squeezes. I want that but know I can't have it.

When my phone rings a minute later, I answer it right away. It's my mom, and it'll be good for me to focus on my regular life.

"Hi, Mom," I say, trying to sound upbeat.

"Hi, sweetie. Just wanted to say hi," she says, and we make small talk as I circle the outskirts of the park. But soon the conversation comes around to her favorite topic. Romance and matchmaking.

"So how's everything with your new beau? When can we meet him? He seems so nice. I read all his press coverage. What a good family man. Did you know he pays for his brother's college? Oh, and he donates to cancer research and animal rescues, and he's such a good one."

My shoulders tense. I'm going to let them down all over again when this silly little pretend girlfriend thing ends. "Yeah, he's great," I say.

And so's the other guy too.

But how would I ever say those words to them? They'd never understand what I'm feeling right now.

She and my dad were high school sweethearts. They had the perfect wedding and have the perfect marriage, the perfect daughter in Cassie.

I'm just...well, me.

29

THE PAGE-TURNER CLUB

Trina

On Friday morning at breakfast, the clock is ticking faster than usual. Just this weekend and then I'm moving into my own place. I want to stop time, but instead, we're making wedding plans.

"Neither one of us has a game tonight," Chase says at the island counter. "We want to take you shopping when you get off work. To Charlotte Everly's. For a new dress to wear this weekend," he says, and whoa.

These guys don't fuck around. She's the new *it* designer. I can't afford her stuff. I can only salivate over it. "I love her designs," I say.

"Good. Then you should wear one of her dresses when you dance with each of us on Sunday," Ryker adds.

"Then when we undress you after here," Chase continues.

"And then we'll spread you out on the bed in your new lingerie we'll have bought for you."

I swoon. "Yes."

I'm fantasizing about Sunday when a notification pops up on my phone. Seriously?

It's Jasper.

The preview pane says *You got to meet my idols. The least you can do is pay me back for those tix you stole.*

I snort-laugh. "Please," I say, then I finally reply to Jasper for the first time since I left him.

With a GIF of monopoly money.

I show the guys and they smother me in righteous kisses. "Our book babe is badass," Ryker says and once we finish breakfast, they walk me to the door, where Chase hands me a brown paper bag.

"You said you had a busy day today so in case you can't get out for lunch, I made you something."

My eyes widen. I'm officially melting before I go into work. "What is it?"

"A peanut butter sandwich with fresh strawberries," he says.

"My favorite."

Though these two guys are my favorites too.

* * *

That evening, Kimora shakes the black and gold paperback in frustration. "Nope. I will never forgive Angus for not burning down the world for Lorelei."

Aubrey sits on the edge of the couch, pointing to the cover with her perfectly polished nail. "He's a hero, not a villain. He's not supposed to burn down the world."

"An antihero," Kimora insists, pointing a dismissive finger at the book in question.

I'm at book club that night, in the comfy "living room" area in a back corner of the store. The ladies and I are hanging out on sofas, eating cheese and crackers while debating the super-spicy football romance—a dark romance—we read recently.

"Maybe we need a romantic comedy for the next book club, and we can debate levels of cinnamon roll heroes," Prana suggests, with a kick of her red flat.

"Only if the book is five chili peppers hot," Kimora insists.

I give Kimora a *c'mon* look. "You know me. I know you know me. You know I'd never give you anything less than the full spicy treatment in a Page Turners pick."

Kimora sighs happily. "All I need is some spice and for the world to leave me alone."

"Amen," Aubrey seconds.

We spend the last few minutes of book club choosing our book for next time, finally settling on *Only One Bang In The Room* from Kennedy Carlisle. Bonus points? The super adorable pink cover with the cartoon couple on opposite sides of the bed.

"Bets on how long the hero and heroine hold out?" I ask.

Aubrey raises a hand. "Ohh! One night."

Kimora flicks her braids off her shoulder. "Two. My money's on two."

Prana weighs in. "Good things come in threes."

Well, yeah.

"May the best woman win a *Fresh Out of Fucks* mug," I say, then hand Kimora the mug prize from tonight. I picked it up at Effing Stuff down the street as a prize for the reader who accurately predicted the chapter for the first bang. Even though my friend didn't like the book, she still deserves the mug.

We all say goodbye, and Aubrey sticks around to help me straighten up. "So, how's life in The Pound Palace?" she asks in a low voice as I crush the cracker boxes so I can recycle them.

A shiver runs down my spine as I think about all the things we've done this week. I check the Edvard Munch-style clock on the wall above the horror section. I'll be meeting the guys at the coffee shop around the corner in ten minutes. Just enough time to share with my bestie.

"It's wild," I whisper, then I tell her a little bit about when they tied me up the other morning. "I swear, I had no idea sex like this was possible."

She fans her face. "I knew it. I knew those dirty books weren't a lie. But rather, a secret roadmap to the promised land. And as God is my witness, someday I will find my way there." She smiles. "Tell me more."

But I don't tell her more about the nookie. Instead, I tell her about the way I felt all soft and squishy from our new pact. My stomach dips, like a roller-coaster car. "And I don't know what to do about it. I mean, this thing is ending, and I'm fresh off a bad breakup. These burgeoning feelings are just..." I wave a hand searching for the words. "Heightened emotions."

Aubrey's uncharacteristically quiet for a moment. "You really like them."

I wince. "Yes."

She brings me in for a hug. "Just have fun. And know that I love you," she says.

That's girlfriend code for *I'll be here for you when your heart gets broken, or even just bent.*

I let go and say goodbye to her, trying to brush aside my feelings.

Best to focus on the way I feel in bed, not out of bed.

A little later, I'm all done, so I say goodbye to Pedro, who's closing up tonight, then head outside, but once I push open the door, it's not my two temporary roomies surprising me.

It's my ex.

30

FIVE CHILI PEPPERS

Trina

Lift my chin. Look him in the eye. Then walk on by.

That's my plan at least, but the second I head down Fillmore Street, Jasper's by my side, keeping pace, his dumb man bun bouncing stupidly. "Monopoly money? Really? I thought you were more mature than that."

I fume, jerking my gaze at him. "Who the hell are you to lecture me on maturity?"

"Who the hell are you to say it was wrong of me to make one mistake, then just go and take something that belonged to me? Two wrongs don't make a right."

Red plumes of anger billow through me. "Did you just equate cheating on me to taking your hockey tickets?"

"I did. You knew how much I wanted those tickets, and you just stole them. They're worth a lot of money."

The gall of him. "Did you need the money for rent, Jaspie?" I ask as we pass Effing Stuff, the mug shop. I'm fresh out of fucks to give, but I'd sure like to throw that mug at his stupid face. "Because that's all you care about."

"No, I care about meeting Weston and Samuels," he says, and I want to shove a bar of soap in his mouth for having the nerve to breathe their names. He's a little man brat, and they're real men. "That was all I wanted. But the way I see it is we could be even, and I could just forget about it if you give the tickets back to me and I'll go to the calendar kickoff," he says, plastering on a nice voice.

I scoff.

But I'm mad at myself. What did I ever see in Jasper the Jackoff? "So that makes us even?"

I power walk down the block, the coffee shop in my crosshairs.

"Yes, and I think you should take my offer. Otherwise I could report you to the cops, you know."

This guy.

I stop in my tracks in front of the shop, fueled by both righteous rage and utter disbelief. "The cops? Seriously? Do you even hear the words coming out of your mouth? Do you even listen to what you say?"

"Yeah, what *did* you say?"

I turn around at the sound of Chase's voice. He's here in the doorway of the coffee shop along with Ryker, cups in hand.

Chase wears a blue Henley and jeans, his bulging muscles evident under the fabric. His brown eyes are fierce as he stares down at Jasper. Ryker is right next to him, a black T-shirt revealing all his tattoos.

"Oh!" Jasper blinks, then smooths a hand down his plaid shirt. *Yes, Jasper tuck it in. That'll impress them.* "You guys are the best and I just really wanted to meet you."

Jasper sticks out a hand. He actually offers his hand, like they'd want to shake it.

Ryker lifts a finger. "Yeah, we're dying to meet you too. Let's get out of the way though so we can chat some more."

His tone is faux friendly and Jasper has no idea.

I'm flooded with anticipation as the two big, broad hockey players walk along the side of the shop to the parking lot behind it, coffee cups still in their hands.

Jasper follows them gleefully.

I do the same.

They stop on the asphalt, Jasper's back's to the wall of the coffee shop.

Ryker tilts his head to Jasper. "So she lifted your tickets. That sucks. What the hell?" he asks, staring at my ex with over-the-top concern.

It takes everything in me to keep a straight face as I stand a few feet away. I won't reveal they're on my side.

Jasper points at me, *j'accuse* style. "Right? Can you believe it? She doesn't even like hockey, and she stole my VIP experience! How could anyone do that?"

Chase shakes his head like he can't believe it either. "Bro, that must have been so tough."

Jasper sighs in relief. "I knew you'd understand. All I want is to come to the calendar kickoff. But hey, maybe you guys could score me some tickets. Help a fan out."

He sounds so pathetically hopeful, and it's wonderfully gratifying to witness. I wish I could record this to play it again.

"Definitely. We'd love to help you," Chase says, then turns to Ryker, like he means everything he's saying. "Wouldn't we?"

Ryker crushes his empty coffee cup ominously, then wings it into a recycling bin before he cracks his knuckles. A frisson of heat rolls down my body as the enforcer in him comes to the surface. "We sure would."

Jasper smiles, still not getting it. "I knew you'd understand."

Chase steps closer. Ryker does the same. They're so much bigger than Jasper.

"We understand a lot of things. And we like to operate with...let's say...*ground rules*," he says, then flashes a smile at Ryker. "Don't we?"

"We love ground rules," Ryker says, stepping closer too, and I want to shout *I adore ground rules*. But I keep my mouth zipped as I watch the best show ever. Bring me some popcorn.

"So here are a couple," Ryker continues, and in a heartbeat, he strips the faux niceties from his voice. His tone is pure feral wolf as he says, "One. Never step foot in either of our arenas."

"What?" Jasper sputters.

Chase crushes his cup now, then tosses it away while giving Ryker a sympathetic look. "Trina said he'd probably have a hard time understanding basic concepts. Let's make it easier for him."

Ryker stares at Jasper like he wants to burn him alive. "You're banned. Unless you want to wear a jersey saying 'I'm The Cheating Asshole.' That'd be your cost of entry."

Jasper quakes. He actually quakes, finally realizing they aren't on his side after all.

"Next," Chase continues, "you aren't coming around to see her ever again."

Ryker tilts his head, staring darkly at my ex. "And if you do, you'll get a VIP experience, all right. You'll feel like you're right there on the ice, like, say, you're in the middle of a hockey brawl. Got that?"

Jasper gulps. "Yes," he mumbles.

Chase sets his hand against the brick wall, towering over him. "Don't show up at her work. Or her home. Don't talk to her. Don't text her. And do not be such a little fucking piece of shit that you ask her for money. You cheated on her, and you could have hurt Nacho too."

Ryker growls. "So do not go near her or her dog ever again." He pauses. "Or else."

The *or else* is crystal clear to me. *Or else we will hurt you.* And it's pretty crystal clear to my ex too, since Jasper gulps and nods vigorously.

"I didn't hear you. Did you understand the *or else*?" Ryker asks in the world's most intimidating tone.

"Yes," Jasper says, terrified.

They smile. "Now, say you're sorry for being a cheating prick," Chase says.

"I'm sorry I was a cheating prick," Jasper mutters, looking at his loafers.

Chase rolls his eyes, then points my way. "Say it to Trina."

They move away from my ex, and Jasper meets my gaze, looking miserable. It's so delightful to witness. "I'm sorry," he mutters.

Ryker curls a hand over Jasper's shoulder. A big, firm hand that squeezes him hard, sending a clear signal—*I could crush you with these knuckles*. "Say *I'm sorry I was a cheating prick who never ever deserved a goddess like you*."

Jasper shakes in his shoes, but then looks at me with watery eyes and says, "I'm sorry I was a cheating prick who never ever deserved a goddess like you."

I smile, and it touches the sky. "That's true. You didn't deserve me," I say, owning that statement with the full force of my badassery.

"Can I please go?" Jasper asks them, sounding devastated and shamed.

Chase taps his chin, like he's considering it. "Unless there's anything else you want to say to him, Trina?"

Actually, there is something. I cross my arms, lift my chin, and smile once more. "Guess what? Turns out I can come like a rock star. Bye, bye Jaspie."

I wave as he runs away.

It's so satisfying.

But what's even better is how ridiculously turned on I am right now from my two guys.

That was five chili peppers hot.

31

___

OUR PRIVATE DATE

Chase

To play pro sports, you've got to be good at a bunch of things. Top among them is spotting opportunities, then seizing them.

I'm staring at one right now.

In the dressing room door of Charlotte Everly's showroom stands Trina Beaumont. She's wearing a teal dress that clings to her curves and a come-hither smile.

The woman is stunning.

We made a private appointment with the designer Ryker's sister had told him about before.

So here we are as Trina models sexy dress after stunning dress. Since Charlotte just left to take a call, the three of us are alone on the second floor. I'm seated on a pink cushion that is so not my style. Ryker relaxes on a dark blue chair.

"Does this work for the wedding?" Trina asks us, sliding a hand down the front of the silky material.

Yup—that's the opportunity. It's like a breakaway, and I'm gliding down the ice. "It's perfect," I say, so hungry for her, like she is for us.

She bites the corner of her lips. "I think I need a little help with the zipper though."

There's no one between the net and me. Except...*risk.*

Briefly, I weigh it. At breakfast the other day, we talked about being cautious. But here we are. Alone. Out of view. And our girl's chest is flushed, her eyes are glinting, and she's clearly got one thing on her mind.

Because I see the fantasy in her eyes and I want this woman to have everything she wants.

The strength of that realization wallops me almost out of nowhere.

My breath strangles me for a few seconds as I gaze at a woman I've known for one week. *One week* and I'm thinking crazy thoughts. Like if I could stop time so Monday never comes...

And these are crazy thoughts that have absolutely no place in my life or my plans.

But maybe, just maybe, I'd make a new plan for her.

And damn, that's just too dangerous an idea. I've got to shake off those thoughts.

Focus on the things that are possible. Buying her all the clothes. Showering her with gifts and lingerie. Bringing her pleasure. Making her feel incredible.

My buddy and I can do that with her for three more nights.

"We better help you undo it then," I say.

With a flirty smile, she turns around, and steps into the large dressing room. We're up and out of our chairs in no time, following her there.

I shut the door, then move behind her. Ryker lifts her hair, running his fingers along the side of her neck, and she trembles as I undo the zipper. Turning her on together is such a high. I get to watch her experience a double dose of pleasure, and she craves that. She adores being touched all over by us.

She lets the sleeves fall, then she turns around and shimmies off the dress.

I groan. She's wearing a pale pink bra and pink cotton boy shorts. She steps close. "I want to say thank you for earlier," she says.

"You don't have to," I say.

"It was seriously our pleasure," Ryker adds.

"But I want to," she whispers, then drags one hand down his chest, the other down mine. Then those ambidextrous hands get to work on our jeans.

"I'm still so turned on from what you did outside the coffee shop," she says as she gets down on her knees and unzips his fly, then mine, freeing our dicks. With a look of pure adoration in her eyes, she licks the head of his cock while she stares up at me.

Lust barrels through me.

Along with a question—how the hell is this my life?

Trina wraps a hand around my dick, stroking me while she sucks him and gazes at me.

If you'd have asked me a week ago if the hottest sex of my life would involve sharing a woman, I would have said no. But over the last seven days, I've become utterly obsessed with her and with the way we fuck.

I've learned new things about myself from being with her. I've always been a giver in bed, like a man should fucking be. But with her, I'm even more obsessed. I want to flood her with pleasure, to watch her get turned on, to arouse her everywhere so her circuits overload.

To drive her wild.

Sometimes what drives her wild is pleasing *us*. The thrill in her eyes when she can take care of us together is like a drug. The way she sparks and sizzles, taking us at the same time, is sexier than anything I've experienced in my entire life. The sheer absurdity of being this aroused as a woman sucks another guy's dick while she strokes mine boggles my mind. And yet here I am.

My body is a fucking torch. And my girl is fire.

Another lick, another deep suck, then she switches, grabbing his shaft, while she gives my dick wicked attention with her magical tongue.

I rein in a groan. My legs shake from excitement. My cock is so damn happy in her mouth. I push her chestnut strands from her gorgeous face so I can watch her suck me while she stares up at him through those red glasses.

I tug on her hair, but say nothing. We're all quiet, just in case. An unwritten ground rule as we steal this moment.

One I've needed since we ran into her ex. Putting that guy in his place was such a rush. Defending her was a thrill I hadn't been expecting. But it was a goddamn gift to let him know that no one, no one in the whole world, fucks with our Trina.

I need this release so badly, and when she takes me to the back of her throat, I nearly lose my mind. Soon, my brain is too scrambled to think and it's a damn good thing. Because I'm starting to picture more moments like this, beyond this week and the next.

More possibilities even though I know I can't have them. I've been pushing toward one purpose for the last several years, and I can't get distracted, no matter how good everything feels with her.

With *us*.

With this unexpected thing we've created. This secret that's just ours.

I close my eyes and let go, savoring the moment fully but quietly as I come down her throat with a shudder.

She lets go and takes care of my best friend, and I don't feel an ounce of jealousy. I just feel joy as I watch her finish him with wild pleasure in her eyes and a hand inside her panties.

Oh, hell no.

No way am I letting her do that by herself. In a heartbeat, I'm kneeling behind her, reaching a hand around, stroking her clit and giving her all the bliss she deserves as she comes a few seconds after he does, her body trembling in my arms.

* * *

Twenty minutes later, Ryker and I buy Trina a ton of dresses—including some with pockets—as well as blouses, shoes, and lingerie, since Charlotte makes it all.

"You're going to look stunning in all of these," the designer says to Trina.

Trina smiles, glancing down for a moment, then meeting Charlotte's eyes. "Thanks. I love your designs. I've been ogling them for a while."

Charlotte flashes a grateful smile as she folds the silky dresses and bright blouses, slides them into bags, then turns to me. "What a lovely thing to do for your girlfriend," she says.

A kernel of guilt worms through me, "She deserves the best," I say, then wrap an arm around Trina, kind of hating that Ryker can't do the same.

Next to me, he's stony-faced though, revealing nothing.

Charlotte turns to him. "And tell your sister thanks for sending you all my way. I'm so glad she thought to do that," she says.

"I will," Ryker says.

Then, shopping bags in tow, we leave, walking out like we walked in. As if the three of us are just one guy with his fake girlfriend and his buddy.

That feels so wrong to me. I wish I could go back in time and redo the moment with my teammates when I said I was seeing her. I wish I could do things differently so I didn't say that she's my girlfriend. Because she doesn't feel like mine.

She feels like *ours*.

But I can't undo it, so I choose a different path forward. "Do you guys want to get a drink before we head home?"

Ryker shoots me a *you'd better explain* look.

"Just a drink. We can get a drink," I say, then glance down the street. No one is near us, so I put myself on the line. "I want to know how it feels. Like it's a date for all of us but we're the only ones who know it," I say quietly, pushing past the discomfort.

The smile on Trina's face is pure magic.

And Ryker's nodding instantly, clearly wanting to please her too.

* * *

We're at a booth in The Spotted Zebra, where the server brings three glasses of champagne. When we're alone, Trina raises her flute. "To the full VIP experience, including our very own private date now," she says, sounding hypnotized on this night, just like I am.

We clink three glasses and it looks too damn right. Everything about this private date feels so damn right.

Enjoy it while it lasts, man, because it's ending.

I take a long, thirsty drink of the champagne, and the three of us laugh, and drink, and talk. After a bit, Trina looks at the clock, then at us, like she's famished.

"You hungry, sweetness?" Ryker asks.

She shakes her head, a coy look in her gaze. "Yes. But not for food. I'm ready for number six."

We're out of there so fast.

32

QUEEN MOVE

Trina

There comes a time in many a woman's life where she asks herself the question—will I ever take a dick up my ass?

And not just in an *ask an existential question with your girlfriends over wine* way.

In a *will I do it* way.

On the drive to Chase's home, I'm lost in my thoughts. Wondering how I've reached the point in my life where I'm desperately craving something that always felt like a bawdy debate topic for a girls' night out rather than a reality.

I never craved two men at once till I met these guys a week ago. What does that say about me? That I've been secretly kinky for all these years and waiting for someone to unlock me?

Or that I never knew my secret self until I met them?

Every day this week I've learned something new. About pleasure. About possibility. About emotions. And about how to talk and how to listen. Once we reach Chase's home, there's something I want to discuss with them. First, though, I let my dog into the little yard then back in. Back in the living room, I turn around and face the men who showered me in gifts and protection tonight.

The one place I don't want protection anymore is in the bedroom. "I'm on the pill. And I've been tested since my breakup. I'm negative. What about you guys?"

"Negative," Ryker says.

"Same for me," Chase echoes.

"Then I want you both...*bare*."

They both gaze at me with beautiful lust in their eyes. There'll be no barriers tonight, and that's beginning to describe my emotions for these two as well.

Chase advances toward me, and curls a hand around my hip. "Good. Then we have another gift for you," he says, like they've got a secret.

"You've been giving me gifts all night."

"And we're not done," he says, and they take me to the palatial bathroom where Chase positions my hands against the wall and pushes up my dress, then slides down my undies.

He takes a small silver plug out of a velvet pouch, then lubes it up, and hands it to Ryker, who slides it into my ass. I draw a sharp breath, adjusting to the new sensation.

"Good?" Ryker asks.

"I think so," I say.

Chase squeezes my ass. "Then how about you go put on that sexy new black lingerie set? Lie down on the bed and wait for us to give you a couple starter orgasms."

Ryker reaches into a shopping bag and hands me some lace. "I want to see your hand inside your panties when we find you. You've got five minutes to get ready."

I fly.

* * *

Hands on my stomach. Lips on the side of my neck. Fingers tracing my thighs. Kisses on the swells of my breast.

My eyes are closed and while I intrinsically *know* who's kissing me and who's touching me, at some point I lose track. As they lavish me with open-mouthed-caresses and tender brushes of their hands, I melt into sensations, and I stop thinking.

I'm just moaning and sighing into their twin touches, and the way they worship my body with their mouths and their hands and the press of their big frames against me.

It's like a sensory overload, this kind of long, lingering seduction. Endless kisses on my belly. Talented fingers traveling over my legs. Hands in my hair. One man is kissing the side of my neck. The other my cheek. Then their hands roam down my body.

Chase grasps one breast; Ryker, the other.

This is so much. I didn't have this on my list. I didn't
even think to put *this* on my list. It's like they're
mirroring each other with their sensual foreplay, and
it's exquisite. My body is popping with electricity. Then
their hands glide over my stomach and they're both
heading for my center. One man tugs up the waistband
of my lace panties. The other slides his hand through
my slickness.

I writhe and I shout, "So good."

Even with my eyes closed, I can feel their wicked
smiles.

"You like that, sweetness?" Chase asks. "You like
when he fingers your sweet, beautiful cunt?"

"I do," I gasp.

"Put some on her lips. I want to taste it," he says.

"Yeah, I want to taste her too," Ryker says. "Right
fucking now."

I open my eyes. I have to watch them. Ryker dips his
fingers against my heat again, then brings them to his
mouth and sucks off my taste. I arch my hips as I watch
him lick each finger. Then, he slides his hand through
my wetness again and rubs my arousal over my lips.
Chase comes up and kisses it off. It's a possessive kiss. I
feel something different in his touch. He's always been
commanding and intense. Now, there's a sense of
ownership and longing in the way his lips meet mine.
Like he'll miss me when I'm gone, or maybe he already
does.

Or maybe I'm just drunk on them. Drunk on him
kissing me while Ryker plays with my pussy.

"I can feel you get wetter as he kisses you," Ryker growls.

As if on cue, I gush.

"Yeah," he grunts. "Just like that."

More kisses. More touches. Until Chase stops kissing me and just lets out a long, lingering sigh. Everything feels dreamy and sexy and buzzy.

Then it feels dirty when Ryker pulls off my panties inch by inch and says, "We're just getting started."

And I no longer have any more questions—existential or practical—about how I got in this bed and what will happen next.

It feels like this is where I'm supposed to be.

* * *

I'm shivering. Panting. Moaning.

They've both already gone down on me. I don't think I could be any wetter. And I seriously appreciate their commitment to the cause of lubrication.

All types of lubrication.

Because Chase removed the silver plug, then opened up my ass more with his lubricated fingers while he ate me out.

Now?

I'm ready and begging for them. Not only was the last hour foreplay. The entire evening has been, from the kisses in the car to the blow job in the dressing room. And to that moment on the street with Jasper. It's been hours and hours of intensified excitement, and now I'm ready.

I push up on my elbows, looking up at two sexy, powerful men with throbbing cocks and hungry eyes. Wanting me. Needing me. I can feel the ferocity of their desire. Their primal need. It's intoxicating, the way they both stare at me like the need to fuck me is their oxygen.

We haven't talked about who's claiming what part of me. Maybe that's because I don't feel like one is the first choice, the other the second. But facts are facts. Someone's going to decide what dick goes in what hole and really, that someone should be me.

I might as well flip a coin, but here goes. Feeling wicked and wonderful and like the best kind of hot mess there is, I sit up and lay out the game plan. "I'm going to ride your dick, Ryker," I say, looking at the grumpy but gentle giant, then at Chase, my outgoing but introspective guy. "And Chase, as you fuck me, I want you to tell Ryker how my ass feels because it's going to drive him crazy."

They both unleash feral moans, then Ryker slides up on the bed, stroking his cock.

Power. I feel it radiate through me as I straddle him, then bring the head of his cock to my aching center, rubbing him against me.

When I sink down on him, we both shudder.

Then I tremble some more as Chase's big hand slides down my spine, then his slick fingers press against my back entrance.

"I've got this, baby," Chase says, soothingly. "You keep riding that dick while I play."

"I will." Slowly I rise up and down as Chase fingers me some more.

But Ryker is unusually quiet as I ride his cock. He purses his lips, like he's fighting something.

It's hard for me to focus on asking him what's wrong though when Chase kneels on the bed. Moving behind me, he notches the head of his cock against my ass.

He presses, barely sliding the tip in.

I groan from the intrusion. It's not entirely pleasant, but it's not painful either.

I'm sweating as I try to relax.

And Chase was right—this *is* work. Especially since the man under me still seems coiled tight. I'm worried. "What's wrong?"

With a guttural groan, Ryker rasps out, "It's just so fucking good. I'm trying to last with you."

Oh. *Oh.*

That's sexy in a way I never anticipated. I'm so used to these guys being able to do anything in bed. Being super-men. The idea that it's hard for him to last because he's so turned on sends a hot, fresh wave of bliss through me.

And just like that, I'm relaxing. Chase pushes in a fraction of an inch more. But what if I hate it? What if it feels terrible?

All at once, I tense and I lock up everywhere. Chase roams a gentle hand through my hair. "If it hurts, I'll stop. If you don't like it, I'll stop."

He's so concerned, and that makes me loosen up. "You will?"

"Of course I will. Anything for you."

"I want to like it," I say, feeling terribly vulnerable. "But I'm afraid."

Ryker touches my face with his knuckles, a reverent gesture. "It's okay if you don't. There's no pressure."

Chase drops a kiss to my shoulder. "You have nothing to prove."

I breathe in all these sensations and emotions. Their acceptance of me. Their desire for me. Most of all, I let my own wishes fill my cells.

I *can* stop at any moment. But I don't want to. I want two men.

I want two men desperately.

I want to feel them both inside my body. I'm climbing this double dick mountain and planting my badass babe flag at the top of Twin Cocks Peak.

I push my ass a little bit against Chase, then crane my neck to look back at him. "Have me."

With a shuddery groan, he eases in inch by inch.

I feel so full. So stretched. Like I can't hold anything else in my body. I don't know if I can last like this.

My desire might not win. My body's limits might prevail.

Until Ryker maneuvers a hand between our slick torsos, down my stomach, and he tenderly strokes my clit. Then Chase presses kisses along my neck. I breathe again and again.

And on the last big breath, I sink down once more on Ryker's dick and back against Chase's, and the pain ebbs away.

In its place comes something all new.

Something deep and powerful. An entirely new kind of pleasure I didn't know was possible.

I'm filled from head to toe, from top to bottom. Before I even know what's happening, I'm moving. It's not easy because I'm sandwiched between them, but I manage as Chase grips my hips and sensually, deliciously drives his cock into my body.

With a possessive growl, then a low rumble, he says to his friend, "You're going to lose your mind when you fuck her like this. She's so fucking tight."

"Yeah?" Ryker sounds desperate. "Her pussy's never been wetter."

"Her ass is so hot. Just looking at her ass taking me is driving me wild," he says.

I tremble and moan.

"I can feel her gushing on my cock," Ryker tells Chase, and I cry out.

Soon, I'm just made of sensations. I'm letting go in a whole new way. I'm giving myself to my two guys as they fuck me and take me and make me theirs.

Words like *tight* and *hot* and *perfect* and *ours* become my whole existence.

And then it's just the slap of bodies.

The slick of sweat.

The pull of pleasure.

And then it's me calling out their names. Begging for release. A deep thrust from under me, another from over me, and I lose my mind to the most intense moment of my life, tipping over into pleasure, nothing but pleasure, as I shatter between them.

I don't know who comes next. I only know my head

and my heart are filled with their groans and their grunts and their need for me too.

* * *

A little later, I'm sore and exhausted but still floaty. Ryker cleans me up in the shower, washing me under the hot stream and the dim lights.

When I get out, he wraps a towel around me as Chase runs a bath then drops in a bath bomb.

Strawberry. They must have bought it for me.

"I haven't had a bath in ages," I say, my voice hoarse.

"Relax, baby," Chase says, then takes the towel as I step into the hot, bubbly water.

I sink down, then turn to look at Ryker. He's wearing sweats; Chase is in shorts.

"Stay with me," I say.

"I'm not leaving you," Ryker answers.

"We're right here," Chase adds.

One man kneels at the end of the tub, the other sits on the floor by the top, and I am their queen.

33

HOW DO YOU DO

Trina

The pine scent of the forest twists around the smell of the ocean breeze as I adjust Chase's sage-green tie on Sunday afternoon, knotting it nice and snug at the collar of his dark blue shirt. We're in the living room, getting ready to leave with Nacho watching from the couch, head cocked.

"Don't ever stop wearing suits. They definitely hooked me the first night I met you," I say, feeling kind of fizzy for them, like I have been all day.

"And I thought it was my charming personality," Ryker deadpans as he finishes looping a knot in the burgundy tie he's wearing. I swat away his hands, taking over.

"I was pretty sure Chase was just a cocky playboy," I continue, reminiscing.

Chase scoffs. "Yeah, not quite."

"More like you're married to hockey," I add, tossing him a hopeful glance.

He says nothing—just gives me a smile that's full of longing.

Maybe he's letting go of some of that all-or-nothing mentality? Or maybe that's wishful thinking.

When I finish Ryker's tie, I set a hand on his strong chest, remembering the first time I did it, when I explored the scar and his ink, then I place my other hand on Chase's shirt, picturing his scratches and cuts.

My two men, with their big bodies they push to the limits to provide for their families. And their bigger hearts.

Everything about this moment just feels so right. Me doing the finishing touches for their outfits. Me enjoying the scent of both of them.

Us getting ready to leave as one.

All day long, I've been borderline sad, thinking about tomorrow and the end of the most unexpected and wonderful week of my life.

Thinking that it's ending like any vacation inevitably does.

Now, with me in the teal dress they bought, with us looking like we belong together, new thoughts—fragile thoughts—circle my mind.

What if this could be my life?

It's a wild thought, but it's taken hold of me as we leave together for the wedding.

* * *

"You must be Trina."

The woman with the piercing blue eyes and bold style—her bright paisley-print dress is eye-catching—can only be Ryker's sister.

"And you must be Ivy," I say, then I gesture to my dress, the one that she helped to pick out, for all intents and purposes. "Thank you so much for that recommendation." Then I quickly add, "I'm so glad you told Ryker, who told Chase."

And shoot. Did it just sound like I was covering something up?

Ivy just smiles, kind of slyly. We're at a gorgeous hotel in the Presidio, in a classy ballroom teeming with white roses, and offering a stunning view overlooking the Pacific. Ivy shifts her gaze from me to Ryker to Chase. The guys are saying hello to Chase's teammate Ledger.

My cheeks flush. And in a heartbeat, it's clear that Ivy knows something.

It took all of two seconds, and I'm positive Ryker's sister knows this isn't a fake date with her brother's best friend.

But before I can figure out what to say next, her brother turns away from the other guys and brings Ivy in for a hug. "How's it going, troublemaker?"

"Fabulous," she says brightly.

Like a hawk, I watch her every move as she chuckles then whispers something in his ear. With a light laugh, he lets go. He says nothing, but there's a smirk on his face.

And I still don't know what to do with this moment

except wriggle away from the awkward. "And I hear you write all about fashion," I say to Ivy.

"I'm kind of obsessed with it," she answers. "I wish I had the skills to design, but I guess I'll have to do the second-best thing."

"I feel the same way about books. I can't write them but I sure know how to read them."

"I'll have to get some book recs from you," she says.

Whew. This is much safer ground. "And you're going to have to tell me what all the trends are in clothes. And then basically how to get knockoff versions at Target," I say as other guests shuffle in, big guys who are clearly from the Sea Dogs and the Avengers.

As the goalie from Ryker's team walks in, Ryker slides past me. "Give me a sec. I need to chat with Dev."

"Sounds good," I say, and now I wonder if that came out awkwardly too. If Ivy or anyone else can read into everything I say to the two childhood best friends.

But what exactly is she reading into it? Does she know I have feelings for her brother and his friend? Does she think I'm some kind of trollop?

My stomach churns. Then it loops when Ivy moves into the aisle and pats the seat next to her. What the hell do I say if she asks me what's up?

I sit, hoping she won't ask prying questions. I gesture to the ocean crashing against the sand in the distance, hoping small talk can save the day. "This is such a gorgeous view, isn't it?"

"I heard you met my grandma."

Well, that small talk didn't last long at all. "I did," I

say evenly since I don't know where she's going with this line of conversation.

Ivy leans closer to me, her voice low. "She likes you."

"Well, I liked her too," I say, wishing I knew what Ivy was getting at. Is she friend or foe? Is she as protective as her brother? Is she going to give me the third degree for being Chase's date but making eyes at the guy who looks out for her?

"I think she sent me here on a matchmaking mission," Ivy says, and whew.

I breathe a sigh of relief. That makes so much more sense. She's Dorothy's soldier rather than my jailer, but still, I don't know what she thinks of unconventional arrangements.

"I do really like her," I say again, and that's completely honest.

"She's convinced that my brother really likes you too."

All I can do is smile. If I speak, she'll hear the emotion in my voice.

Mercifully, the guys rejoin us, scooting into the aisle. I'm dying to ask Ryker what on earth is going on, but then he turns around and says, "Hi, Mom."

My heart climbs into my throat. What the heck do I say to the woman who raised him? I turn, too, as he gives her a big, adoring hug.

I melt into a puddle.

Then, I go even squishier when Chase embraces his mother with a "Hey, Mom."

And my head fills with confusing thoughts as I fall even harder for both men.

* * *

My mind is a train depot at rush hour, racing with ideas I never expected to entertain. I barely pay attention to the ceremony, but when Erik pledges to love Lisette for the rest of his life, my throat tightens. Tears prick my eyes.

Can't help it. I don't even know them and I'm overwhelmed with emotions and with hope.

Maybe I am a big old traditional romantic like my parents. Or maybe I'm a romantic in a whole new way. Here I am with a heart that's being stretched between two men.

With a hope that's making me think everything is possible.

When the officiant asks the all-important question, the bride gives a joyful, "I do."

"You may kiss the bride."

Erik cups her cheeks and kisses her, and my mind races way too far ahead.

How can three people even be together? How do you get married? How do you do Thanksgiving? How do you have kids? How do you do life? What do you say to others? *These are my boyfriends, and this is our girlfriend*? What will everyone think?

These thoughts dog me as the wedding ends and we make our way to the reception, where the photographer snaps pictures of all the guests. Chase and I stop and smile for the camera. Then Ryker and his sister, and so on.

Finally, before we can head into the glittery room, I pull the guys into an alcove and I whisper to Ryker, "I think your sister knows," as a warning.

He winces, like he feels bad, but he nods, resolute. "I think so too."

"What do you think she knows?" I ask, my nerves high and kicking through me.

"That you're not *my* girl," Chase cuts in. "That you're *our* girl."

God, that word—our.

It makes me crave a brave new future so badly. And in a way, it's a relief that Ryker's sister isn't cringing or saying *get the hell away from me with your polyamory.*

But on the other hand—the more important hand —I'm not their girl for much longer.

Only one more night.

Sure, Chase means what he says in this moment. But could he ever mean it beyond tonight? Beyond tomorrow?

I won't know unless I put myself out there, and now isn't the time to do it. Maybe later though. I can't wait much longer. I feel like I'll go mad if I don't ask them if they want to be together with me.

For the moment, I focus on brass tacks. "Do you think she cares?"

"No, I don't," Ryker says, giving a simple answer to a complex question.

He's so lucky to have a sister like that. I can't even imagine.

"She told me what she thought was going on when I first saw her before the ceremony," Ryker adds.

Ah, when he laughed and smirked after that hug. I'm so relieved, I can't even be mad that he didn't save me from the *what if* questions in my head.

Then, a throat clears, and I turn around and it's Chase's mom, all sun-kissed brown hair and a simple yellow dress. I blink, then automatically smooth a hand over my dress even though it's not messed up.

We step out from the alcove, adopting, I'm sure, overly innocent expressions. "Hi there," I say, my voice uncertain. Will she hate me for liking another man too?

"You're the girl with the cute little dog," she says, and that's a promising start.

"I am."

"Join us."

My pulse spikes. Suddenly, my fake date's mother is guiding me to her table, and the guys hang back to chat with teammates, and I'm sitting between Ryker's mom and Chase's mom. Ivy is across from us, as well as a younger version of the fashionista, who I learn is Ryker's other sister, Katie. Am I in for the grilling of a lifetime?

"So, I hear you run a bookstore," Chase's mom says.

"I just manage it."

"Well, that would be running it," Ryker's mom says in the same laconic tone of her son. She has a tattoo on her wrist. A simple circle of black ink, and the word *strength.*

"That's so fantastic," Chase's mom says. "To spend

the day surrounded by stories. To help people find stories. And you run Page Turners Book Club."

"You know about that?" I ask, surprised she's aware of my whole CV.

"I might have looked you up," Ryker's mom adds playfully. "When Chase called me about the photos you wanted."

Right. Of course. How could I forget that?

"It's good to see him on social. I can spy on him more now," she says dryly, and I know where Ryker gets his sense of humor.

We chat some more, and no one lambastes me. No one gives me the third degree. No one asks when I'll pop out babies either.

It's a nice, normal conversation.

I might be foolish but maybe *this thing* could work. Perhaps their mothers being so cool is the sign I needed.

Maybe it doesn't matter if my family doesn't understand me. I've become used to that. But I've found my own family with Aubrey and Nacho and my book club, and maybe now with these two guys.

I try to let go of all the noise in my head. All of the questions chasing me. I relax into the moment as we talk about the city, and hockey, and books, and dogs, and weddings, and flowers, and how happy Chase's cousin is with his teammate.

Every now and then someone else from Ryker's team or Chase's team stops by to say hi, and it's so endearing to see all these players playing nicely with the parents. The women are warm and welcoming and treat them like family too.

With every minute that passes, I'm feeling like maybe the impossible is possible.

When the band begins to play, Chase swoops by and pulls me out to the dance floor. We slow dance, and he looks at me with soulful brown eyes that seem to understand me in a way my own family doesn't. When he looks at me like that, my heart thumps.

But I'm careful to keep some distance between us.

I want to pull him close—too close. I definitely want to. But I don't feel right doing that *just* with him. I don't feel right doing that unless I can declare myself as theirs.

When Ivy and Ryker swing by, Ivy gives me a friendly nod. "Let's switch. I need to dance with Chase."

We trade off, and I'm in Ryker's arms, and this feels right too. My heart beats hard all over again.

Somehow, a few weeks after my dog ate another woman's underwear, I've fallen deeply for the two men who helped give me sweet revenge.

But with them, I've found so much more than sweet revenge. I've found a Golden Retriever and a grump who like me just the way I am.

Maybe, just maybe, I can put myself out there at the end of the night.

34

HOOK, LINE, AND SINKER

Ryker

As the wedding winds down, Ivy waves me aside. She tugs me along the corridor and into the alcove again, then stares at me, like she can see inside my soul.

"You're in love with her," she declares.

What the hell? She *can* see inside my soul.

"No," I say, bristling.

Ivy rolls her eyes but says nothing.

"I'm not," I add.

She scoffs.

"Seriously."

She smirks. "You just denied it three times."

"Because you said it," I point out, annoyed, but not with her. Annoyed with myself for being so transparent even when I've tried to show nothing.

She pokes my chest. "You big lug."

I narrow my eyes, hating that I'm cellophane with her. "Why are you talking to me about this here?"

"Because it's so obvious."

I blow out a harsh breath, then I defend myself. "I danced with her, and Chase danced with you. So how did you realize it?"

She flashes me an impish grin, like only a little sister can. "I figured it out the same way Grandma did."

"And how's that?"

"By knowing you. This is how you were when you met that—"

"Don't say her name," I hiss.

But Ivy goes quiet for a long beat. "Actually, no. You're not like you were with Selena. This is different."

I can't leave that word hanging by itself. I have to know what she thinks is *different.*

"In what way?" I don't bother to mask the desperation in my tone. I feel desperate for Trina.

"This is kind of hook, line, and sinker. And I'm pretty sure Chase is all in with her too." There's no judgment in her voice. No condemnation over the unusual nature of this arrangement. Just a simple question comes next. "So what are you going to do?"

That's the rub.

Nothing. Absolutely nothing. "There's nothing to do."

"Because of the three of you?"

"Well, yeah," I say, with a *life sucks* shrug. Even if my sister's cool with us, would others be? My teammates? The rest of my family? And really, most of all, would Chase and Trina want to be in a relationship? Maybe they like it for a week, but asking someone to be a throuple is more terrifying than facing down blood-thirsty teams on the ice.

"Please. You love who you love," she says, emphatic.

I don't disagree but I won't get my hopes up. "Regardless, she just got out of a bad breakup. She doesn't want anything more than something casual. She said as much. So even if I had a modicum of feelings—"

"You don't have to be so Mister Vocabulary to cover up your feelings." Ivy snorts.

"An iota," I say tightly, refusing to give in.

"More like a fuck-ton."

Fine. I hold my hands up in surrender. "Even if that's true," I continue, "there's nothing I can do about it. She's here with Chase, and he's not into anything more, and..." What's the point? The cards are stacked against us.

I drag a hand through my hair, wishing there were another way, wishing I didn't have a pact, wishing I could somehow lay my heart on the line for Trina and not lose my best friend in doing so. "It doesn't matter. I'll get over her."

But it will hurt, because in one stupid, annoying, amazing, incredible week, I've fallen in love with a girl who stole her ex's tickets and then my heart.

* * *

A little later, we leave, but once we reach Chase's home there's a message blinking up at me on my phone.

. . .

Ivy: Call me when you get this.

That's not foreboding at all.

In the garage, I step away from the two of them and dial her. "What's going on?"

"Your ex did a podcast with the shit-tastic reporter. And it's about Trina."

I want to kill them before I even listen.

35

BAD LUCK CHARM

Chase

The three of us are gathered at the kitchen counter, the site of so many fantastic dinners and breakfasts over the last week. The place where we've gotten to know her, where we've laughed, and argued, and shared. Where we made the new pact.

Now, with dread crawling through my veins, I open my podcast app. I'm bracing myself for the worst. Trina's face is pale. Ryker is a stone, and I've got to keep my shit together since that's what I do.

I keep it together, no matter what happens.

"It's going to be fine," I say tightly, then I hit play.

The reedy voice of a one-time hockey podcaster fills my home. "Bryce Tucker in the house. You might know me from my sports coverage, but celeb coverage is way more fun. So let's do it. I have a fantastic guest here today. The Stuntwoman."

Abby laughs. Or Selena, or whoever she is. It's a familiar sound, one I used to liken to bells, but now, it's the sound of deception wrapped up in a pretty package. "Hey everyone, this is your girl Selena here, AKA The Stuntwoman. And no, friends," she stage whispers, "that's not my real name."

"Never give up your name," Bryce says. "Now, I hear you have an interesting story for us."

"I sure do."

I rub a hand across the back of my neck. This is going to be bad. Trina's fidgeting with her nails, picking at her cuticles. I've never seen her do that before. It's so unlike her. I don't even know what to say to reassure her.

If I can say anything.

"Remember a week or so back when that hockey game made the news for the VIP evening?"

Oh, shit.

This is going to be worse than bad.

Trina purses her lips together. Ryker stops pacing and sets his hands on the counter, like he's going to rip it out from the floor.

"Well, I did a little digging about the guest. And want to know what I found out?"

No, just no.

"So this woman who *won* the tickets to hang out with Chase Weston and Ryker Samuels, and is now *supposedly* dating Weston?"

"Supposedly. That's a fighting word," Bryce says, clearly amused by his guest.

"So, on Friday night she goes to the game. The next

night, she's at the dog park with him. A couple days later, she's hanging out with the *other* guy at her bookstore and then the library, and then she goes to a wedding with Weston tonight? Something is sus. I mean, earlier in the week she was clearly posting pics on Samuels' social feed?"

"Wait. Wait. I have to ask, how is she clearly posting pics?"

She sighs like *c'mon*. "He didn't even have social beforehand, and then there's a shot of him at her bookstore, along with team shots and so on? She's got to be some kind of image consultant for Samuels, for sure," she says, and I wince.

Way to hit the nail on the head, though of course Trina's so much more.

"All right, so your conclusion is?" Bryce asks.

"She's a prop. She's an engineer. She's a provocateur. Because she's also a, wait for it, fake date."

Trina's breath comes sharply.

"No way is she his real GF. Guarantee it's fake," my former girlfriend says.

Trina swallows roughly, then drops her head in her hand. I rub her shoulder. Ryker lets go of his irritation long enough to smooth a hand over her back.

"And you're sure because?" Bryce asks.

"Weston is a pro athlete. No way did he go from VIP night to suddenly saying she's his girlfriend. The only logical answer is she's posing as his girlfriend all while she's managing Samuels' surly rep. And together that tells me she's some kind of puppeteer. Pulling all the strings. She's up to something. If it looks like a stunt, talks like a stunt, and quacks like a stunt, it's a stunt. She's running some sort of great experiment too and I have a feeling what it is."

"What is it?"

"Well, I have a little more intel," she says, sounding like the cat who ate a box of canaries. "I spoke to her ex a week ago..."

Trina gasps, then presses her lips together even harder, as if she's holding back tears. "Sweetness," I say gently, trying to make her feel better during what's sure to be the worst part.

Then, Jasper's voice fills the room. "She was mocking hockey when she broke up with me. She hates the sport! Every time I watched a game she was insulting it. Now she's spending all her time with pros? She's up to something. She's always up to something."

"You ass," Trina seethes, and I want to wring that guy's neck all over again. He might have laid off her if Abby had called him yesterday, but this was a week ago.

"So this proves what?" Bryce asks.

I don't have to see Abby to know she's drawing a deeply satisfied breath as she says, "I'll be waiting to see what her endgame is. Launching a PR company? Announcing her own podcast? Because this is how you do it. With something bold and public, and with two celeb studs at your disposal. I mean, they were useful to me. I dated both of them during my How Many Boyfriends stunt earlier this year."

I hiss.

Ryker slams a fist against the counter.

Trina breathes fire.

"Oh, damn!" Bryce calls out with a cackle.

"Either way, girl, if you're listening, let's do something together! We can conquer the world. Find me and we'll join forces."

I hit end. That's enough. That's fucking enough. I don't care that she named me after all. That she named us. But I care deeply that Trina's getting dragged through the mud.

In her beautiful teal dress that clings to her curves, she's frozen, drawing deep breaths.

This is not okay. I can't let this spiral. I step away from the counter, jaw clenched, running my hand through my hair, trying to devise a plan, stat.

"I'll fix this," I bite out.

"It's okay," Trina says softly but her voice is empty. She's clearly shocked. "I'll be fine."

"No. This is not fine," I say, anger rising inside me, but also determination. I've spent my whole damn career as the good guy. I'm the player who's friendly and outgoing, who plays well, wins games, and loves the sport.

I don't fucking cause trouble.

But this? This is trouble.

And I have to fix it for everyone. For her, for me, and for my friend. He's trying to rehab his rep, and I won't let this blow up all his good work. Besides, we made a pact to be friends in public.

Time to implement it.

Before anyone can say a word, I spin around. "Look. You're moving out tomorrow anyway," I say to her. "If anyone asks, we'll say we became fast friends. No one needs to know the date tonight was fake because it's none of their fucking business. I'll tell my teammates not to say a word and they'll have my back. But I'll let the press know you're a friend. That's the truth. We're all friends."

Ryker shakes his head, his eyes filled with fire. But he's quiet.

"What? We are. No one fucking knows what we did. We presented to the world as friends. So we went on a date. Big deal. We'll just say we're friends. This is why we made a pact, guys. We made a pact the other morning to act like friends, to be friends, to effectively look out for each other as friends, right?"

Ryker breathes out hard but nods like it pains him.

"Yes. We did," Trina says on a rough swallow. "This is the pact," she says, getting it, like she always has. "But what about Charlotte?"

I cycle back to Friday, but I feel okay about it. "We never did anything in public. We don't have to say a thing. People made assumptions. Abby is making assumptions. We're just friends."

Trina looks at me like she's eaten something sour, but she says in a hollow voice, "Friends."

Ryker crosses his arms. "That's bullshit and you know it."

I fling my arms up. "Someone has to triage. I don't want our girl taking the fall. Do you, man?"

Ryker's jaw ticks. "Of course I fucking don't. But that's not what this is about."

I don't need this shit right now. "Then what is this

about? I'm trying to fix the problem. What are you doing?"

"Oh, excuse me. Like you gave anyone else a chance. You're just deciding that this is the way it is."

Seriously? He wants to argue when we have all this stuff to deal with? I am not in the mood. "I've had three shitty games in a row. Now the press is saying terrible things about Trina. I'm trying to fix it. The last thing we need is this blowing up and someone saying she's a bad luck charm for me. Saying it's her fault my team's losing," I say, breathing hard, like I ran a race.

Trina snaps her sad gaze to me. "They would say that," she says heavily.

See? She gets it. She gets *me*. "They love to find an enemy. That fan account that loved you the other day will hate you when the team doesn't play well. I need to play well." I also need to calm down. A few deep breaths and I'm settled. I'm the team captain. I need to handle this thoroughly and well. "Look, if you need a PR firm to run interference, I'll find you one."

Ryker rolls his eyes. "She doesn't need a fucking PR firm."

"What does she need then?"

He doesn't answer—just gives me a *you're a dick* look.

I turn to Trina, wishing I could erase the situation I've put her in, all because I didn't want to be set up at a wedding. "Look, I made a mistake. I should have just gone to the wedding solo. No big deal. This is my fault and I'm sorry, but I want to fix things. You get that, right? You understand me?"

I feel a little desperate. She's always understood me. I hope to hell she still does.

She hesitates. But not like she's unsure, more like she's weighing everything, then she says, "Is this what you want?"

Like what I want matters. I want her. I want *this*. But if this thing between us could get toppled so easily...

"This isn't about what I want. It's about doing the right thing," I say, emphatic and resolute.

But just so I'm not a unilateral dick, I turn to my buddy. "You good with this?"

He sears me with his eyes. He's the grump all over again. The guy in the limo with the hard edge. The one who doesn't trust people.

I can't fix that right now though.

I turn to the woman I was falling for to see what she wants to do tonight. But she's already down the hall, and when I follow, I find her throwing shirts and dresses into her suitcase, gathering her things.

That's clear then.

36

DRESS HANDKERCHIEF

Trina

Rushing through Chase's home with an aching heart, I stave off a torrent of tears as I grab my lotion and toothpaste, then send a quick text.

This is so ridiculous, the way I feel. It was nine days. I shouldn't feel a thing, and yet my throat is terribly tight from fighting off all these emotions.

I call a Lyft, then beeline into Chase's gigantic room, squinting so I don't have to see every single corner of the place that feels like my new home. I grab the few shirts I left here, then I hightail it back to the guest room I never used. I toss my clothes into my duffel bag, then a few books, and I stop, frozen as I stare at all these gifts.

What do I do with these dresses they bought me the other night? I hold up a red one with pockets. Ugh. I want to bury my face in it and use it as a handkerchief to soak up all the waterworks I'm holding back.

"Take them. They're yours," Chase says from the door behind him.

I squeeze my eyes shut. *I want more than dresses, you idiot.*

"But you don't have to leave tonight," Chase adds, perhaps trying to lessen the blow.

Good luck with that, buddy.

"It's fine," I chirp.

"Trina, I didn't mean to suggest you had to go now," he says, trying again.

But I do. I really do. I stuff the dresses into the bag. "It's no problem."

He sighs, then asks, "Can I help you with anything?"

This is who he is. The helper. Giving me a place to stay, helping with my sex woes, and then offering to sort out this new mess.

It's hard to be mad at him for not wanting me the way I want him. For not falling for me the way I fell for him.

His heart is in the right place, but I still shake my head, squeaking out an "I'm fine" as I shove the rest of the clothes into my duffel.

I shouldn't be upset because no one made any promises. No one offered me a single thing. Both of these guys were totally upfront from the get-go. This was just sex. This was just a week of fun. This was just a to-do list, and we did it all and more.

I'm the idiot who got caught up. I'm the one who

saw a happy ending that was definitely never on the list. And I won't overstay my welcome ever again.

After I zip the bag, I rush back to the living room, scoop up my dog and snap on his harness, then hunt for his leash as he tilts his head, as if asking *what's up*.

I stop to pat him for a sec. It's not his fault I was rejected. "I love you," I whisper to my trusty companion.

From the kitchen, the too-familiar voice of Ryker says, "Let me drive you. It's safer that way."

Nope. Don't need it. Don't want it. He'll see me cry then. They can't know that I was about to put my foolish, silly, anything-goes heart on the line for *both of them*. "My Lyft will be here soon," I say, as breezy as I can.

But as I hook on a leash to my pup, Ryker comes to my side, the remnants of his forest scent tugging on my aching heart.

"I'll carry out your stuff," he says as Chase returns to the kitchen and Ryker shoots him a damning look.

I shake my head adamantly as my phone pings, telling me my Lyft is pulling up. "I've got it."

I don't need an escort to this relationship execution. I won't let him play the part he wants to play. The protector. Like he's protecting me from Chase now. They are exactly who I thought they would be and I can't fault them.

"It's all fine," I add, then press my lips together so I don't let other words fall out like *I fell in love with both of you*.

With my loyal dog by my side, I march to the door,

my life packed up in a matter of minutes. In the entry-way, Chase gives me a pleading look. "I didn't mean to make you feel that you had to leave tonight," he says, trying once more.

"It's all fine," I say brightly, as brightly as I possibly can. "I have things to do. It won't be a problem."

A second later, my hand is on the knob, my heart is in my throat, and the most wonderful week is circling down the drain. This is over. It's over exactly how it was supposed to be—with me leaving. But in a flash, I know if I walk out the door like this, it'll be as if these nine, eye-opening, earth-shattering, heart-expanding days never happened.

An hour ago, I was ready to put my heart on the line. Now I know they don't feel the same way. There was never a future.

I'm not going to walk out that door denying what I learned about myself with the two of them. Yes, I found a Golden Retriever and a grump. But I found myself too.

Our time will fade into the past, but I'm going to own who I am. Chin up, I turn around and look them both in the eyes, and I say, "Goodbye. I was falling for both of you."

Before anyone can say another word, I leave, slam-ming the door behind me. As I walk down the front stoop to the car that's cruising down the block to save me, the tears start to come. They sting the back of my eyes first, prepping to slide down my face. But the door creaks from behind me.

I hold my breath.

A voice calls out, "You forgot his toy."

Oh. My shoulders sag.

Ryker's bringing me a dog toy. That's all. I don't even turn around. When he reaches me, he hands me the stuffed monkey. When I finally raise my face, he's holding my gaze like he's trying to say something without words. Something important. But the only word that comes out of his mouth is a sad, broken "Trina."

I shouldn't say anything. Truly, I shouldn't, but I do anyway. "Was this as good as I thought?"

His gaze is as intense as his voice when he says, "Best week of my life."

Somehow my heart hurts even more. "And now it's over."

He says nothing as I grab the door and get in the car with Nacho. We head into the night, away from my two loves.

Away from my best friend too. Aubrey's out of town for the night, and I have no other choice but to go to my sister's place.

When I arrive, I am a mess in every sense of the word. Tears are streaming down my face, my makeup is ruined, and my heart is broken as I set my dog down on Cassie's perfectly polished hardwood floors.

To her credit, she doesn't flinch at the sight of a pet in her home.

One hand on her giant belly, Cassie lets me in, with an *I knew you'd wind up here* look on her face. "I'm glad you texted. You know you always have a place with me," she says.

And the sad thing is, I do know that. She is constant.

"It's only one night. I'm moving into my place tomorrow," I say, since this is just a stop gap.

"Stay as long as you want," she says, perhaps wanting to save me from me.

"I'm fine. I'm fine. I'm fine," I say, but my voice is breaking.

She ushers me into the living room and hands me a tissue. "You don't look fine. What happened? I knew that guy would break your heart. I knew it was a bad idea. I just knew it," she says, like she's going to beat up those jerks on the playground.

Only, she doesn't know there were two jerks who did this to me. With a sigh that breaks me, I just let out a raw, "I know."

"Let me give you a hug," she says.

I let her because she's here with an open door and at least in her own bossy, annoying, judging way, she's fighting for me.

The men I fell in love with did not.

37

I'M THE DICK

Ryker

In the kitchen, I glare at my best friend. Right now, he feels like my enemy. "You're a fucking dick," I say.

Chase is ice as he stares right back at me. "Oh, I'm the dick?"

"How could you do that to her?"

"Do what? Try to fix things? Try to solve the problem?"

I stab the kitchen counter with my finger. "Make her feel like she's nothing."

He rolls his eyes. "Oh, I'm sorry. How did you try to make her feel like she was everything? I didn't see you doing anything. You fucking stood there and grunted."

A plume of anger rises inside me. "Because you'd already decided how it was going to be," I say, seething. "Like you did before."

"We're still on that? We're still negotiating that

fucking issue?" he asks, shaking his head, then wheeling around and yanking open a cupboard like he'll rip it off the hinges.

"Because you're still doing the same shit," I say.

Shaking his head, Chase grabs a bottle and a cup, pours a few fingers, then knocks it all back. He sets down the glass with an angry clink. "And you're one to talk. What did you do? You were just Grumpy Ryker. Angry Ryker. Growly Ryker." He holds his arms out wide. "Well, Growly Ryker didn't solve the problem."

I clench my fists. "And you didn't either, Mister Fix-It," I bite out, then turn around and stalk down the hall.

He's seconds after me. "It's easy to get mad at me, isn't it? It's easy to wrap yourself in this whole persona you've created. The guy who's unfazed. The guy who's so tough, he just grunts. That's what you do. You create this whole illusion. And then you use it when it suits you. When it's fucking convenient."

I whirl around, fuming now. "And you're better? You just stand there and take over. You try to fix everything before you even think about what it means. Before you even consider how anything comes across."

"I didn't see you trying to fix it," he says, missing the point entirely.

"You don't give anyone else a chance," I roar.

"So what did you want to say that I didn't let you say?" he asks, sweeping out a hand. "The floor is yours."

Fuck him and his empty gestures. "How magnanimous of you."

"*Magnanimous.* So typical. You say that stuff to just cover up how you really feel."

With narrowed eyes, and righteous rage in my heart, I step closer, poking his chest. "And I know what you do. You try to make everything right to cover up how you really feel."

He pushes my finger off his chest. "Well, Mister Expert. Tell me how I feel then? Or hey, better yet. How do *you* feel?"

I didn't tell Trina that I was falling in love with her. No way am I going to tell him. No way am I going to say *I wanted to make a go of this crazy thing we built.* Because no matter how angry I am at Chase right now, I made a deal with him. He's not interested in a relationship. So what am I going to do? Go after her and confess my dumb heart? Ask her to be with just me? Not an option. I promised that I wouldn't let a woman come between us and I won't, even though he's a world-class fuck-face right now.

"Forget it," I say, because I'm not giving him the satisfaction.

I head into the room I didn't use and grab my shit. Three minutes later, I'm out the door too and in my car. My floors are fixed. They've been fixed since Thursday. I didn't tell him. I didn't tell Trina. I didn't need to stay here any longer.

I chose to.

But I'm leaving because I'm not only mad at him, I'm mad at myself. Chase is one hundred percent right.

I hid behind the image I've created, not the new one Trina helped shape. I didn't stand up for her.

* * *

The next day in Seattle, I'm stepping off the plane with Dev, debating whether we should get Korean barbecue or check out some cool new sushi spot in Capitol Hill. The argument is better than being alone with my incessant thoughts of the woman I can't have and the friend who I don't want to talk to.

"Apparently, the sushi is so spicy your mouth will be on fire," Dev says, making his pitch.

"Please. Sushi has nothing on Korean barbecue," I say, but mostly I don't want fish and rice since it reminds me of the first gift we gave Trina.

"Sushi's closer to the hotel," Dev adds when Oliver catches up to me on the jetway.

"Got a sec, buddy?" he asks in his upbeat tone.

He's always upbeat. That's the job. He's chipper when he gives you bad news and when he delivers good news. The last twenty-four hours, though, have been all bad. My agent, Josh, called this morning when I boarded the flight, wanting to know what the hell had happened. "This podcast episode is everywhere," he said, sounding like he wanted to track down Bryce and my ex and give them a piece of *or else*.

"That's great news," I'd deadpanned.

To his credit, Josh also asked if there was anything he could do. But since muzzling Selena was not a viable answer, I said, "Nothing, man. But I appreciate the check-in."

What else could I say? In one podcast episode, all the work Trina did for me during the last week crumbled to dust. If the team didn't like my rep before, they'll hate it now. Oliver's probably about to let me know I'm on the shit list.

"Sure," I say to him, since what's the alternative? I've got to own my mistakes.

Dev laughs. "If the debate's over, that means sushi after the game."

"Nope. Sushi is not the answer," I say.

But Dev shoots me a cocky grin. "Fish it is," he says, then continues on his way. Un-reprimanded. Lucky fucker. But at least he didn't mention my clusterfuck of a reputation on the flight. Or ask for any details about what went down with Trina.

I'll chalk that up as a small victory.

I turn to Oliver as we continue down the jetway, bracing myself. "What's up? Nothing good, I presume."

"Well, it's not great," he says, diplomatically. "There was a lot of coverage of that podcast. *But*," he says, and it sounds a lot like a *here's the but* coming my way. "I get —and the Avengers' front office does too—that it's not your fault."

What? I jerk my gaze to him. "They do?"

"You didn't cause this problem," he adds.

"But that piece. It was grist to the sports news mill."

"It was. But like I said, not your fault. It's not Trina's fault either," he says, and the sound of her name rips at my tattered heart. "We don't blame you, or Chase, or the VIP guest," he says, and she's so much more than a VIP guest, but I shut my mouth about that. "It's just a situation that got out of hand. We do appreciate what you did to work on your socials. We appreciate, too, that she helped you out." He shrugs, but it's not a help-less one. "You can't control what others say."

True. But still. "I thought you guys wanted the whole *good guy* image," I say, doubtful.

He laughs lightly. "Of course we *want* positive press. We want our players to present well online. You did all that. And then this happened, but there's nothing you can do. We'll just keep on moving forward. How does that sound?"

Like I don't buy it.

"Sus," I admit as we head into the airport.

He chuckles. "Love your 'trust no one' attitude. It's great for a hockey player. But seriously, it's fine, Ryker. I swear."

"What was the point then?"

He stops and I do too. Oliver's young, but in this moment, he seems wise beyond his years as he meets my gaze straight on. "The point was to let your fans know who you are." He takes a beat, still intensely seri-ous. "Someone who loves his family, who cares about his sisters, his mom, his grandmother. Someone who gives books to a library. Who gets a jersey signed by teammates and helps donate it to rescue dogs. That's who. The rest? You can't control it. Sometimes you let it go and focus on what you can control."

I didn't have *get good life advice from the PR guy* on my bingo card today, but I'll take it. I ease up on my doubt. "I appreciate all that. Thank you, Oliver," I say genuinely.

"If you want to sit out of any press conferences, that's fine with me."

"I'll think about it," I say.

But mostly, I spend the day thinking about all the things I don't think I can control. And trying to figure out if I can control any of them.

Then I get on the ice, and I play my best, blocking passes, rattling the other team, not letting up even an inch, and doing everything I can for the Avengers for all three periods.

It's a tight game, and it comes down to the wire as they attack in the final few seconds. But I'm all focus as the Seattle center flies down the ice like he's hellbent on tying it up and forcing overtime.

Nope. Not today.

I'm there, blocking the shot before he even reaches Dev, and the buzzer sounds, signaling our victory.

* * *

Later, I don't take the easy way out. I retreated last night. I won't do it again. I talk to the press after the game and I don't grunt. I don't swear either.

I do say we played hard against a tough opponent. "But I'm glad we won," I add, even though I still feel empty.

But I keep that part all to myself.

38

DIDN'T SEE THAT COMING

Chase

Here's the thing about New York fans. They don't just hate you. They really fucking hate you.

Which is why it's that much sweeter that I'm finally in the zone again with, count 'em not one, but two goals over the New York Rogues in their famed arena on Wednesday night. And the rabid fans have not let up with their chants of *bad luck charm*.

Yeah, real creative.

Pisses me off. But makes me play even harder. Trina wasn't a bad luck charm. Not one bit. She is fucking incredible, but nope.

Can't think about her on the ice.

Not during the game. Not at all. And I won't get cocky even with our three-goal lead.

With only a few minutes left, I'm skating hard. Ledger has the puck, and he's racing to the net. He takes aim, and then it comes: a mighty shot that smashes into the net's twine and pads the lead.

The boos are deafening but still crystal clear.

Bad luck charm.

A few minutes later, when the horn sounds, signaling the end of the game, the jeers intensify, the brand-new insult rising in volume.

It's not even apropos given we won, but that's beside the point. I knew someone would say it. It started online a few days ago and picked up steam. But at least we're winning again, and that's all that matters.

On the way to the locker room, I rip off my helmet and Andrei high-fives me. "Nice work," he says, then smacks palms with Ledger too. "And you too, old man."

Ledger thumps Andrei's head. "Where was your goal tonight, kid?"

Andrei laughs it off and the conversation moves on to the next game and the one after that.

And that's the thing—it was one game, and anything could have happened, but it was a relief to play well. The bigger relief? My teammates haven't said a thing about the podcast blowup and the big *she's your fake girlfriend* bit.

In the hallway, Gianna catches up and says she wants Ledger and me for the post-game press in ten minutes.

"I'll be there," I say, and a few minutes later, after I take off my skates and jersey, we head to the media room. Along the way, Ledger shoots me a thoughtful look. "Don't let that shit get to you. That bad luck charm stuff. I don't think you are, but I just wanted to say it."

And I spoke too soon. They noticed. Or at least, he did.

"Me, let something get to me? Never," I say, keeping things light even though I don't feel that way inside. I haven't since Trina walked out. I know it's for the best. Truly, I do. But I miss her more than I'd expected. Too bad there's nothing I can do about it.

Ledger gives me a dubious look, but there's no time to dig deeper since Gianna's ready and waiting outside the room. Which means I need my armor since it's New York and the press here has fangs.

After a couple easy questions about the game, a reporter in the back barks out, "Joe Cotton. *New York Press*. So you dumped the bad luck charm?"

And I burn inside as the gloves come off. I hate that he called her that. But I can't let on. I'm all smiles as I say, "C'mon, Joe. You know you can't believe everything you read. She's a friend."

"That's not what I heard," Joe presses. "She was your pretend girlfriend. Why'd you need a pretend girl-friend? To improve your play?"

And yup. I had a feeling this would happen, but I'm staying on message because it's the right thing for her. But Gianna cuts in, leaning toward the mic at the table. "We'd like to keep the questions focused on hockey."

"Fine. How was it dating someone who hates the sport?" someone else asks.

Clever. Real clever.

"That's not hockey related," Gianna corrects, but I can't let her handle this mess for me.

"Actually, she knows a helluva lot about hockey," I say. "Picked up the nuances real fast. And if you're interested in nuance, you might want to consider reading a romance novel. You might learn a thing or two. Next question?"

Gianna seems to stifle a grin, and she lets the questions come. I handle them all. I might not be able to have Trina, but I can protect her even from afar.

Later, when the battering session is done, I return to the locker room with Gianna and Ledger. "It'll die down soon. And then you'll be like me, and they'll just ask when you'll retire," he says.

"Not on my watch," Gianna warns him.

"Or mine," I add. I rely on this guy. I don't want to think about playing without him. Just like I don't want to think about being back in my home without Trina when I return to California in a few more days.

That's going to suck big time.

Sucks, too, that I can't call or text Ryker to get a beer and play pool. We're not really talking, and that's all kinds of messed up.

But for now, I'm the hassle to the team, and I hate being that guy. "Listen, Gianna. This should blow over soon. I'm going to do everything I can to make sure we can just keep on sailing," I say, staying cheery.

"It's okay. My job is to smooth your path, not the

other way around."

"Thank you," I say, wishing I didn't need the help.

When she heads the other way, Ledger holds up a stop-sign hand. "Chase," he says and shit's getting serious if he's using my first name.

"Yeah?"

"I told the guys not to say anything. About the podcast and your...*friend*. And everything that went down."

Oh.

I scratch my jaw, a little embarrassed that it came to that, him cleaning up my mess. But this explanation makes sense—explains why the guys said nothing. They listen to Ledger since he speaks from years of authority.

"Um, thanks," I say.

"Anytime," he says, then clears his throat. "But I did it because you seemed happier before."

Ledger doesn't usually give relationship advice. "That so?" I say with a smile.

"Yeah, that doesn't fool me. That smile," he says, calling bullshit. "If the bad luck charm makes you happy, get her back. We all know it wasn't fake."

He turns around and heads into the locker room, leaving me stuck with that piece of advice.

Get her back.

As if it's not the thing I want most. And the thought I've been trying to avoid since I let her go on Sunday night.

* * *

Alone in my hotel room that night, I lie in bed, staring at the ceiling, the words *get her back* echoing in my head.

Nice idea, but it seems impossible. Ledger doesn't know it wasn't just her and me. There was someone else in the mix too, and we both want the girl. We both want to share the girl. But I'm not even talking to Ryker. Not so much as a single text. So getting back the girl seems harder than pulling off a hat trick.

I need to keep my head in the game, even if my heart's on the other side of the country.

But as the trip goes on, the missing doesn't ebb even as we keep winning. It intensifies. Every day. Hell, every hour. By the time the trip ends, and I'm boarding the plane back to San Francisco, my chest is tight, my muscles are tense, and my head is a mess. I can't separate thoughts of her from thoughts of anything else.

I can't focus on a single thing that's not her, knowing I'll be in the same city as her again.

I'll be close to her store. Close to her. She's all I can think about. She's the only thing on my mind. And she's filling up every hollow space in my heart.

I can't fix this feeling. I can't solve this feeling. I can't paste on a smile and make it all go away.

I just want her, no matter how hard I try to be the same guy I was before.

Because maybe I'm not the same guy anymore.

39

IT'S COMPLICATED

Ryker

When my Saturday afternoon game ends, I meet Ivy for an early dinner in Hayes Valley. We're at a trendy spot she picked out that serves Mediterranean food, and I wish she'd told me in advance since it reminds me of Trina. But then again, everything does.

That's just my life.

Ivy and I catch up about her work and Grandma over hummus, but a few minutes in, she sets down her mojito. "Enough of this small talk. What's going on with Trina and you and Chase?"

"Someone doesn't mess around," I say with a low whistle of appreciation for her candor.

She's unflinching. "Talk. It's that thing people do with those they trust when something's on their mind."

But where do I even start? It all feels so big, so

consuming. I drag a hand over my beard, hunting for a way out but knowing I won't find one. Or maybe I don't want one anymore. Maybe I'm ready for...connection.

"So, after the wedding, we had this huge fight," I begin, then tell her what went down. What I said, what Chase said, how she left, how I left, and how I haven't talked to Chase since and can't get Trina out of my head.

"First, you're pissed at him. I get that," she says. Then she tilts her head, studies me with those deep blue eyes. "It sounds like you really miss her."

Part of me wants to deny it, even though I know that's pointless. Ivy knows me too well and can see right through me. So I just nod instead.

"I miss her like I'd miss breathing," I finally admit, taking a sip of my beer as if it might give me some courage to go on. "But it's complicated."

She laughs at that but shakes her head. "Ryker, of course it's complicated. That's why you need to talk to Chase, and then you need to figure out how to breathe again."

I close my eyes for a second, picturing Trina, how I felt with her. Understood. Accepted. Most of all, I felt trust, coming both ways. From her, from me, and then, honestly, with my best friend too.

It's so strange, wanting all of that. Wanting to have her both to myself but also with him. Wanting to love her but not just alone. Wanting to give her more love like she deserves.

Would he even want to though? And would she

want to hear from us again? No idea, but it's time to fix everything that's wrong.

I can't avoid him much longer. And I don't want to.

40

WHAT IF IT DOES?

Trina

The door to my studio apartment swings shut as Aubrey and I step inside on Saturday evening. It smells of paint and freshness, and finally I feel some joy in my own space. It's starting to look like home, especially when Nacho scrambles around my feet to say hi. I scoop up his cuteness and give him a kiss in greeting. "Missed you, but we were only at the farmers' market for a half hour," I say.

In dog time, that's forever, so he takes another minute to kiss me before settling into his bed with a satisfied huff.

I head to the kitchen counter where Aubrey sets the daisies we bought in a vase, then takes a step back to survey the room.

"There," I say since it's finally come together, and Aubrey's been helping me make it look like home. My little home with my little dog. Just us. "Looks good. Thanks to the flowers."

Aubrey takes in the scene with an approving eye, but then turns on her eagle-eyed-friend vision. "The place looks great, but now that we're alone, tell me—how are you really doing?"

My heart aches in response. "Sad," I admit, before quickly pushing away the thought and forcing a more optimistic tone in my voice. "But you know what? It'll be okay. Eventually it will be okay."

"You don't have to be a tough girl with me," she says as she heads to the couch that came with the place. Furnished studio for the win.

"It's been almost a week. I'm fine. I'm just fine," I say, staying strong, keeping my chin up.

"Are you though?" she asks, not letting this go.

She pats the couch, and I join her, slumping against her, grateful to admit the full truth. "I miss them still. I have all week. So much it hurts. But what can I do?"

I sit up, exhaling, trying to let them go once again like I've done every day for the last week. I've had no luck though. There's a Chase-and-Ryker-sized hole in my heart, and it shows no signs of mending.

"Well," she says, meeting my eyes, "you could talk to them."

I shudder. "Talk. Ugh. What is that? That sounds terrifying."

She laughs, but then quickly turns serious again. "You could though, Trina," she urges.

"But I did. I literally told them," I say, and she knows because she's heard the story. She heard it the day I drowned my sorrows with her in nachos—well, they're a favorite—and cheap wine and friendship. "And Chase said nothing, and Ryker basically said *hey, I had a good week*."

"I know, but I just think with everything that went down, maybe Chase was really rattled. I think he was truly trying to help. And I think Ryker was pissed because he's already madly in love with you."

I wish I had her optimism. Truly, I do. "That doesn't mean he wants to be with me. And it's fine. I mean, who finds their two true loves a few weeks after a horrible ex cheats on them? That stuff doesn't happen."

The stuff that does happen is this—longing, missing, wanting. But then, figuring out how to move on. I'll have to do that, even though I ache terribly for the two men I never expected to fall for.

"But what if it does?" Aubrey asks, encouragingly.

The question is too tempting. Too alluring. It's a question for book club. A question for starry-eyed dreamers. One I'll ask the ladies tomorrow night.

In the real world? No matter how much I wish it were true—and I wish for it from the bottom of my soul —it can't be.

I used to think the three of us couldn't be a thing because of my family. Because of my sister. Because of all their unmet expectations of me. But sometime in the week I spent with Chase and Ryker, I learned to let go of their life plans for me.

To embrace my own *un-plan*.

I came to accept myself, and my own quirky, messy, making-it-up-as-I-go-along choices. Including the one to fall for two men. To imagine a future with two men. To see that as a bright, new possibility, with me and my two guys.

I was ready that night after the wedding. Ready to say *screw the world, let's be together anyway.*

But I told them I was falling for them, and they didn't see it the same way. I'll have to keep moving forward into my own messy future, full of unpredictable choices.

Even though the question Aubrey asked plays on repeat for the next day.

What if it does?

41

THE BIG IF

Chase

The text arrives when I'm walking to my mom's home for the lunch she planned last week—the one with the guy I used to call my best friend.

> Ryker: Let's talk. Today.

That's a relief. I was about to send him one saying the same thing. I hit reply.

> Chase: Agree. Let's do it in about ten minutes.

.   .   .

But the rest of the way, I'm still a powder keg. Too many emotions swirl inside me. I'm still pissed at Ryker for the attitude and a half that he gave me a week ago. I'm filled with regret for letting go of Trina. And then, there's this brand-new emotion that's jostling all the others like bumper cars.

Obsession, I think?

But that doesn't feel quite right.

Sure, I can't stop thinking about Trina. Yes, I can't stop wanting her. But I also want to shower her with gifts and pleasure and kisses and sex and adoration and so much more.

Is that obsession?

Hell if I know, but the question is driving me mad. It was driving me mad when I was in New York and then in Boston. It's reached a boiling point now that I'm in the same vicinity as she is. I'm itching to go see her, to find her, to tell her I wake up thinking of her, I go to bed and dream of her, and I spend all day wanting her.

I don't know how to contain all these feelings. But I know this—I no longer want to.

It's time to deal.

When I reach my mom's home, she swings open the door. I relax for a second, giving her a hug and handing her a three-bean salad I picked up at the gourmet shop she loves.

"Good to see you, Mom," I say.

"You too. You look good. But out of sorts," she says, reading me right away.

"I feel out of sorts," I admit.

She nods sagely. "It's about a girl, isn't it?"

"Yes," I say, relieved.

"Well, sort it out, kid," she says, and on that simple piece of advice, I head inside, feeling a little less tightly wound. I breathe in the lavender scent of her home— one she owns fully, thanks to the money she and my dad put away. She's been able to do that partly because I pay for college for my brothers, so she never had to worry about that.

But as I walk through her bright, cheery home, it hits me—*we've* done it. Mom and me. She's made it through the tough years. I helped her like my dad asked me to. But she helped herself too.

Now, she's secure and my brothers are set. Maybe it's time to take care of me finally.

I'm ready at last. Hell, that's probably why I'm obsessed.

In the kitchen, I find Ryker's mom pouring a glass of chablis. "Hi, Chase. You better have brought a good salad this time. I still have nightmares about the egg salad from last month," she says, then shudders.

I smile, grateful for the levity, then give her a hug. "This one is good. I promise."

I don't sit though. I'm antsier than I ever have been for a simple lunch. More out of sorts than when I've stepped onto the ice during playoffs.

For all my time spent taking care of people, I'm clueless about romance.

But maybe it's like hockey. When the puck drops, you go after it. Seconds after Ryker rings the bell then comes inside, I don't waste time. "Excuse me, ladies," I say to the moms, then I tip my forehead to the patio. "We need to talk."

"Yes, we do," he says.

But before he heads outside with me, he looks to his mom, then mine. "Nice to see you. I guess I've been summoned."

His mom shoos him off. "Wish I could get my popcorn and watch, but you boys probably need to figure out your girl situation on your own."

Our moms are both smiling, and maybe, just maybe, they're on *our* side. That's a wild thought. But I'd better not put the cart before the horse.

Once we're on the back patio, I dive in. "I'm mad at you, but I'm mad at me too."

"Welcome to the club," he says.

"Everything is a mess, and we need to straighten it out," I say, determined, like I was the night of the wedding but in a whole new way and for a whole new goal.

"That's what I was telling you a week ago. But then you didn't even ask me what I wanted with Trina and, for fuck's sake, with the three of us, man," he says, but he doesn't sound angry now. He sounds pissed but vulnerable, and that's a different beast. I can work with this beast. Hell, I am this beast too. "You just decided how it was going to be. You didn't even ask what I wanted or what she wanted."

"That's fair," I say honestly, taking it on the chin, letting go of my anger like he's let go of his. "I'm sorry I was a unilateral dick."

He nods, accepting it. "And sorry I was a turtle dick."

"What?"

"I retreated. Like a turtle."

"You do know turtles and dicks aren't the best comparisons?"

"They kind of are though."

I laugh, and it feels good to laugh again with him. But the laughter dies quickly.

There's business to deal with. The business of love.

Ryker stares me down. "Let's try it again. What do you want?"

I appreciate that he's taking the lead on fixing things, but I should be the one asking him. That's what I didn't do last time. "What do you want?" But while I *should* wait for him to answer, I also need to be more honest with myself, so I start now and I say the hard thing. "Since we're both in love with the same woman."

His eyes widen with a surprise I've never seen before, then he grins a crooked grin. "Took you long enough to figure it out."

I laugh. "No, dude. You were easy to figure out. I knew you were in love with her by the second day. Easily."

He shakes his head, laughing. "That's not what I mean, dickhead. Took you long enough to figure out you're in love with her too."

I shrug, but it's a hopeful one. For the first time since I behaved like a control freak, I feel hope. "That's probably true too."

And this obsession? It's not only obsession. It's love,

and it's terrifying, but it's also thrilling. "So what are *we* going to do about it?"

Ryker grins like a cat. "At last, he gets it. That's what I wanted to talk about."

I've needed this talk so badly. I want to share her love so much—if she'll have us and that's a big if. "So, talk. Since I talked too much last time."

Ryker's easy to read this time as he runs a hand through his hair, like that unwinds his tension. "A lot of things pissed me off that night. First, I made this promise to you that I wouldn't let a woman come between us, and I didn't. So I let her go, and that damn near killed me. It devastated me to let her walk out. It's been eating me up inside. But I don't just want her." He takes a deep breath, then pushes on. "I want us both to have her."

Yes! Holy fuck, yes. I can't erase this stupid grin because I want that too.

"I want us to share her," I say, my voice full of wild hope. "I want us to love her together. She lights up with both of us. She's like a flower, and she needs two suns. She needs her two men. She thrives with you and me."

But Ryker's smile disappears. "But if I were her, I don't know that I'd even remotely consider seeing the two of us idiots ever again."

My heart drops. "We really fucked up, didn't we?"

"Big time."

I pace the patio, scrubbing a hand across the back of my neck. "Why the hell didn't I figure it out sooner?"

"It's a little complicated," he says dryly.

I chew on that for a minute. "It is but it's also not."

"How do you figure?"

"Because," I begin, and I strip down my defenses. I let down my guard. "Because she told us she was falling for us when she left, and we let her walk away."

Ryker practically bolts for the door. "We need to get our girl back. And we need to do it right away."

"Yes, we do. But we also have to do it the right way," I say.

Good thing I have some excellent ideas.

42

BOOK BOYFRIEND MOVE

Trina

I say goodbye to Prana, then hand her the victory mug. "Well done. Your bang sense is most excellent."

She clutches it to her chest. "It's my top skill."

The romance lover and nookie prognosticator waves goodbye and heads out of the store. Aubrey sticks around to help me finish cleaning up, then flicks a strand of hair off her shoulder when we're done. "I have an early blowout. Which always sounds dirty no matter how many times I say it," she says, breezily.

"I hope you enjoy your *blowout*, you dirty girl," I say, then give her a hug and say goodbye. It's closing time in a few minutes and the store is mostly empty on a Sunday night.

I make a few laps, straightening books that are sticking out of shelves and realigning them when the bell tinkles at the door.

Pretty sure it's nine, which is when we close, but if someone wants a book, then dammit, they should still get it.

"Let me know if you need anything," I call to the customer, glancing over my shoulder to the entryway.

I turn back to the shelves when my brain catches up with my eyes.

Was that...?

"We do." Two voices. They speak in unison, and the hair on my arms stands on end.

No way. It can't be them.

But I'm too full of traitorous hope. They disappeared from my life. It's just my imagination playing tricks on me. Cautiously, I turn around and...

Oh.

Wow.

They're here. Together. In my store. Chase in jeans and a dark Henley, his soulful brown eyes locking with mine. Ryker, in a trim T-shirt, glorious arms on display, with those midnight blues that see inside me. The guys I love.

Wait. Hold on.

These are *also* the guys who broke my heart.

All at once, my hurt rushes to the surface. My throat tightens. The heartache I felt this last week pummels me all over, and I want to grab the nearest hardcover. Like that one right here—*Paris Off The Beaten Path*. I want to grab it and fling it at them.

But I've let my emotions get the best of me before. I won't let that happen again. Instead, I adjust my glasses, lift my chin, and plaster on a customer service smile. "You must be looking for *Ten Ways to Break Up with A Woman And Make It Look Like It's For Her Own Good*. I can show it to you," I say brightly. "We also have *Five Great Lines To Use When Dumping Her Gently*. And the perennial favorite, *But We Can Be Friends, Right?*"

I bat my lashes.

Chase blows out a breath. Ryker mouths *oh shit*.

"I'm sorry," Chase begins, setting down a canvas bag he's been holding.

"I'm so damn sorry," Ryker continues, dropping his bag too.

"Cool. Apology accepted. You'll find that title on the self-help shelves. It's called *Fool Me Once*," I say, staying strong, even as they step closer, walking past our bright and bubbly romance bestsellers display, full of pastel covers and delicious stories THAT ARE ALL A LIE.

"Trina," Chase says again, but I back up. Toward the shelves. Toward the safety of books. "Can we please talk to you? There's a book boyfriend move we have to do."

"And it's called The Grovel," Ryker says.

Oh. Wow. They're serious. This is real. They're not just here to say they're sorry. They're here to grovel? I've never seen a real grovel.

"I fucked up badly the last week," Chase begins. "I tried too hard to solve a problem, and I didn't stop and think about what the gorgeous, amazing, incredible woman right in front of me actually needed."

"And I just let you walk away," Ryker says, jumping in. "That was the worst decision of my life. I should have fought for you. I should have tried to keep you.

Because you're incredible, and I can't stop thinking about you."

And as they come closer and the scent of pine mingles with the smell of the ocean, my defenses start to weaken.

Ryker's gaze is so vulnerable. Chase's voice is so earnest. Their words are so outrageously romantic.

But they still hurt me so much. They left me. "You really broke me," I say, looking from one to the other, my tone as tough as can be. "Both of you. So much."

"We know," Chase says, never looking away. The intensity of his gaze strips off another layer of self-protection. "I want to make it up to you. *We* want to make it up to you," he says, gesturing to Ryker.

The bearded, broody man swallows roughly, then says, "I'm crazy about you, Trina. I have been since probably the night I met you."

"You hated me," I say, challenging him.

"Only because I liked you from the start. You were fun and feisty, and you called me on my attitude and you never stopped doing that. And even when I tried not to fall for you, you did all these things—wanting to help me, wanting to know me, wanting to meet my family. I don't trust easily, but you showed me what it's like to trust completely in just a little over a week."

God, my heart is mush. Where are my defenses going? They are crumbling like weak bricks.

"And when I met you, I thought we had this dog bond going," Chase picks up the dialogue. "I thought that was our thing. But really, our thing was understanding each other, accepting each other, wanting to help the other see that...*you're enough*. On your own, Trina, you're enough no matter what your family thinks. Just like you showed me that I'm enough even without hockey."

That's official. It's melted. My heart is a puddle on the floor. I'm trembling and my bottom lip is quivering, and I'm so glad there are no customers here because I'm about to cry stupid tears of happiness.

"I love you," Chase continues.

"And I love you," Ryker says, then takes a beat. "And we want you to be..."

In unison, they say, "Ours."

Gasping, I cover my mouth with my hand. This is too much. Too romantic. Too good to be true. Except, it is.

"I love you both too," I blurt out, and then they're both coming toward me and wrapping me up in their arms. Chase is on one side, Ryker on the other, and I can feel it—all of their love, all of their protection, all of their promises.

I have no idea how we'll make this work. What I'll tell my family. What they'll say to the world. But in this moment, I don't care. They're here with me.

Where they belong.

When they let go, Chase retreats to root around in one of the bags, and Ryker in the other. Anticipation thrums through my cells.

A gift is coming my way, and I do like their gifts. Always have.

Chase goes first, handing me a fancy, festive, studded dog collar with a bow on it, and a shiny dog tag. I take it, curious why they're giving me a dog collar, besides, well, the obvious. I have a dog.

But when I see the name and address on the tag, my breath catches. "Is this—"

Before I can finish, Ryker hands me a velvet pouch. I dip my fingers into it and take out a simple, silver key.

My heart gallops so fast. My throat clogs with emotion. "Are you—"

"Move in with us," Chase says. "You and Nacho. We don't want to go back to separate places. We want you with us."

I look to Ryker, confused. "But you have your own place."

"My place is with you," he says, then shrugs helplessly. "I want us to share a home."

Share.

That word has become my whole entire heart.

"What do you say to that?" Chase asks, so hopeful.

I'm hopeful too. "Yes. I say yes."

And I let go of the hurt. I step into my future with my two guys.

43

THE BAND'S BACK TOGETHER AGAIN

Trina

As Chase kisses the back of my neck, I gasp.

The sound turns into a long, low moan. Because Ryker thrusts deeper into me at the same time. I'm in bed, on my side, face-to-face with Ryker, who's fucking me, while Chase is spooning me, his strong body holding mine.

Pleasure twists through me as Ryker reaches for my thigh then hooks my leg over his hip, all while Chase slides a hand down my back, caressing me.

With their twin attention, I lose my mind and soul to bliss.

Minutes later, after I come down from that first high, I'm on my other side, looking into Chase's eyes as he takes me. He rocks into me while Ryker lies behind me, buries his face in my hair and inhales me, nipping my neck and palming my ass.

It's everything I never knew I wanted.

It's a deluge of sensation. It's them together with me, giving me so much more than I thought I had a right to ask for. Than I ever knew I wanted.

But now in bed, they're taking turns making love to me, cherishing me, worshiping me.

Making me the star of the night.

Well, I suppose they've always treated me like a VIP.

* * *

After I shower, I pad out to the kitchen in a tank top and shorts I picked up during a quick stop at my apartment.

Now I'm here in *my* kitchen. That's a strange thought, but it's also a cozy one that warms me up. I feel at home as I head to the sink and fill a glass with water. As I drink, a metal tag jingles and my little dog trots into the kitchen, wagging his tail, looking up at me, as if he's asking, *"What's up?"*

"This is our new home," I answer as I scoop him into my arms.

He sighs happily against my chest, snuggling up to my boobs—his happy place.

But we're not alone for long. My guys join me after their respective showers. Ryker's wearing low-slung heather-gray pants while Chase is dressed in a pair of basketball shorts.

"It's the shirtless chefs," I say, giddy at the sight of my men.

"I guess the band is back together again," Ryker says

as Chase yanks open the fridge and asks, "Pancakes, anyone?"

"Only if our girl can show us my second-favorite party trick," Ryker answers.

I can, and I do, flipping the pancakes high in the air.

Once the breakfast-for-dinner is ready a little later, we head to the counter.

The canvas bag Ryker was carrying in the store is perched on the end of it. Chase grabs it and waves it toward me. "We have one more thing for you."

"Another gift? You guys are really spoiling me."

They look at each other with intensely serious expressions. "And the problem with that is?" Chase asks.

"It's a lot of gifts," I say, a little overwhelmed by their generosity.

"And I'm still not hearing a problem," Ryker deadpans.

"No, it's not a problem. I'm just not used to it."

Chase nuzzles my neck. "Get used to it."

I sit straighter, soaking in their attention, letting myself enjoy it completely as I take the bag from Chase. "I will."

After they met me at the bookstore, we went to my studio for Nacho. My studio is a month-to-month lease, so I won't give it up right away. But I don't plan on living there again.

My home is with these guys.

When I pull out the gift, my throat tightens in all the good ways. It's a jersey. On the front it says, "The

Hockey Guys." On the back, there's a numeral one, and the word above it is *Ours*.

I never thought I would cry over a sports jersey. But once upon a time, I never thought I'd fall in love with two men who love me just the way I am.

44

AT THE SAME TIME?

Trina

I feel like I've drunk ten cans of Monster Blitz drinks, even though I've had nothing. But I'm shaking with nerves on Tuesday morning and about to breathe into a paper bag.

Aubrey grabs my wrist. "You can do it," she says, reassuring me.

I take a calming breath and nod. She's at my home —my new home—and the guys are off at the gym.

I'm about to leave to meet my family for an early breakfast before work. "I can do it," I say.

"You're going to nail it," she says, then winks. "Just like they nail you."

"Actually, they double nail me."

She narrows her eyes. "I hate you. All I want is a damn good nailing."

"Some girls dream of unicorns. Some dream of unicorn dick," I say, then we leave together, and she walks with me through my new neighborhood and over to Fillmore, then says goodbye when I reach Mindy's Café.

I smooth a hand along my shirt, then gulp. I head inside, spotting my family immediately in a booth. I make my way over and join them, sitting next to my sister, who I swear is going to be pregnant forever.

"Forty weeks—so you're pumpkin size now, right?" I ask, focusing on her since I need to wade my way into the *I'm in a three-way relationship* pool.

"Forty weeks, two days, and five million hours," she says with a miserable moan. "Which makes me house size."

I pat her shoulder sympathetically.

My mom laughs. "At this rate, you're going to be a mansion."

"Maybe even an entire complex," my dad says.

Cassie frowns. "I'm a whole city." Then she turns to me. "But thank you again for all the books on my registry. That was cool."

I smile, thinking of Chase, buying out all her books at Target. He's such a good boyfriend. I *can* do this. I can tell them. Any second now. "Glad you like them. Can't wait to read to my niece or nephew," I say, and as those words come out, so does a new realization. I will be an awesome aunt for *that* reason. I can read my ass off to the baby.

"But how are you doing?" Cassie asks, her bossy voice back. "How's the studio? Are you okay? Is the neighborhood safe? Do you want to come back to my place?"

There it is. My chance. "That's what I wanted to talk to you about," I say, even though the nerves are now a whole battalion in my belly. "I'm involved."

That's a start, but *only* a start, since I haven't used the plural pronoun yet.

My mom beams. "Oh, you got back together with the guy from the dog park? So it's serious?"

She can't even hide the hearts and flowers in her voice.

Just say it.

"Yes, and his best friend too. I'm in a relationship with two guys," I say, putting it out there for them at last. *This is me. Take me how I am.*

Cassie's brow knits. Mom tilts her head. Dad's face is blank. And I keep going. "I don't expect you to understand it. I don't expect you to even like it. But I like it. And I love them, and they love me. And I want you to know that this is me. This is real. This is who I am."

Cassie's jaw drops, and you could probably fit a mansion in her mouth now. But she says nothing. She's shocked speechless. That's a first.

My mother recovers her voice first. "You're with both of them?" It comes out as a clarifying question, like she can't possibly have heard me correctly.

"Yes. We're together. I'm with both of them, and each guy is with me."

"Oh," she says, then tilts her head the other way. "Ohh." She blinks. "At the same ti—" She slaps a palm over her mouth.

My dad raises a stop-sign hand at Mom. "That goes under things I don't need to know, honey."

Yeah, I agree, Pops.

Chagrined, my mom looks at me. "I'm so sorry."

I scripted this morning a million different ways, but never did I think my mom would apologize for accidentally asking if I take a double dose of dick with my morning coffee.

"It's no big deal," I say, even though they've got two very big deals.

Cassie lifts a finger, speaking at last. "That's why you were so upset the night you came to my house?"

"Yes," I admit. "I didn't think it was going to work out with them. But it did after all."

"You didn't tell me. You only said it was one guy. Why didn't you tell me the truth?" she asks, hurt in her tone.

Is that a real question? "Because you don't like most of my choices?" I say, but it's more of a question. How is this a surprise for her?

"I don't care if you're with two guys," she says, and is that honesty in her eyes? It sure looks like it. "I care if somebody hurts you. I never want anybody to hurt my little sister. And if they hurt you, they'll have me to answer to."

"That's sweet," I say, as unexpected tears prick the back of my eyes.

"It's not supposed to be sweet," she says briskly. "It's supposed to be threatening!"

Mom laughs, then Cassie and I join in, and I guess her personality type is the one I added—the protector.

Like Ryker. That helps me understand Cassie a little bit more. "So you wouldn't have judged me for being in love with two guys?"

She's quick with an answer, like she always is. "I think it's strange. I don't understand it. I don't get it. But you brought me pound cake and called me when you needed someone, and you came to my shower with books. I think that's all I can really ask for in a sister," she says, and I suppose that's as good as it's going to get with her.

"Thanks," I say, meaning it.

My mom clears her throat. "I have questions though."

"Darling, please don't ask *that* again," my father warns, his tone stern.

"Not that," Mom says, staring intensely at me. "More like what should I call them when I meet them? Will they both come over for Thanksgiving? I don't understand how any of this works. It doesn't make a lot of sense to me, but I understand it was a big deal for you to tell us. So I'll have some questions. Like when I introduce all of you, should I say *This is my daughter Trina and her boyfriends*?"

And I was today years old when I learned my romantic mother is highly practical too.

I guess people have a way of surprising you. "Yes, that would work."

EPILOGUE

TWO RIVALS AND THEIR GIRLFRIEND

Trina

A week later, I head to the park with my three roommates—my two boyfriends and my pervy little dog. We walk through the streets of Pacific Heights like, well, a throuple.

Along the way, Chase says, "So, I was watching this new dog video from the vet dude, and he was talking about dog DNA, and I thought we should get Nacho's DNA tested. How fun would that be?"

"Only the most fun ever," I say, because that sounds like Christmas and my birthday all at once.

"Make sure he didn't just eat any panties when you swab his cheek," Ryker says dryly.

I jerk my gaze to my bearded boyfriend, alarmed. "Is that your way of telling me he ate some undies?" Nacho's been lingerie-less for several weeks now. I'm seriously proud of his panty-free diet. But he could relapse at any moment.

Ryker shoots me a reassuring grin. "Sweetheart, we hung your hamper five-feet high. In a laundry room. With a door that shuts," he says. "That's our job in the household. To make sure that boy is safe."

He nods to the pooch leading the way, and I love that Ryker, a self-declared *not a dog guy*, has added Nacho to the inner circle of those he protects.

Chase clears his throat. "Speaking of household, did you know the word *ménage* comes from the French word for household?"

We all stop in our tracks, Ryker and I staring at Chase. "Is that you or did a word nerd take over your body?" Ryker asks.

Chase blows on his nails. "I live with a couple word nerds. Gotta hold my own."

I squeeze his arm, gleeful. "And you did."

We enter the park and head to the tents, where the guys from the two teams are gathered for the kickoff event for the Hockey Hotties calendar. It's a *bark in the park* for rescue pups, with dog treats, toys, pools, and jumps. As we walk up the grassy hill, I've got Chase's hand in one of mine, Ryker's hand in the other. Some of the athletes stare at us. Then, most of the athletes.

I squeeze both their hands, but they don't seem worried. Just ready. Like me. When we reach the Sea Dogs' tent, Chase holds up my hand, joined with his, and says, "This is my girlfriend, Trina."

Right next to that tent is the one for the Avengers. "And this is my girlfriend, Trina," Ryker adds. "Got it?"

There's silence for several weighty seconds as gears turn in heads. Then Erik draws a triangle in the air. "Like a three-way?"

"And you can count," Chase says as Ledger pushes past the guys and joins us, gesturing to Chase as he talks to me. "So glad this guy listened to my advice."

I smile. "Is that so?"

"Yeah. I told him to get the girl," he says, a little cocky, a little proud. His smile disappears, and he delivers a scathing look to Ryker. "But this changes nothing. We're still going to destroy you when we play you." Ledger turns back to Chase. "Right?"

Chase scoffs. "Like we'd do anything else."

Ryker just rolls his eyes. "I'd like to see that happen."

Dev, the goalie from Ryker's team, heads over, stopping to give the three of us a long, appraising look. "So it's two rivals sharing a woman?"

Ryker and Chase make a show of pretending to think on the question and then they nod.

Dev cackles, then thrusts his arms skyward under the San Francisco sun. "Dude, thank god for the two of you, because we will never have to deal with the press again with what you guys are gonna have to handle."

All the hockey guys at the park crack up. "Talk about taking one for the team," Ledger puts in.

"Yeah, that's why I did it," Chase says dryly.

Their teammates give them hell the whole afternoon. I never knew there were so many sandwich jokes. Meatball ones too. Then, Erik ups the ante asking if I'm the marshmallow between the graham crackers and the chocolate bar.

"I do like s'mores," I say, and he laughs, but some of their teammates are quieter. Some say nothing. Some just give us curious looks.

Maybe this is just the way it goes, but I want to make sure my guys are good with everything.

Concerned, I pull them aside under a tree. "Is this okay? Does it bother you that some are looking at us funny?"

Chase shakes his head. "No. We did what we needed to do. We told them. It's not a secret. We can finally be ourselves."

I relax some. We were never hiding because of worries over his teammates, or honestly even the press. We were secretive because we didn't want to look like a pair when we're three of a kind.

"And the rest is out of our hands. Can't please everyone," Ryker seconds, then presses a reassuring kiss to my cheek.

"But what about the press?" I ask, because their teammates think that'll be a field day.

"That is definitely out of our hands," Chase says, and it's clear the comment comes from experience. "But we'll handle it."

"You're worth it," Ryker adds.

I breathe a deeper sigh of relief. Whatever comes next I can handle. I did the hard thing—I told my family. That was always my biggest concern.

Beyond that, I'm lucky to work in a field that embraces love, in all its shapes, sizes and forms, including unconventional arrangements. The women and men I interact with don't judge who you love.

Soon, some of them will be here—part of my found family and I can't wait to share some of my love story with them.

But first, I have one more thing to say to my boyfriends. "I love you two," I say, and the worries fade away even more.

* * *

A little later, Aubrey joins me at the launch. Ivy and Katie are here too, along with some of my friends from book club. Nacho's parked at my feet in the grass, rolling on his back, showing off for the ladies as they ask me lots of questions.

Unlike my mother, they have no qualms about asking the *at the same time* question.

But I don't kiss and tell. I just give a coy shrug and they move onto other queries.

"Do you always go out together?" Kimora asks.

"We're figuring that out, but no, not always. Sometimes I hang out with Chase. Sometimes Ryker. And sometimes it's the three of us."

"And do your parents know?" Prana asks.

"They do, and they're not totally freaking out. Just partially freaking out."

"And their parents?" Aubrey asks, pointing to the guys.

Ivy laughs and raises a hand, swiping her dark hair from her cheek. "I'll take this one. Our mom is completely cool with it and so is Chase's. But they also were used to those two sharing toys when they were kids," she says with a wicked grin, like she's been dying to make that comment for some time.

"Well played," Aubrey says approvingly, then the conversation returns to more questions.

"Do people look at you when you all go somewhere?" Prana inquires.

I nod to the big packs of burly men several feet away. "Well, they all did. But I suppose I would too," I admit, then my gaze snags again on that group of men.

I could be wrong, but I'm pretty sure Ledger's checking us out with obvious interest in his eyes. But is he looking at Aubrey or Ivy or one of the other gals?

I'm not sure, but I see sparks in his dark eyes from a distance.

I'll have to talk to my guys later and ask what they think, but for now, I chat more with my friends, then I join my boyfriends for a picture.

Later that night, as we're all settled in on the couch, I prep it to post on Ryker's social feed with the caption *Two rivals and their girlfriend*. But I add a heart.

I show it to him and he arches a brow. "Really? A heart emoji?"

Chase cracks up. "It's just an emoji."

"It's a whole new image," Ryker grumbles.

"It's a whole new world," Chase corrects.

I look from one man to the other. "Yes. Yes, it is."

* * *

I don't wake up to a welcome wagon on social media. There are plenty of questions, side-eyes and WTFs from hockey fans. At breakfast, Ryker's and Chase's notifications are blowing up with questions, and requests from the media—not even the hockey media. But from Page Six, and other celebrity sites.

It's still so weird to me. So surreal.

I do worry about them. They're mine after all. I can't *not* worry. I set a hand on Ryker's strong arm. "I hope this doesn't mess things up for you with the team, and with everything we were trying to do," I say. "Especially after the podcast thing."

"It won't. The team wasn't even upset about that. They get that we can't control the media. They just wanted me to show more of myself online," he says, then faux shudders.

"You still hate that," I say, laughing.

Chase laughs too. "He probably always will," he says.

"Damn straight," Ryker confirms. "But I'll do it anyway. Since it matters to the people I care about. Like my team."

And I fall a little harder for him.

Then I turn to Chase. "Is this going to distract you? What if I was the bad luck charm?"

He scoffs. "Sometimes you win, sometimes you lose. And the thing is, you showed me there's room in my life for hockey and love."

My heart thumps louder for him too.

"The real issue is this," he adds, as he shows me his phone and his social feed. Right alongside the WTFs and the *freaks* are comments like *cool*, and *can I come to the wedding,* and *whatever works, as long as she doesn't root for the Sea Dogs.*

Ryker stares sternly at me. "See? That's all that matters. You're an Avengers fan now, Trina."

Chase clears his throat. "She's a Sea Dogs fan, and that's that."

"Avengers."

"Sea Dogs."

And I suppose that really is the biggest concern. Which means, it's time to set our phones down, and not worry about the world, and all the things we can't control.

I have my guys, my dog, and some books to read. The rest is just noise.

ANOTHER EPILOGUE
THE DOUBLE WAG

Trina

A year later, I'm torn.

This is seriously hard. I'm in the VIP suite, wearing my special jersey, nibbling on avocado bruschetta but feeling like I'm being ripped in half.

"Nobody in my throuple support group warned me about this," I joke to Aubrey, but I'm not really joking.

Loving two players from two teams does a number on your sports loyalties. Mine have shot sky high in the last year since I've gone from hockey hater to hockey lover.

The year hasn't been all smooth skating. Like my two men, I've been subjected to a fair amount of scrutiny from the media—but we take it all in stride, and most of it is behind us now. All that's important to me is that my guys are happy, and that our families accept us —which they do.

Besides, what goes on behind closed doors isn't

anyone's business but our own—and the stuff that does go on behind closed doors? It's all so very worth it. Everything with them is because I love Ryker and Chase, and they love me.

But I don't just love my guys. I fell hard for the game too. I dare anyone to claim it's not the best sport there is. But right now, the score is tied in the game as the Sea Dogs and Avengers vie against each other on the ice.

"What do I do?" I ask. But it's a question for the universe. An unknowable one.

"Well, obviously blow both of them regardless," Aubrey deadpans.

"That's a given, but still," I say, staring down at the ice as the guys fly by at rocket speed. But when there's a media time-out, I pull my focus from the rink and turn it straight to my friend.

She'd been telling me about a new guy in her life and how very complicated the situation is. I listen, then give her my best advice, hoping it's as good as the advice she gave me when I desperately needed it a year ago.

The last year has been a good one for many, many reasons. The book club has tripled in size. Business at the store is terrific. We raised a good amount of money for Nacho's rescue with the jerseys. And my boy won his most recent agility competition.

He's seriously the best dog ever. He's also cut way down on his underwear snacks.

Oh, and also, Selena-slash-Abby was exposed. At first, I'd thought some industrious reporter had tracked her down. Then I'd thought maybe the book club had put their clever heads together and found out who she was. Because they could do that with their big brains.

Finally, I'd imagined the guys on the Avengers or the Sea Dogs had exposed her.

But nope. I was wrong on all three guesses. It was my sister. Cassie put her determination to use and found out who The Stuntwoman was.

Pretty sure it'll be hard for the boys' ex to pull off her tricks now—on anyone—now that *everyone* knows her name, and her face, and her voice.

Such a shame.

As for Jasper, I heard through the book club grapevine that he keeps getting on the apps, and getting shut down once women learn who he is—the guy who cheated on his girlfriend in front of her dog.

It's the kiss of death, it seems.

Good.

I'm just glad he never came around again, and I haven't seen him once at a game.

Well, I have excellent seats at both arenas. Perks of being a double WAG.

Later, when the game ends, I wait in the corridor for my boyfriends, watching as they stride down the hall in their suits to take me out for a VIP night on the town. These two have been the best part of the past year. I don't see them every day or even every night, and coordinating two hockey schedules with my own is like a game of Jenga. But it's worth it. When we're together we make the best of it, playing poker with Ryker's grand-mother, having lunches with their moms, visiting my family for the holidays, where my mom finally got to say *This is my daughter Trina and her two boyfriends.*

I'm pretty sure every one of my extended family looked at us thinking *at the same time?*

But no one said it.

Now, it's only me and my guys tonight, just the way I like it. "Want to play pool?"

Ryker groans. "So you can crush us?"

"Exactly," I say.

Chase shakes his head, sighing deeply. "Never should have taught you. Now you're way better than we are."

They carried through on their first night promise and taught me the game. They even bought me a pool table for Christmas so I could work on my skills.

Though mostly, I think they got it for, ahem, *other reasons*.

"C'mon hockey guys, take me on."

And they do. They take me on at our home that night on the pool table.

We don't talk about who won or lost the hockey game.

Because, really, we all won.

THE END

Can't get enough Trina, Chase and Ryker? Scroll below for access to an exclusive bonus scene of their life together! But first, mark your calendars for October for

PUCK YES, and as you wait for that spicy and hilarious hockey romance to hit KU, be sure to grab **PLAYS WELL WITH OTHERS** for free NOW in KU. That fake-dating, best friends-to-lovers, spicy standalone romance has a dirty talking sports hero who falls first while he shows the heroine how a man should treat a woman in and out of bed! Read on!

* * *

Click here for the Double Pucked Bonus Epilogue!

* * *

Plays Well With Others excerpt

Carter

"Please just fuck me. Can I make it any more clear?" she demands, and there she is again. Bold Rachel. I like all Rachels, but I do like this forward side of her in bed.

A lot.

"No, but maybe I can," I say, then finish stripping off her jeans and her panties as she watches me with avid eyes. "Since I'm gonna fuck the last shreds of doubt right out of you." I take her hands, bring them to the button on my jeans. "Take out my cock."

Then her hands are eagerly sliding down the zipper, pushing my jeans down, right along with my boxer briefs.

My dick springs free and is so fucking happy to see her.

And yeah, maybe I did want her to walk in on me last night. Because of *this*.

Her reaction. The wide eyes. The parted lips. *The moment when her mind asks the question.*

The thing is—I'm a big guy. I'm supposed to be big to do my job well. For whatever reason—call it luck, good fortune, or just proportionalism at play—I was blessed with size *everywhere*.

She gulps. "Will it...fit?"

That's so fucking hot to hear her say.

But it'll be even more fun for her to find out. I take her hand, wrap it around my shaft. "That depends, Sunshine," I murmur, then I sigh happily as she fondles me. Up, down, then over the head.

"On what?" she asks, trance-like, on an upstroke.

"How wet you are. And if I've got you worked up enough to take me all the way," I say, then slide a hand between her thighs, gliding my fingers through all that slick wetness. Mmm. Yes. She's silky and hot, but I need to get her even wetter. Drive her wild. She lets go of my dick, lifting her hips for me as she grips my shoulders.

That's it. That's the way to find out.

I stroke her eager clit till she's moaning and arching on the counter, offering me her wet pussy.

Just to be sure though...

I slide a finger inside her and she gasps. I crook it, then draw a delicious circle on her clit with my thumb as I stroke inside and out. I add another finger. She's soaked. Then I nip her earlobe. "What do you think, Sunshine? Think my cock will fit now?"

"I don't know. Maybe you could give me a lesson in size as you fuck me," she says, biting her lip.

I go up in flames. "You are a fast learner," I say as I ease out my fingers, then bring them to my lips, sucking off her taste. "Fuck, you're sweet."

"And you're dirty," she says, her lips curving up.

"I think you like my kind of dirty." I grab a condom from my wallet, then toss the billfold onto the counter. As I open the foil, I play the part of gentleman for a second, asking, "Want me to fuck you on your bed? Will that be easier?"

The woman knows her mind since she shakes her head adamantly. "I've never been fucked on a kitchen counter," she says in a whisper full of wicked delight.

My cock throbs as I cover it, eager to give her a first. I tug her closer to the edge of the counter, keeping the apron under her bare skin. I line myself up and rub the head against her slick heat. She can't seem to tear her gaze away from the place where we meet. Her eyes are locked on us.

"You like that? The way we look when we're about to fuck?"

"I do."

I take my time. Pushing in just an inch or two.

Her hands shoot out, grabbing my shoulders.

"Does it hurt?"

She winces as she nods. "But I like it."

My brow furrows. "You sure?"

She digs her nails into me. "Yes. Give me more."

Well, I won't deny her.

Keep reading for more hot sex on the kitchen counter, in front of a mirror, and on the couch...as well as fantastic fake dates, he's-great-with-kids moments, and witty banter as he falls first in: **PLAYS WELL WITH OTHERS**

BE A LOVELY

Want to be the first to know of sales, new releases, special deals and giveaways? Sign up for my newsletter today!

Want to be part of a fun, feel-good place to talk about books and romance, and get sneak peeks of covers and advance copies of my books? Be a Lovely!

ACKNOWLEDGMENTS

I am so grateful to Sharon Abreau, AKA the hockey goddess. Sharon is a life long hockey fan and she graciously read the entire book and checked all the hockey details. Any mistakes in hockey are entirely my own. Sharon, let's do it again!

Big gratitude to Melanie Harlow, who encouraged this project from the start and provided the much needed *do it*. Abiding thanks to KP Simmon for her tireless support and early reading and feedback. Thanks to Kim Bias for final tweaks, and to Lauren Clarke for taking this over the finish line. Kara Hildebrand, Sandra Shipman, Claudia Fosca, Karen Lawson, and Virginia Carey were immensely helpful with eagle eyes and eager spirits.

I am also grateful to Laurelin Paige for her guidance on this book and on all books, Kayti McGee for her creativity, Anthony Colletti for his acumen, and Sawyer Bennett and Sarina Bowen for hockey guidance.

Thank you to Kylie Sek for the fantastic cover and her endless patience in getting it just right. You're a dream, Kylie!

Most of all, thanks to my family for believing in me, and thanks to my dogs for inspiration.

But last and certainly not least, I am deeply, truly, madly grateful for YOU. The readers. You make everything possible. Thank you.

MORE BOOKS BY LAUREN

I've written more than 100 books! **All of these titles below
are FREE in Kindle Unlimited!**

The Virgin Society Series

Meet the Virgin Society – great friends who'd do anything
for each other. Indulge in these forbidden, emotionally-
charged, and wildly sexy age-gap romances!

The RSVP

The Tryst

The Tease

The Dating Games Series

A fun, sexy romantic comedy series about friends in the city
and their dating mishaps!

The Virgin Next Door

Two A Day

The Good Guy Challenge

How To Date Series (New and ongoing)

Four great friends. Four chances to learn how to date
again. Four standalone romantic comedies full of love, sex
and meet-cute shenanigans.

My So-Called Sex Life

Plays Well With Others

The Anti-Romantic

Blown Away

Boyfriend Material

Four fabulous heroines. Four outrageous proposals. Four chances at love in this sexy rom-com series!

Asking For a Friend

Sex and Other Shiny Objects

One Night Stand-In

Overnight Service

Big Rock Series

My #1 New York Times Bestselling sexy as sin, irreverent, male-POV romantic comedy!

Big Rock

Mister O

Well Hung

Full Package

Joy Ride

Hard Wood

Happy Endings Series

Romance starts with a bang in this series of standalones following a group of friends seeking and avoiding love!

Come Again

Shut Up and Kiss Me

Kismet

My Single-Versary

Ballers And Babes

Sexy sports romance standalones guaranteed to make
you hot!

Most Valuable Playboy

Most Likely to Score

A Wild Card Kiss

Rules of Love Series

Athlete, virgins and weddings!

The Virgin Rule Book

The Virgin Game Plan

The Virgin Replay

The Virgin Scorecard

The Extravagant Series

Bodyguards, billionaires and hoteliers in this sexy, high-
stakes series of standalones!

One Night Only

One Exquisite Touch

My One-Week Husband

The Guys Who Got Away Series

Friends in New York City and California fall in love in this
fun and hot rom-com series!

Birthday Suit

Dear Sexy Ex-Boyfriend

The What If Guy

Thanks for Last Night

The Dream Guy Next Door

Always Satisfied Series

A group of friends in New York City find love and laughter in this series of sexy standalones!

Satisfaction Guaranteed

Never Have I Ever

Instant Gratification

PS It's Always Been You

The Gift Series

An after dark series of standalones! Explore your fantasies!

The Engagement Gift

The Virgin Gift

The Decadent Gift

The Heartbreakers Series

Three brothers. Three rockers. Three standalone sexy romantic comedies.

Once Upon a Real Good Time

Once Upon a Sure Thing

Once Upon a Wild Fling

Sinful Men

A high-stakes, high-octane, sexy-as-sin romantic suspense series!

My Sinful Nights

My Sinful Desire

My Sinful Longing

My Sinful Love

My Sinful Temptation

From Paris With Love

Swoony, sweeping romances set in Paris!

Wanderlust

Part-Time Lover

One Love Series

A group of friends in New York falls in love one by one in this sexy rom-com series!

The Sexy One

The Hot One

The Knocked Up Plan

Come As You Are

Lucky In Love Series

A small town romance full of heat and blue collar heroes and sexy heroines!

Best Laid Plans

The Feel Good Factor

Nobody Does It Better

Unzipped

No Regrets

An angsty, sexy, emotional, new adult trilogy about one young couple fighting to break free of their pasts!

The Start of Us

The Thrill of It

Every Second With You

The Caught Up in Love Series

A group of friends finds love!

The Pretending Plot

The Dating Proposal

The Second Chance Plan

The Private Rehearsal

Seductive Nights Series

A high heat series full of danger and spice!

Night After Night

After This Night

One More Night

A Wildly Seductive Night

Joy Delivered Duet

A high-heat, wickedly sexy series of standalones that will set your sheets on fire!

Nights With Him

Forbidden Nights

Unbreak My Heart

A standalone second chance emotional roller coaster of a romance

The Muse

A magical realism romance set in Paris

Good Love Series of sexy rom-coms co-written with Lili Valente!

I also write MM romance under the name L. Blakely!

Hopelessly Bromantic Duet (MM)

Roomies to lovers to enemies to fake boyfriends

Hopelessly Bromantic

Here Comes My Man

Men of Summer Series (MM)

Two baseball players on the same team fall in love in a forbidden romance spanning five epic years

Scoring With Him

Winning With Him

All In With Him

MM Standalone Novels

A Guy Walks Into My Bar

The Bromance Zone

One Time Only

The Best Men (Co-written with Sarina Bowen)

Winner Takes All Series (MM)

A series of emotionally-charged and irresistibly sexy
standalone MM sports romances!

The Boyfriend Comeback

Turn Me On

A Very Filthy Game

Limited Edition Husband

Manhandled

If you want a personalized recommendation, email me at
laurenblakelybooks@gmail.com!

CONTACT

I love hearing from readers! You can find me on Twitter at LaurenBlakely3, Instagram at LaurenBlakelyBooks, Facebook at LaurenBlakelyBooks, or online at LaurenBlakely.com. You can also email me at laurenblakelybooks@gmail.com